BE MINE

Also by Rick Mofina
in Large Print:

No Way Back

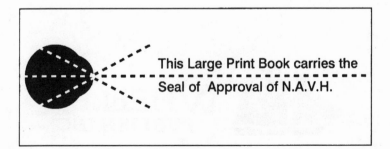

This Large Print Book carries the
Seal of Approval of N.A.V.H.

BE MINE

RICK MOFINA

Published in 2004 by arrangement with Pinnacle Books, an imprint of Kensington Publishing Corp.

Wheeler Large Print Softcover.

The text of this Large Print edition is unabridged.
Other aspects of the book may vary from the original edition.

Set in 16 pt. Plantin by Ramona Watson.

Printed in the United States on permanent paper.

Library of Congress Cataloging-in-Publication Data

Mofina, Rick.
    Be mine / Rick Mofina.
      p. cm.
    ISBN 1-58724-781-X (lg. print : sc : alk. paper)
    1. San Francisco (Calif.) — Fiction. 2. Stalking victims — Fiction. 3. Police murders — Fiction. 4. Journalists — Fiction.
5. Large type books. I. Title.
PS3613.O37B4 2004
  813'.6—dc22
                                             2004053586

For
Inspector Eddie J. Erdelatz,
San Francisco Homicide Detail (Ret.),
who has been a friend since the day
I walked into room 450 at
The Hall of Justice

National Association for Visually Handicapped
----------------------- *serving the partially seeing*

As the Founder/CEO of NAVH, the only national health agency solely devoted to those who, although not totally blind, have an eye disease which could lead to serious visual impairment, I am pleased to recognize Thorndike Press★ as one of the leading publishers in the large print field.

Founded in 1954 in San Francisco to prepare large print textbooks for partially seeing children, NAVH became the pioneer and standard setting agency in the preparation of large type.

Today, those publishers who meet our standards carry the prestigious "Seal of Approval" indicating high quality large print. We are delighted that Thorndike Press is one of the publishers whose titles meet these standards. We are also pleased to recognize the significant contribution Thorndike Press is making in this important and growing field.

Lorraine H. Marchi, L.H.D.
Founder/CEO
NAVH

★ Thorndike Press encompasses the following imprints: Thorndike, Wheeler, Walker and Large Print Press.

And I gave my heart to know wisdom, and to know madness and folly: I perceived this is also vexation of spirit.

For in much wisdom is much grief: and he that increaseth knowledge, increaseth sorrow.

— Ecclesiastes 1:17,18

1

Waiting alone at Jake's Bar & Grill in North Beach, Molly Wilson finished her second diet cola, then pressed redial on her cell phone. Four rings. She got his machine again. Damn.

"It's me. I'm at Jake's. Where are you? Call me."

Nearly an hour late and not a word. This was not like Cliff. Maybe he'd left her a message at work. She tried her line there.

"You've reached Molly Wilson of the *San Francisco Star.* I'm either on the phone or —"

She keyed in her password. No new messages since she'd left the newsroom. Just two hang-up calls. She'd been getting a lot of those lately but nothing from Cliff. She ordered another soda and brooded.

In the time they'd been together Cliff had never been late. Except tonight. Maybe he'd sensed that she'd reached a decision. Cliff was a great guy. She'd never set out to hurt him. She'd set out to have fun and they were having fun. But she didn't want to move in with him. Wasn't ready for it. She wanted to do cool things. See other people. She was going to tell him tonight. She was going to thank him for his offer and return his key.

If only she could reach him, she thought on an exhale.

She didn't like this. She tried his cell phone, wanting this night to be over so she could retreat to her apartment, soak in her tub, listen to some Phil Collins, then eat a gallon of butterscotch ripple. No answer. She drummed her glossed nails on the table. Then stopped.

Someone was watching her.

She pushed back her auburn hair and inventoried the after-work office crowd. Nothing unusual until she noticed two men nearby warming stools at the bar, ties loosened, stealing glimpses of her, then the big TV overhead.

Of course. She was on *Eyewitness 24-Hour Action News.* It was her weekly eight-minute spot with Vince Vincent, host of *Crime Scene,* when they talked about crime trends in San Francisco.

The show was taped at noon. Molly was still wearing the same sweater and matching blazer, which complemented her eyes. There she was with Vincent at a studio desk against San Francisco's skyline at night discussing the latest justice department figures.

". . . but what about violent crime, like murder?" Vincent asked.

"The odds of your being murdered, or a

victim of a violent crime, are very remote," she said.

Watching the set over the bar, Molly shook her head. Vince was worried. No sensational crimes in weeks.

"But violent crimes do happen here, Molly. We've got gangs, drug wars, murders of every sort. The city is still reeling from the recent jewelry heist homicides."

"Sure, but the fact is, your likelihood of being victimized by such a crime is virtually nil."

The two guys at the bar were now grinning, offering Molly little waves. She shrugged them off.

She'd been on the show for over a year. She loved doing it but there was a downside. It was more than a magnet for jerks like those two. Since *Crime Scene* had been picked up by a statewide cable network it had attracted more whack jobs. Sickos of every description tried contacting her. *Comes with the territory.* She shrugged.

Molly could handle the pair at the bar. There was little she couldn't handle. But not tonight. She wasn't up for these two. Not now. One was headed her way. That was her cue. She grabbed her bag, tossed a few bills on the table.

Outside, an evening breeze rolled up from the bay and she was struck by an odd sensation. It was as if somebody was just waiting for her to leave Jake's.

And now they were watching her.

This was stupid. She took stock of the street. Nothing but a few window shoppers. She was being silly, put off by those drunks at the bar. And Cliff. Where was he? She waved it off and flagged a cab.

"Upper Market," she told the driver.

The lights of San Francisco rolled by and Molly thought of Cliff. He was so good to her. Nothing like some of the creeps she'd dated and dropped. Like the hair puller who called her a "stupid bitch" and the weirdo who went mute and just glared at her. She bit her lip wondering if cooling things with Cliff was a mistake. He was considerate, intelligent, had a sense of humor. A decent handsome guy. Nothing was wrong with him. They'd only started dating a few months ago. She just wasn't ready for a long-term relationship.

She considered her friend Tom Reed, the reporter who sat next to her at the *Star*. Look at what he had with Ann, his wife. The real thing. They had Zach, their beautiful son. They were far from perfect but they had a fire that could melt steel. They'd endured heartbreaks and emerged stronger. Maybe someday she'd find something like that. She just wasn't ready to settle down yet.

"Miss?" the driver said. "The address, please."

Molly recited it as the cab climbed the

neighborhood's serpentine hills. She liked the way the fog rolled up the steep streets of Cliff's little oasis. He'd joke about being sheriff when she pointed at the community signs that demanded suspicious persons be immediately reported.

The creak of brakes echoed in the stillness as the cab stopped at the small Queen Anne–style house. Cliff's apartment was upstairs at the back.

"If you shut off your meter and wait, I'll go back with you," she told the driver.

"How long, miss? I gotta make a living."

"Not long. Please. I need to see if my friend's home."

He slid the gearshift to park and killed the motor. It ticked down.

Molly approached the front. The exterior lights were on, but the place seemed oddly dark. No interior lights. The wrought-iron gate squeaked as she took the tiled walkway to the rear stairs. The yard was lush, private, bordered with rosebushes, shrubs, eucalyptus trees. A couple of sturdy-looking palms.

Her footsteps echoed as she ascended the wooden staircase to his door. Inhaling the fragrance of the flowers rising from the boxes on his balcony, she pressed the buzzer, heard it sound through his apartment. Then nothing. She buzzed again. Waiting, she put her ear to the door. Not a hint of movement. She knocked. Waited. Nothing.

Strange. She reached into her bag for her key to his apartment, slid it into the slot. It went in too fast. What the — The door was unlocked. She turned the handle. It opened. Inviting her to enter.

"Cliff?"

No one responded from the darkness. She reached inside, flipped on a light.

"Cliff?"

The first room was the kitchen. She saw his jacket draped over a chair. His car keys were on the counter, along with his cell phone, wallet, loose change, unopened mail.

"Cliff, it's Molly."

She moved to the living room. In the darkness the red message light of his answering machine was blinking like something terrified. She switched on a lamp.

It was too quiet.

Something began to stir deep in her gut, telling her this was all wrong. The next room across the darkened hall was his bedroom. Instinct warned her to leave now but her hand hovered over the doorknob. The driver out front had blasted his horn and her skin nearly exploded.

"Jerk."

She took a breath and opened his bedroom door. The room swam in a surreal dim blue glow from the digital clock on his nightstand. Her stomach tightened.

Oh God.

Cliff was on the bed. Facedown.

She inched toward him.

He was dressed in jeans and a T-shirt. A huge damp, dark blue halo encircled his head. Something resembling wet raw meat had erupted from the side, glistening in the eerie blue light.

Resting on Cliff's lower back was his service weapon, a .40-caliber Beretta. Next to it, open for display, his official San Francisco police identification. It read:

CLIFF HOOPER
INSPECTOR OF POLICE
HOMICIDE DETAIL

2

Across San Francisco, Walt Sydowski looked upon his father sleeping in the hospital bed.

Johnny.

Born a Polish peasant, he was a potato farmer and village barber who'd kept his family alive in a labor camp during the Second World War by cutting the hair of Nazi officers.

Now his heart was deteriorating. The doctors gave him a year.

Sydowski saw San Francisco's skyline glittering in the night. Several years ago he'd lost his wife, Basha. She died in this very hospital calling his name. His first years without her were dark. He nearly gave up. His daughters helped get him through it, visiting from the East in shifts. Sydowski wished they'd visit more but he'd endured. Kept going. He had his work. It was his salvation.

Visiting hours were over. He kissed his old man's head. Then popped another Tums into his mouth. As he neared the hospital's main exit he nearly bumped into his partner, Linda Turgeon, as she was rushing in.

"What's going on?" he asked.

"Leo said you might be here."

"What's wrong?"

"It's Cliff."

"What about him?"

"He's dead."

Sydowski steadied himself against the wall. Turgeon gripped his shoulder.

"It can't be. How?"

"Appears he was shot. In his apartment."

"In his apartment."

"Leo wants you to be the primary. We have to go now."

Sydowski stared at Turgeon, not believing what she'd told him. Then they hurried to where she'd parked their unmarked Chev. A crumpled tissue was on the passenger side. She drove.

"A few hours ago in the detail Cliff's goofing around, holding my coffee mug hostage for a Hershey bar, *and now he's dead,*" Turgeon said.

Alarm bells screamed in Sydowski's ears until he got control of himself. He ran his hand over his face, then shook his head.

Hooper's dead. Christ almighty. Hoop.

The city blurred by like Sydowski's life. Over twenty years in San Francisco's homicide detail. Four hundred and ten murder investigations. The highest clearance rate in the state. He could retire anytime. And some days he thought about it. Dreamed of a fishing cabin in British Columbia, and raising

17

his birds. But no matter how he looked at it, he could not get his head around the idea of hanging it up. He needed the job. It was how he defined himself. Yet, he knew it wouldn't last forever. Nothing does.

His wife. His old man. His job. Now Cliff.

Sydowski had investigated the deaths of police officers. Some were his friends. But nobody this close.

In the coffee room that afternoon, Cliff had patted his shoulder. "My best to your old man. See you tomorrow."

In the Upper Market, Sydowski and Turgeon came upon a knot of radio cars, their flashing lights painting the rubberneckers who'd crowded at the yellow scene tape cordoning off Hooper's house. As he stepped from the car, it dawned on Sydowski: Cliff's girlfriend was Molly Wilson, one of the *Star*'s crime reporters. He pulled out his notebook and started a case log as he and Turgeon approached the first officer on the scene, who briefed them from his own notes.

"His girlfriend found him. Came to check on him when he didn't show for their date. Cabdriver called it in." The officer recited the times and names. Sure enough, Molly Wilson. "And we confirmed no sign of life. No weapons there, except his."

"How's that?" Sydowski looked up from his notebook.

"It's not a suicide."

"How about we let the investigation determine what it is or isn't?"

The officer understood. "Look, we know he was in your detail."

Sydowski and Turgeon stared hard at the officer.

"I just want to say I'm sorry."

The officer lifted the tape. Sydowski and Turgeon started down the walkway, nodding to the uniform posted at the back. They ascended the staircase at the rear to the landing, pulled on latex gloves and shoe covers.

"All set?" Sydowski's hand gripped the doorknob.

Turgeon nodded and they entered.

They studied the kitchen, making notes, taking stock of the sink and trash.

"Walt?"

Turgeon pointed her pen to a dime-sized hole in the kitchen wall, about five feet from the floor. Sydowski drew his face close, shone his penlight into the hole, then glanced back to the doorway. He tapped his knuckle on the wall.

"There's a slug in there. Looks like it's lodged in the stud."

Nothing looked out of place in the living room. Turgeon went to the answering machine, listened to the messages, all from Molly Wilson. She noted the time and the

19

number on his call display. The scene techs would scour everything. She joined Sydowski at the doorway to the bedroom where he took a moment to prepare himself for what awaited them beyond the door. He'd come upon murdered children, slain families, the scenes of rampages by insane gunmen, satanic ritual killings, and the suicides of retired cops, many of whom he'd known. But beyond the door was a colleague, a friend, and, Jesus, he swore he could still feel Cliff's hand on his shoulder from only a few hours ago.

"My best to your old man. See you to-morrow."

Turgeon took a breath. Sydowski opened the door and entered. For the longest time, he stood over Hooper's corpse, saying nothing, absorbing the scene. Hooper's open eyes met his from his death mask. Turgeon took note of Hooper's gun and ID left on his back by the killer.

"Ready?" Sydowski asked.

Working from opposite sides of the body, Sydowski and Turgeon slid their gloved hands under it to explore for any concealed evidence. The odor was not strong. They felt nothing.

"He's still warm," Turgeon said.

Sydowski examined the blood pool around the head. Then using his flashlight he probed along the bedsheet, the floor, and to the wall as if following a trail.

"What is it?" Turgeon asked.

Sydowski went to the adjoining bathroom, inspected the sink, checked a dampened towel and the floor under it, then returned to the bedroom wall. Turgeon was on her hands and knees, studying the floor.

"Looks like tiny blood drops and water," she said. "Looks like somebody tried a fast cleanup."

Sydowski stood before the spotless blank wall, examining it.

"Here too. They tried to wash it off the wall," he said. "Something written . . . looks like blood."

3

Tom Reed tensed the instant he walked into the *San Francisco Star* newsroom. No one was at the far corner monitoring the city's emergency radio scanners this morning.

Listening to them was an inviolable duty.

This was why the *Star* was getting killed by the *Chronicle* on breaking news, he thought, casting around the metro section.

No one useful in sight.

No clink of bracelets from Molly Wilson, who sat across from him. Where was she? No sign of Acker, the assignment editor. Something was happening out there. Tom could feel it in the voices of the police dispatchers. It was Bobby's job to sit by the scanners. That's what interns did. Where was he? Unable to ignore the transmissions, Tom went over and listened.

". . . they're booked out at the 187 . . ."

". . . ready to copy? It's in Upper Market . . ."

A 187. A homicide. In Upper Market. You didn't get many there. *Surely, Irene Pepper knows about this,* he thought, heading directly to her glass-walled office.

Pepper, the *Star*'s new metro editor, was standing at her desk taking notes, phone wedged between her ear and shoulder. She'd landed her post five months ago after Bob Shepherd, a legend in the craft, left for the *Los Angeles Times*. Irene was a strange blend of American-British-Canadian upbringing, in Toronto, London, New York, and Marin County. She'd been a freelancer in Washington, D.C., where she'd married the *Star*'s Washington, D.C., bureau chief. After he transferred back to San Francisco, Irene joined the *Star*, writing and editing fashion features.

Two years later she became editor of Special Sections, the ad-driven pages about homes, recipes, lifestyles, and things to do on weekends. After that, she became national editor before taking control of Metro, the paper's largest editorial department. Installing Irene there was something of a head-shaker, given that she had precious little news experience. But as a manager, she never overspent her budget.

"Excuse me, Irene?" Tom knocked on her open door. "We know about this murder in Upper Market, right?"

"Just a sec," she said into the phone. "Bobby checked it out this morning. It's a suicide."

"No, it's a homicide. Where is he?"

"I'm sure it's a suicide. Bobby wasn't

feeling good. I let him go home."

"So no one's on the scanners?"

"The new intern comes on in an hour. I've got to finish this call."

Back at his desk Tom took a deep breath, then dialed a police number. While it rang he searched through his clutter for a fresh notebook and came across the managing editor's recent memo demanding to know why the *Star* was missing breaking news stories. *Irene Pepper is why,* he thought. She didn't think it was important to keep the interns handcuffed to the damn scanners like Bob Shepherd and every other editor in the country did.

"Vickson," a voice growled over the line.

"Hey, man, it's Reed. I need a favor."

"Don't we all?"

"Buddy, can you help me out on a 187."

"And how may I enlighten you?"

"I'm hearing some chatter on one in the Clayton, Short area of Upper Market. Can you tell me, is that one a grounder or what?"

"Hold on. I've got to put you on hold."

Tom took a hit of Colombian coffee from his FBI mug, then looked back at Ann, and their twelve-year-old son, Zach, smiling from framed pictures. God, the hell he'd put both of them through over the years.

Some days Tom questioned if his job was still worth it as he reflected on the keepsakes at his desk. The faded clip from the *Tribune* in Montana with the head FORMER GREAT

24

FALLS NEWSPAPER BOY PULITZER PRIZE FINALIST. Tramping through Great Falls, the *Trib* bag knotted over his shoulder, the smell of crisp editions, newsprint blackening his hands with each paper he'd deliver. Dreaming under the Big Sky of being a big city crime reporter. Some of the happiest days of his life.

There was the old snapshot of a younger Tom in front of the Golden Gate Bridge with the gang from AP's San Francisco Bureau. The Associated Press was his first major job in the business after college where he'd met Ann. They got married and moved to San Francisco where she started her first children's clothing store and he started with AP. It was where his reporting on West Coast crime networks earned him a little glory as a Pulitzer finalist.

Then the *Star* hired him.

It was funny. In the last few years Tom had reduced his inventory of treasured tearsheets. Gone were the grisly front-page stories he'd displayed like blood-dripping trophies. He no longer needed the validation. His success at covering tragedies had bestowed him with its own honors: the healed scars of a fractured marriage and a craving for Jack Daniel's whiskey whenever a trip into the abyss overwhelmed him.

During his worst time Ann had begged him to quit news reporting, stay home, and write books. But he couldn't quit. Ever. Yes, his job had exacted a toll on his family. But over the roller-coaster years since he'd become the *Star*'s chief crime features writer he'd gotten a handle on his life. He'd broken a succession of major exclusives. Most drew national recognition for the paper. He was good. Once he locked on to a story he was relentless. It was in his blood. Being a crime reporter was what he'd dreamed of doing since he was a kid delivering newspapers in Great Falls.

"Still there?"

"Still here."

"That 187 in the Clayton and Short area is a homicide at the home of an SFPD officer."

"What?"

"You heard me. Here's the address."

"Is the officer the victim or the suspect?"

"Victim."

"Who is it?"

"That's all you get from me. I advise you to get over there. It's getting old. Every news team in town has been there for hours."

Tom slammed down his phone, turned, and saw Pepper headed his way.

"That 187 is a police officer murdered in his home in Upper Market. We missed it. Everyone's there but us. I'm on my way."

Tom thrust the managing editor's memo into Irene's hands. Her face reddened as she folded it.

"It's early," she said. "Lots of time to catch up."

Tom's cold stare threatened to rip open old wounds from ancient battles with Pepper but he didn't have the desire or the time to get into it now.

"A murdered cop," she said. "What else do you know?"

"That's it right now. Since we're behind I could use some help."

"This is sensational. *Simon!*" Pepper waved another reporter over. "We need to be strong on this story, it'll be huge. People will eat this up. Who's the victim? Any other details?"

"Nothing yet. Where's Molly?"

"I don't know. You go. I want you on this."

Simon Lepp, the paper's science writer, joined them at Tom's desk.

"I'm putting you on a breaking murder story with Tom. You're going to learn from our master crime specialist."

"All right."

"Your job is to guarantee the *Star* owns this story. You do whatever Tom needs to make it happen. I'll put more bodies on it. But you're both on this murder until I take you off. Got it?"

"Sure." Lepp nudged his round rimless glasses as Pepper strutted away.

Tom shook his head, struggling to find a fresh notebook while concealing his disgust at the whole thing. And why assign Lepp to this story? No offense but he'd prefer a seasoned crime reporter like Molly or Della Thompson.

Lepp was a soft-spoken bookish type who'd covered the science beat for years. He'd never touched a crime story. The guy seldom left his cubicle way off in a far-flung corner. The thing was almost overrun with Boston ferns and spider plants. He was bright. His family had moved around a lot when he was a kid. His father had been some kind of research genius. Lepp had won a slew of awards for producing page-eating eye-glazers about things only Nobel winners at Berkeley and Stanford understood.

"You sure you want to do this?" Tom asked.

"I'm sure. I've become a little bored with science. I've watched what you and Molly do. I told Irene I thought a switch to breaking crime news would be exciting."

Tom looked at him. No one else was available to help at the moment.

"Want me to deputize you?"

"Just tell me what to do."

After making a few quick calls, Tom jotted details on a page in his notebook, then tore it off. "There's a press conference at ten-thirty at the Hall of Justice, police commission room. You go to that. As soon as they release a name get the library to search for stories on any cases the dead cop may have handled. Track down the victim's detail, or district, academy buddies, search the newsletters, call POA and OCC."

"POA and OCC?"

"Police Officers Association. You've got time to swing by there before the newser. They may know about the victim and friends. OCC, the Office of Citizens' Complaints, may know of any beefs against the cop. Get them to speculate on whether it could be linked to anything. We'll get our court guys to ask about cases too. We'll cast out a wide net and see what we get."

Tom reached for his jacket just as his desk phone began ringing.

"Right, that's good. Where're you headed?"

"I'll poke around here and there with sources. You go ahead without me. Make sure your cell phone's on."

Tom reached for his phone hoping it was Sydowski. If anyone had data on this thing, it would be him.

"Hey, Reed," Vickson said. "All I've heard is the dead guy's an inspector. A detective."

"An inspector. Which detail?"

"Don't know."

"Thanks." Tom gulped the last of his coffee, slipped on his jacket, then headed for the news reception area. The switchboard was ringing as the elevator doors opened.

"Tom," Tammy, the receptionist, said. "You've got a call."

"I have to go."

"Hang on," she said into the phone. "Tom, it's Molly."

"I'll take it." Tammy passed the phone to Tom. "Molly, where are you?"

"The Hall of Justice. Homicide."

"You're on this? You're covering the story?"

"No." She choked on a sob. "Tom, can you come and get me, please?"

"What's going on?"

"It's Cliff."

"What do you mean?"

The elevator bell chimed. Tom felt something brush his arm.

"Cliff Hooper. He's dead. I'm the one who found him."

A homicide detective. Molly's boyfriend. Tom struggled to grasp it.

A delivery of flowers came to reception.

"Okay, Molly, hang on. I'm on my way."

Tom passed the phone back to Tammy, who was smiling at the spectacular arrangement of white roses.

"Aren't these lovely?" she said to the deliveryman. "Who're they for?"

"Says here, Molly Wilson."

4

The Hall of Justice is a grim Stalinesque building rising from Bryant Street amid the low-rent units, office towers, and struggling high-tech firms in San Francisco's Soma District. It houses the D.A.'s office, courtrooms, jails, and the headquarters of the San Francisco Police Department. It is also the home of punishment, or righteous wrath, depending on your bank account, Tom thought after parking.

He hustled up the steps of the Hall's grand entrance to the polished stone lobby for a security check and a walk through a metal detector. Riding the elevator to the fourth floor and room 450, the homicide detail, Tom recalled Cliff Hooper. He'd met him at murder scenes, even hunched over a few late night coffees with him. Hooper was a former wide receiver for San Jose State who'd studied philosophy and law. A good guy. A smart, honest homicide cop. Molly's boyfriend.

Who'd want him dead?

Stepping from the elevator, Tom saw a deputy chief go down the crowded corridor to the detail. He followed him, threading his way through the detectives and uniformed officers, bumping into handcuffs and holstered guns. Keeping his head down, he moved respectfully, for he'd now entered a hallowed zone: cop land in mourning.

Inside, Linda Turgeon was consulting a report with a huge detective. No sign of Molly. Craning his neck, Tom glimpsed Hooper's partner, Ray Beamon, sitting at his desk across from the empty one that was Hooper's. High-ranking officers circled him. Upon seeing Tom, Turgeon seized his arm. "Out. Press conference in thirty minutes."

"I'm looking for Molly."

Emerging from an office with a report in his hand, Sydowski caught what was happening. "I'll take care of this."

Lieutenant Leo Gonzales stepped from his office, head in a file, approaching Sydowski: ". . . just heard that ballistics is having a little computer trouble and will need more time and Crime Scene is —"

"Hold on, Leo," Sydowski said. "Come with me, Tom. I want to talk with you." He took Tom down the hallway. "Molly's with a crisis worker."

"I'm sorry about Cliff."

Sydowski nodded.

"How's Ray Beamon doing?"

Sydowski deflected his question with another.

"How's your wife doing?"

"Ann? Oh, her sessions are helping." Ann had been the victim of a terrifying abduction not so long ago, and the repercussions were still being felt.

"It takes time."

Neither of them said anything more until they came to a room where Molly was at a table with a middle-aged woman clutching a crumpled tissue. Two ceramic mugs sat untouched between them.

"Hi." Molly sounded far away.

"Thanks, Fran," Sydowski said.

Taking her cue, the woman left her card. "Remember, you call me anytime, dear. Doesn't matter. Anytime."

"Thank you."

Tom embraced Molly.

"It's going to be all right," he told her. "Just hang on."

She nodded as Sydowski lowered himself into a swivel chair. Like her, he hadn't yet slept. "Everyone's hurting but what I'm going to tell you is critical." Sydowski paused to hold Tom in his stare. "We know Molly was close to Cliff and she's your friend."

Tom searched her eyes for any signal.

"Look at me. This is critical," Sydowski said. "She found him, you're both reporters. She knows things you'll want to report."

"What are you getting at? Censorship? Muzzling me?"

"I'm asking you to exercise judgment here."

"I'm going to write what I know. It's my right."

Sydowski's gold fillings glinted as he winced. "That's just what I'm getting at."

"I'm sorry for everyone's loss here. I know this hits us both hard, your squad and my newsroom, but I can't give you special treatment."

"That's not what I'm asking."

"And I can't afford to get beat on this."

"Give me a break," Sydowski said.

"All right, all right. How about we 'cooperate' where we can? Given the *Star*'s connection here?"

"I won't make any deals with you. I never have."

"But things have worked for us before."

"I've got concerns about this one."

"What is it?"

"He doesn't —" Molly interjected. "He would like us to be careful about not releasing details about the items I saw or how they were arranged."

Items? Tom felt ice roll up his spine. "What items? Is this a ritual?"

"Just listen," Sydowski said. "We can't let details out. We've got to hold back. Molly's going to hold back. I'm asking you not to make this any more difficult than it is."

Tom looked at Molly as Sydowski continued.

"If you weaken the case with your re-

34

porting it could reduce our chances of an arrest, let alone endangering prosecution down the road. Understand?"

"My job is not to make yours easier. That's what you always tell me."

"You of all people know how critical this is right now."

Tom's focus bounced between Molly and Sydowski.

"We'll work things out as we go," Tom said.

"I've got your word?"

"You've got my word we'll work things out."

"All right. Take Molly home. There's a news conference set for the Police Commission Hearing Room in fifteen minutes."

"You got a suspect or recover a weapon?"

"It's too soon. Take Molly home."

Before they took the elevator down, Ray Beamon caught up with them in the corridor. Although Beamon had joined the detail a few years ago, the others considered him the rookie. His hair was messed. Lines of anguish were carved into his face.

"Molly." His red-rimmed eyes found hers. "If you remember anything —"

"It's okay. I told her," Sydowski said.

"He was my partner, you know."

Molly gave Beamon a hug.

"He thought the world of you," she said before stepping into the elevator with Tom.

During the ride down she put her head on Tom's shoulder. He put his arm around her, smelling traces of perfume in her hair.

When the doors opened Simon Lepp stood before them.

"Hey, guys, what's going on?"

"I'm taking her home," Tom said. "You've got the news conference."

"Yes, but what's going on?"

"This isn't a good time," Tom said as they headed for the door.

"Wait! Do you have a minute?"

"I'm sorry," she said. "I can't talk now."

Lepp walked with them. "They're saying you knew him."

Tom and Molly stopped.

"Before I came here," Lepp said, touching his glasses, "I swung by the scene. The TV people and a guy from the *Chron* are floating the rumor he was a detective. Some were saying you're the one who found him. That he's the cop you were dating."

Tom and Molly exchanged glances.

"Holy cow," Lepp said. "It's true. That's why you're here."

"We can't say anything right now," Tom said.

"We work for the same paper, don't we?"

"It's complicated right now. I'll catch up with you later," Tom said.

Molly nodded to a KGO-TV crew that had its camera trained on them.

"We have to go," Tom said.

"Wait." Lepp's face was filled with concern for Molly. "It must've been horrible, finding him. I mean, I just cannot imagine." He touched her shoulder. "Are you going to be okay?"

She closed her eyes and shook her head.

"We have to go," Tom said.

Molly lived alone on the top-floor apartment of a restored Victorian mansion at the edge of Russian Hill. It had a view of the bay and Golden Gate Bridge.

"I need a hot shower, then we'll talk," she told Tom. "Help yourself to anything. Let the machine get any calls."

Ever since she was hired from a small Texas daily, Molly had been Tom's partner at the *Star*. They sat next to each other, worked with each other, knew the details of each other's lives. She had a master's degree in English literature and was an outstanding writer and reporter.

Tom had first become her mentor, then her friend and confidant. During his darkest drinking days when Ann took Zach and moved out, Molly made no secret of her willingness to help him through his nights. That was long ago. He never acted on it. Instead, he repaired his life and his marriage while managing to keep his friendship with Molly intact.

He dropped his notebook on her kitchen table. Strange he thought, gazing at the bay. They'd been through so many stories together, nightmares that turned their world inside out. Now this one. Man, it was brand-new territory. He took in her living room, the bookshelves with the framed picture of Molly standing between her mother and father, clutching her degree. There was a plaque for her Texas statewide creative writing award, a framed print of her first front-page newspaper story, a feature on a blind farmer. Then a small photograph of her between Cliff Hooper and his partner, Ray Beamon. The *Star* would kill for that one, he thought as it hit him full force.

This was a murder among friends.

5

After a few hours of sleep and refueling on coffees from a McDonald's drive-through, Sydowski and Turgeon guided their unmarked Impala back to Hooper's neighborhood for more legwork.

They came to an uphill house overlooking Hooper's staircase, the sixteenth address on the list. The woman who answered the door was Dora Mahoney, a sixty-nine-year-old retired high school history teacher who said well, yes, come to think of it, maybe she did see something last night.

"I'm pretty sure I saw a man leaving the apartment. I'll show you."

Dora led them through her home to French doors that opened to a rear balcony. It offered a stunning view from her terraced yard. In the distance, over a thick hedge, a stand of eucalyptus trees framed Hooper's building and the stairway to his upper apartment.

"It was dusk. I saw a man going down those stairs."

"Describe him, please." Sydowski pulled out his notebook. And as her cat threaded its way around his ankles, he took down every detail he could squeeze from Dora.

A white man. In his thirties. Wearing a T-shirt and jeans.

It wasn't much but it was something, Sydowski told Gonzales when they returned to the homicide detail.

"All right. Good."

"Hear from Crime Scene or the M.E. yet?" Sydowski asked.

"Not yet."

"Where's Ray, I want to talk to him."

"I sent him out. Would you step into my office now?"

His tone alerted Sydowski. Whoever was in his lieutenant's office was going to make for an unpleasant meeting. He popped a Tums in his mouth and rolled up his sleeves.

"You know Ms. Sareena Fortune with the Office of Citizens' Complaints."

She was a civil rights attorney. Wore an expensive tailored power suit. Had hair styled like Cleopatra.

"My condolences, Inspector."

"And Dan Taylor, with Management Control."

"Everyone sends their best," Taylor said.

As he shook hands, Sydowski's guard went up at the presence of Fortune with Taylor, the SFPD's assassin who probed internal affairs. Taylor practically worked foot in boot with OCC, to plant it on the neck of most

40

cops who failed to say "have a nice day" while arresting psychos who tried to kill them. Sydowski grinded on his Tums.

Fortune said, "Inspector, it's no secret the department and OCC have been at odds lately." Fortune picked a thread from her suit. "I thought this was a critical time for my office to show its support and pay respects to the people who risk their lives every day for this city."

"And here I was afraid I'd misread this as OCC trying to exert some warped sense of its mission that might be defined as obstruction," Sydowski said.

"Walt," Gonzales warned.

"Did some sewer dweller complain already? Or are you just hopeful?"

"Walt."

"It's a little early to get in my face. Cliff's not even in the ground yet."

"Inspector," Fortune said, "you're taking this the wrong way. This is a visit of compassion."

"Ms. Fortune," Sydowski said, "do you personally, or does your office, have any information that has a direct bearing on the homicide of SFPD Homicide Inspector Clifford Hooper?"

"No, Inspector."

"Does OCC have any blue folders that relate to, or could in any remote way be material to, the homicide of Inspector Hooper?"

41

"None." Fortune smoothed her skirt.

"Thank you for your heartfelt support," Sydowski said. "Dan, does MCU have anything to offer us on this case?"

Taylor held up an SFPD personnel folder.

"This is Hooper's file. That's the extent of what I'm here for."

Fortune stood, indicating they'd finished.

"Again, our sympathies. Lieutenant. Inspector," Fortune said before she left with Taylor.

Gonzales closed the door behind them. Sydowski shook his head. "What in the hell was that?"

Gonzales leaned back in his chair, his weary eyes going round his cramped office to the file cabinets, vacation and duty schedules, the bookshelf jammed with departmental regs, the Penal Code, California statutes, then his poster of the Rockies.

"It's politics and bullshit," Gonzales said. "Plain and simple. A detective is murdered. It sets the stage for agendas, so the watchdogs come out. Automatically smell corruption. They figure Cliff *had* to be doing something wrong to just go out and die like that." Gonzales gritted his teeth and looked at the mountains.

"Well, if they know something we don't they'd better damn well tell us." Sydowski turned the pages of Hooper's file. " 'Cause there's nothing in here. He was in Narcotics,

42

Vice, the tac team, worked in Taraval, Mission, Ingleside, the Loin, before coming here. Spotless record. By all accounts, he was outstanding."

"He was." Gonzales blinked. "Now you know why I sent Ray out. It would have been a bad scene with him."

Getting back to work, Sydowski slapped Hooper's file on his desk. Turgeon was on her phone, taking notes. Sydowski was helping himself to coffee when Beamon returned.

"How you doing?" Sydowski asked.

Beamon hesitated for a beat as the older detective looked into his bloodshot eyes. The guy was a mess. Gonzales had ordered him off the case and called the staff psychologist, but Beamon had put off talking to her.

"I had to step out to take care of some things. I talked to Cliff's sister."

"How'd that go?"

"She's taking it hard. She's all the family he had. She's a paramedic. On her way up from Los Angeles with her husband to make arrangements as soon as the M.E. releases the body."

"Shouldn't be too much longer. What'd you do to your fingers?"

Beamon was rubbing the knuckles of his right hand, feeling Sydowski's attention on them.

"This? Oh, I was working on my car."

"Your Barracuda?"

"Yes. Changing the plugs. I must've skinned 'em. Funny. I was going to drive over and see him last night. But I stayed home."

"You didn't see him after your shift?"

"I never left my house."

"Look. I know you want to help us."

"I want to find the mother who —"

"All right. Take it easy," Sydowski said. "I saw you last night after you'd finished. You ran after Cliff, chased after him to the elevator."

Beamon listened for a question.

"What was that about?"

"I just wanted to see if he was up for a beer."

Sydowski's eyes traveled all over Beamon, absorbing his body language and his eyes.

"What was Cliff's demeanor like?"

Beamon shrugged and said it was fine.

"I noticed you were in the hall for a minute or two. What did you and Cliff talk about?"

"What did we talk about?"

"Yes. Your last conversation with him. What did he say? What was on his mind when he left the detail last night?"

"He was going out with Molly. That's why he didn't have time for a beer."

"That it? That's all you talked about? He didn't mention any problems, or beefs with anybody?"

"No. I just don't know who or why anyone would do this."

Sydowski stared at Beamon.

"It might be better if you took some time off."

"No, I just can't."

"Okay, why don't you go back over all your cases? Think of anyone you took down who had it in for Hoop. Anybody who made threats, anybody who wanted to take a run at you. Think you can do that?"

Beamon nodded.

Sydowski stood to his full height, drawing himself up until his shadow fell over Beamon. "And you better damned well tell me now if Cliff was into anything."

"What do you mean?"

"You know what I mean. No one was tighter to him than you and Molly Wilson, so if you know something you damn well tell me now, because I'm going to find out. I usually do, Ray."

"Jesus. You know that Cliff was a Boy Scout," he said. "And I —"

Sydowski tuned his radar to its maximum and wouldn't release Beamon from his concentration, taking in his face, his bruised knuckles. "Want to go in an interview room and tell me what's on your mind?"

"No, it's not that. It's —" Beamon looked at Hooper's empty desk and chair, the notes Hooper had scribbled on his calendar about court dates, 49er games. "It's like, this didn't happen. This isn't real . . ."

Sydowski let the silence play for a while, giving Beamon the chance to fill it. Finally, he placed his hand on Beamon's shoulder. "If you want to tell me something, you call me. Anytime. Understand?"

"Yes."

"Excuse me." Turgeon finished her call and indicated she needed a private moment. They went downstairs to the cafeteria where she opened her notebook.

"I spoke with the M.E., Crime Scene, and Ballistics. The full autopsy will be completed tomorrow, that's when they'll recover any rounds from the body."

"What about the round in the wall?"

"They got that but it's badly damaged," Turgeon said. "They need more time. All they can confirm at this stage is that it's a .40 cal."

"A .40?" Sydowski repeated.

Worry crept into the corners of Turgeon's eyes and she lowered her voice to a whisper. "Not just a .40. It looks like it could be an SXT Talon, 180-grain. The exact type issued to every cop on the force."

6

It was late afternoon when Tom left Molly's apartment and returned to the *San Francisco Star.*

The newsroom was humming.

He enjoyed a small private victory. An intern was now fused to the police radios. *That's better,* he thought. Editors and reporters were working at their keyboards or taking notes over the phone while news flickered from TVs on overhead shelves, harmonizing with clatter as the first deadline loomed, along with Irene Pepper.

She was making her rounds, clipboard in hand, gathering story updates for the editors' news meeting to decide tomorrow's edition. Spotting Tom, she raised her taut chin, signaling that she was still smarting from their episode over the scanners.

"What've you got?"

"I spoke to Molly."

"Good. I've been trying to reach her. How's she doing?"

"She's shaken up pretty good. I took her home."

"I'll call her later."

"Meeting!" the deputy managing editor called from the boardroom doorway. Pepper glanced at a newsroom clock.

"I don't have much time. So fill me in."

"I interviewed her. It's an exclusive."

"She give you a lot of detail?"

"I got mostly color and time line. She couldn't provide a lot of details."

"Why not? She's the one who found him, according to Simon."

"That's true but as you can imagine, she's pretty shaken up."

Pepper frowned.

"But what I have is good," Tom said. "It's really good. And it's all ours."

"They have any suspects?"

"It's too soon."

"Motive?"

"Again, too soon."

"What about old enemies?"

"It's early in the investigation. They're pretty tight-lipped."

"Can you get someone to speculate in print as to who would want to kill a homicide detective in his home?"

"Sure, but speculation's meaningless."

"Readers love to play amateur detective."

"I know some profs at Berkeley who could do some psychological profiling."

"Good." Pepper glanced at her notes. "We've got a pretty strong package coming. Simon Lepp's got a bio on Hooper that looks really nice. We've got a Winston Jones column coming and Della's doing Bay Area cop killings. Mickey Chang got some nice shots of you and Molly leaving the Hall of Justice. Henry Cain has some great crime scene art."

Pepper waved to acknowledge the impatient deputy managing editor who was gesturing for other editors to move more quickly to the meeting room.

"Tom," she said, "I want you to think about an idea I have for Molly."

His stomach began to tighten.

"Did she go to pieces? Or can she write a story for me?"

"You want a story from *her?*"

"A first-person account, taking us into the cop's death house."

"Meeting!" the deputy managing editor called from the boardroom doorway.

"She's in no shape to do that for you today."

"No. Not today. But soon."

"I don't know."

"This is the biggest story in the state right now, we own it, and I'll be damned if we're going to blow it." Pepper checked her watch.

At that moment Violet Stewart, the managing editor, interrupted them on her way to the meeting. "Excuse me, Irene." Stewart turned to Tom. "I heard how you recovered our fumble on the detective murder. Nice work."

"Thanks."

Before leaving them, Stewart shot a cool glance at Pepper, who responded to her supervisor with an equally cool smile.

After Stewart was out of earshot, Pepper said to Tom, "I want Molly to do a first-person feature."

"I think you're overcompensating for us missing the jump on the story."

"Watch it, Tom. Just remember to inject your piece with emotion."

"Emotion."

"Make readers feel something," Pepper said. "Put them in her footsteps when she makes her sensational discovery. Take them where the competition can't. Give me every minute detail. Make my hair stand on end. Got it?"

Tom nodded and went to his desk where he loosened his tie and went to work crafting a lead. The minutes ticked by as he carved out the first sentences. He paused to consider them along with Molly's empty desk and the bouquet that had arrived that morning. Letters and gifts were common in the newsroom and Molly received more than her share — Tom assumed because of her great looks and regular TV spot. But these flowers were unusually gorgeous and expensive for your run-of-the-mill reporter groupie. Where did they

come from? he wondered, just as his computer beeped with a story sent to him from
Simon Lepp.

A cradle-to-grave 1,200-word obit-bio on
Hooper. It had tributes from academy buddies,
guys who'd played football with him at San
Jose State, Hooper's sister, and a high school
teacher. It even included his hobby of collecting Civil War postage stamps and his
shooting score at the range. It wasn't bad,
Tom thought, as Lepp stopped at his desk.

"Irene said to send you a copy, so you
could pull what you like for your piece."

"It's good, thanks. I'm sorry we brushed you
off at the Hall earlier. It was crazy, you know."

"How's Molly doing?" Lepp slipped on his
jacket.

"Well, she's pretty tough."

"It's terrible what's happened to her, but
she'll survive it."

"Hope so."

"You two are pretty close, huh?" Lepp adjusted his tie.

"Yeah, we're good friends. We've been
through a lot on this beat. She's a good reporter."

Lepp nodded, nudged his glasses while
taking stock of Molly's desk.

"Didn't you guys date for a bit?" Tom
asked.

Lepp's face flushed, and he smiled as he
looked off self-consciously.

"Yeah. It was a long time ago. We went out several times. She was so nice. It was fun." He shrugged.

"She's dated a lot of guys. But I thought she was getting serious about Hooper. They'd been going out for a few months, but in all the time I've known her I don't think she was ever as serious about anyone."

"I guess that's what makes this so tragic."

Tom nodded until something occurred to him.

"There's a group from the paper going to see her shortly." Tom wrote Molly's address on a clear notebook page.

"Thanks. I'll be over to offer my condolences, see how she's doing."

Tom resumed writing, incorporating a few lines of Lepp's material into his piece. Then he came to the point in his story where Molly had entered Hooper's bedroom. She'd said she'd found items placed in a certain way. *What were those items?* She'd refused to tell him. Didn't want to jeopardize the investigation.

"Hey, big guy, you'd better hurry up and file."

Della Thompson stopped to smell the flowers on Molly's desk. She was one of Molly's closest friends. Grew up in Sunnydale where she'd helped raise her little brother after her father walked out on her sick mother. Della had worked as a waitress and a UPI stringer to put herself through college before becoming one of the *Star*'s best reporters.

"Irene said to send you my stuff."

"Got it. Thanks."

The history of Bay Area cop deaths. It started with the case before Hooper. The cop who was killed during a jewel heist in the Richmond District several months ago. That one was still fresh in Tom's mind.

"Who sent Molly these roses?" she asked.

"Don't know. They came this morning as I was heading out."

"This morning? That was early." She hunted for a card. "I'm going over to Molly's now with Carmine. You coming?"

"I've got to finish this. Maybe I'll catch up."

"All right." She collected the flowers. "We'll bring these with us."

It took nearly an hour before Tom wrote the last sentence and sent the story to the metro desk editing queue, minutes under the first edition deadline. The night editor asked him to stick around in case they had any questions. Standing to stretch, he spotted the small card that had accompanied Molly's flowers and retrieved it from the carpet. He looked at the little envelope, contemplating his temptation to open it.

Finally, he decided he'd give it to Molly later.

Unopened.

7

"Even if it turns out we pried an SXT Talon from Hooper's wall, it doesn't mean a whole hell of a lot right now," Sydowski said. "It's a commercial caliber, not exclusive to the SFPD. If that's what you're thinking."

"To be honest, I don't know what I'm thinking anymore. It's nearly three-thirty in the friggin' morning."

Turgeon dropped off Sydowski at his home in Parkside after a futile night of recanvassing in Hooper's neighborhood.

Might as well look in on the birds. Sydowski headed for the aviary he'd built under the creaking oak tree in his backyard. His grandchildren loved how it looked like a tiny cottage from a fairy tale. His late wife had made the curtains. Twenty-five years ago, a friend had given them a singing finch, which eventually led to Sydowski's love for breeding and showing the birds.

He flipped on a soft light to check the water and seed supply of his newest fledglings. Fife fancies, less than two weeks old, about the size of a baby's thumb. He was optimistic for this group. He didn't like the trend toward gargantuan budgerigars. He was a traditionalist who favored graceful, tiny treasures, classic original border canaries. Everything looked good.

He deposited himself into his recliner to rest amid the tranquility. He always found comfort here where the velvety cooing soothed him while he analyzed his darkest cases.

Like this one.

Sydowski remembered the time Hooper had accepted a rare invitation into his aviary after a Niners game. "This is your little fortress of solitude." Hoop slapped him on the back. "I always knew you were Superman."

This case hit him in the heart. And with OCC and Management Control perched like vultures on his shoulder, Sydowski, for the first time, didn't know if he had the strength for this battle.

"I always knew you were Superman."

Nothing ever remained the same. Time was a thief, stealing everything sweet in his life. The girls had moved away. Basha was gone. His old man was in death's grasp. Now Hooper. He was too tired to even dream of happier times.

A few hours later, he was at the Hall of Justice, in the medical examiner's autopsy room. Clifford James Hooper's naked corpse lay on a stainless steel table. His clothing had been examined, his body had been weighed, measured, and X-rayed prior to the procedure.

Male. White. Six feet one inch. One hundred eighty pounds. Forty-one years old.

In San Francisco, homicide detectives were not required to witness an autopsy. But Sydowski's reputation for thoroughness usually meant watching, if it was his case. He and Turgeon said little as Julius Seaver, the forensic pathologist, performed the procedure.

Right off, the autopsy yielded a revelation. There was a large contusion on Hooper's lower left jaw. Given the body's posture, the detectives wouldn't have spotted it at the scene, Seaver said.

On Hooper's right side, Seaver began examining the bullet's entry into the head. He noted that the star-patterned contact wound had seared into Hooper's right temple. Then he started his bone-cutting saw and opened Hooper's skull to track the course of the bullet and retrieve it. It took several moments before Seaver located the spent round. It had not been damaged much and clinked like a coin when he dropped it in the stainless steel tray.

Sydowski never liked the autopsies. Maybe it was the chilled room, or the overwhelming smells of formaldehyde, ammonia, the eggy odor of organs, their shades of red and pink, or the pop when the calvarium was taken, opening the skull to reveal the brain and dura, or seeing the primary Y incision across the chest, as the pathologist worked through the examination of the body.

Sydowski knew autopsies were critical. He just never liked them. Later, when the procedure was completed, they all met in Seaver's office, where he set the bullet in its plastic evidence bag on his desk.

"Looks like a .40 cal. A Talon," he said.

"Like the one Crime Scene dug out of the wall," Turgeon noted. "What can you tell us?"

"The victim died of a single gunshot wound to the head. No other gunshot wounds, defensive wounds. Nothing."

"Except for the bruise on his jaw," Sydowski said.

"Correct." Seaver checked his notes, then entered and retrieved data from his computer. "The contusion would be consistent with someone punching him."

"There was a fight?"

"Well, there were no defensive wounds. No scarring on his knuckles."

"Sucker punch?"

Seaver shrugged. "The contusion appears to have been recent and could easily fall within time of death."

"Can you give us more?"

"Theoretically the bruise on his jaw would fit with a right-handed person slugging him, like this." Seaver closed his right hand into a fist and touched it to Sydowski's left jaw. "It's conceivable the person who hit him would have bruised or scraped knuckles."

Like Ray Beamon, Sydowski thought.

8

In the moments before she woke, Molly struggled between consciousness and her lingering nightmare that Cliff had been murdered.

Only a bad dream, she told herself until reality seized her from the fading darkness and forced her eyes open. She was in a field of white crumpled tissues. Dozens. Like headstones in a cemetery. This was no dream. It was true. Cliff was dead. The images of his apartment swirled. She struggled to keep from screaming.

It's real.

Through her bedroom doorway she focused on her living room sofa bed, unfolded, covered by a thick comforter with Della Thompson's hair spilling from the top.

"No use in arguing. I'm not letting you face this alone," Thompson had said last night as Molly assured her friends she'd be okay after they left.

It was a lie and she was glad Thompson had stayed. You could count on that girl, she thought, pulling on her robe, padding to her bathroom, then to her kitchen to make morning tea.

Molly tried to remember the last words Hooper had spoken to her, but it hurt because she must've loved him in some way. Her thoughts drifted to the distant spires of the Golden Gate, the twinkling red and white lights of its early morning traffic. As the kettle boiled she ached to be in someone else's skin.

She summoned the courage to go to her door for the *Chronicle* and the *Star*. She glanced at their front pages. Cliff's murder was the lead story. She touched her fingers to Hooper's smiling face. Setting the papers on the coffee table, she slid into her favorite chair and pulled her knees to her chest, sipped her tea and tried not to think of anything.

"How you holding up, hon?" Thompson said from under the blanket.

"I don't know. I made tea for you."

"Thanks. You feel like talking?"

"I'm just numb. It doesn't feel real."

"Yolanda from Human Resources told me to tell you that they can set you up with a shrink if you want. Want me to call her?"

"I don't know. Maybe. Hold off. I don't know."

The two women sat in silence with their tea. It was calming. Thompson examined the *Star*'s front page.

"You know, Irene was leaning all over Tom to torque his story right up to final deadline, saying how she wanted the paper to own it because of your connection to Cliff."

Molly changed the subject.

"I think I want to go for my morning run."

"It wouldn't be against the rules to miss today."

"No, I need to run. I think it will help."

"Want company?"

"No, thanks. You've been great pulling duty like this, giving me a shoulder. I'll go alone."

"You sure you're good with that? I mean feeling safe and all?"

"It's my neighborhood. It's practically full light, I'll be damned if I let whoever did this take everything from me." Molly stood to go change when a sob exploded from her, doubling her. Thompson caught her.

"Oh God," Molly gasped. "I just can't believe it. It was horrible."

"Hang on." Thompson held her tight.

"It was so cold-blooded and Cliff was such a good man. A decent man. I don't understand."

"I know."

"And the way I found him. Why? Who would do this? *Why?*"

"It makes no sense."

"And it all happens just when I —" Molly stopped herself.

"What? It all happens just when you what?" Thompson asked.

Molly shook it off, regained her composure. "I should run. I need to run."

"All right."

"Would you do me a favor?"

"Name it."

"Stay here, until I get back, see how I'm
doing?"

"Sure."

Molly left Thompson to digest the papers
and catch the breakfast newscasts. By the
time she emerged in her jogging clothes,
Thompson had finished reading the *Star*'s
stories on Hooper.

"Tom did a nice job."

"I have to go," Molly said, collecting her
keys, heading for her door just as her phone
rang.

"I'll screen it for you," Thompson said.
"It's probably a reporter."

"Hello . . . yes . . ." She covered the
mouthpiece. "It's Cliff's sister, you want to
take it?"

She took it in her bedroom.

"This is Molly."

"I'm sorry for calling so early. I've been up
most of the night."

"Me too." Molly had never met Hooper's
sister, Andrea Carroway. She lived in
southern California. "Are you in San Francisco, Andrea? Would you like to get together?"

"We're downtown, at a hotel. Gosh, I don't

62

even know the name. Molly, I'm calling because the medical examiner is supposed to release him to the funeral home here this afternoon. I would like it if you would help us with arrangements later today."

"Me?"

"His partner is joining us. You know Ray?"

Molly squeezed the phone. "Yes. I know Ray."

"I don't mean to put you on the spot, it's a difficult time for all of us," Andrea said. "We would like it if you'd consider saying something at his eulogy."

"Of course I'll help. Please give me the time and place where I can meet you."

Andrea gave her the information, then before ending the call she said, "Molly, I was talking to him on the phone a few days ago. He always talked about you. I know he loved you. You made him happy. So happy."

She squeezed her eyes shut.

Why, why, why did this happen? Molly asked the sky as she ran through the steep streets of Telegraph Hill, her feet pounding in time with the clanging of the cable cars. Gulls cried as she weaved through her neighborhood, drinking in the bay views, inhaling the morning air, taking stock.

Dear God.

Who would do this to Hooper? Commit such a cold-blooded act. Such an outrage.

Anger shuddered through her as her feet hammered the street. He was executed in his home. His gun and wallet displayed like some sort of twisted victory memorial.

The story stared back at her from the newspaper boxes she passed. Like a Greek chorus. Sydowski had to hunt the animal down and bring him to justice. Emotions swirled through her. Hooper was her boyfriend. Last week he'd asked her to think about moving in with him.

"Just think about it is all I'm saying, Molly."

Why did he have to push it? She liked him. Maybe even loved him. She must've loved him a little. But she wasn't ready to move in with him, or anyone else.

A horn blast pulled her from her thoughts and she veered from a car she hadn't seen while she skirted North Beach. None of that mattered a damn anymore. Molly came within inches of colliding with an elderly Asian woman carrying bags laden with vegetables.

"Sorry."

She kept running, nearly finishing her route, knowing that it was stupid to feel any guilt. Yet she did. Or maybe she felt bad because she was going to end things with Hooper that night. God. She punched at the air, gaining a second wind, driving herself with a ferocity she'd never known.

Yes, she'd wanted to tell him that she

wanted to cool things. See other people. But there was more going on. The truth was she'd already started seeing someone else. *Ray Beamon.*

She'd committed no sin. But now their date, their one date, haunted her and it was all so stupid. Come on. She'd warned Hooper not to expect a serious relationship. And now he was dead. Who the hell did this? Molly covered her face with both hands to keep her fury from escaping.

That's when she noticed it.

The sedan parked down the street. The same one she'd almost stepped into. Had that guy been following her? She stared hard at the car, at the guy behind the wheel. She couldn't make him out. His face was in shadow. He was wearing a ball cap and dark glasses. Who was that? A cop? Molly held her gaze. By his body language he knew she'd made him. A reporter? Sydowski had said there was nothing to indicate she was in danger, but they might ask district people to swing by her address.

This was odd.

Molly had been on the crime beat long enough to sniff out an unmarked police car. She'd settle this right now. She'd get the damn plate. She started toward the vehicle, half a block away. She saw a flash of hands, heard an ignition.

"Hey!" She jogged toward it.

Tires squealed, the car lurched from its spot, pulled a 180-degree turn, then disappeared.

9

The clerk at the twenty-four-hour corner store stared at his early morning customer, thinking how the dude was transfixed by the newspapers he'd just bought. Look at him, just standing there reading.

"Yo, sir?" The clerk scratched his eyebrow, the one pierced with the captive bead ring. "Your change."

"Keep it."

The customer rolled his papers, tucked them under his arm, and left.

His home wasn't far from the store. Sipping take-out coffee, he walked in fear and anticipation. Recent events had unleashed forces beyond his control, propelling him toward the point in his life where soon he'd unmask the truth about himself.

For now, he had work to do.

He quickened his pace until he reached the place where he lived. It was quiet. He liked it here but was prepared to relocate if circumstance compelled him to do so. He was adept at moving fast.

Inside, he kept the curtains drawn, blocking out the sun. He preferred darkness as he sat alone before his television, finishing his coffee by the light of Bay Area morning newscasts. He assessed each paper's reports on Inspector Cliff Hooper's murder. The *Star*'s headline stretched six columns above the fold. HOMICIDE DETECTIVE FOUND SLAIN AT HOME.

Both the *Star* and *Chronicle* had full coverage with front-page reports, keying to more stories and pictures inside. He locked on a photo in the *Star* of Tom Reed with his arm around Molly Wilson at the Hall of Justice.

The veins in his neck spasmed.

Take it easy.

He looked away in time to catch another TV news update on the homicide. This one carried file footage from Vince Vincent's show, *Crime Scene*, and focused on Molly Wilson.

His heart rate ascended.

Molly.

Look at her.

She took his breath away. Her face, her hair, the fragrant softness of her skin, the sound of her voice. The way she moved. Something celestial lit her from within. His stomach knotted whenever he imagined being with her.

Again.

Why had he been condemned to this torment? If only they'd never met. Molly had resurrected an entity he thought he'd entombed years ago in the darkest catacombs

68

of his mind. With her touch she had brought a dangerous ghost to life.

Bleeder.

Go back. Please. There has to be another way. He rubbed his sweating hands on the cushioned arms of his chair. He feared Bleeder. Bleeder controlled him. He struggled but it was futile. *Bleeder, please. Please, Bleeder, stop. There's still time to go back before any more harm is done. Please. After what happened with Amy. All those years ago. You promised you would never come back. Never. I'm begging you to leave, before you make things worse.*

Bleeder cackled from the darkness.

Forget about that old business, sport. Amy was a mistake. Amateur stuff. Still, no one ever found out, did they?

Leave me alone.

Now, Molly. She's different. And I'm wiser.

Shut up.

Look at her. You've never known anyone like her.

Stop.

She's the reason you sent for me. You need me.

That's not true.

Don't lie to me, sport. She's triggered your unfulfilled desires and you will not relent until you possess her totally. That's where I come in.

Stop.

Too late. No turning back now. Look at the news. You've set it all in motion.

No.

Molly's rightfully yours. She stepped into your world just like Amy did. It went bad with Amy. A mistake. But don't worry, we won't let that happen with Molly. I'm back to help you get it right this time. In fact, I'll take over from here.

Bleeder, please, I'm begging you. Don't.

Relax, sport. You do your job. I'll do mine. And nothing will stand in our way. We'll give Molly a little more time to put the pieces together. To realize that what we did to Hooper, we did for her.

She's the prize.

Soon we'll claim her.

10

It was the first bunch of flowers that puzzled Tom.

Those long-stemmed roses for Molly that had arrived in the newsroom the morning after Hooper's murder. He'd practically bumped into the delivery guy at the elevator. If they were sent in condolence, how had they arrived so soon? More flowers came later but that was to be expected. It was a bit strange, he thought, knotting his tie before his bathroom mirror.

What did the card say? *The card.* Where'd he put it? Tom sifted through the closet laundry hamper for the shirt he'd worn yesterday. Looked in the pocket. Not there.

"Dad, check this out." Zach called Tom into his room where a model of U.S.S. *New Jersey* was under construction on his desk. He was impressed with Zach's craftsmanship. No glue blobs anywhere. As Zach got older his work had become flawless. Tom had taught him to use patience with his model building and the pieces would eventually all come together. The way most of his stories did.

"Looking good, son. Real good."

"Do you think you can help me with the superstructure later, Dad?"

"You bet." Tom bent down to examine Zach's neat work on the turrets and guns. He patted Zach's shoulder and his son beamed.

"Tom." Ann approached them from the hallway. She was wearing a tailored suit. He loved how the fine gold necklace he'd given her for their last anniversary looked with her V-neck top. "Phone. It's Irene Pepper." She passed him their cordless. "Zach, honey, go finish your breakfast."

"Hi, Irene," Tom said.

"Nice job on today's piece. Have you seen the paper yet?"

"Not yet." Tom resumed rummaging in a futile search for the card.

"We absolutely killed everybody. Good work. You think Molly might give us a first-person account today?"

"I don't know. It just seems early. Have you talked to her?"

"Just briefly. I never raised the story with her. I was wondering if you, being close to her, would sound her out on it?"

In the silence that followed Tom felt the heat of Pepper's determination to pull a story from Molly. He forced himself to hold his tongue.

"Dad!" Zach called from the kitchen. "You're on TV!"

72

"Irene, can I talk to you when I get in?"

She let a beat pass.

"Fine."

In the kitchen, Tom saw himself on the portable TV on the counter. Zach lifted his face from his cereal bowl and boosted the volume.

"We have to get going, Zach," Ann said from the table where she was going through the morning papers as *Live Action Bay News* broadcast the last of its interview with Tom Reed, senior crime writer, the *San Francisco Star*, according to the graphic under his head.

"And tell us, Tom, do police have any suspects in Inspector Hooper's homicide?"

"No. Not that they're saying. They'll examine everything at the scene, retrace Hooper's final steps —" he said as the item ended.

Zach thudded down the hardwood hallway. Ann collected her keys and her bag. "I tried to call Molly last night," Ann said. "Her line was busy. How do you think she's doing?"

"Holding up, I guess. You know how these things go better than anyone."

She nodded and he stroked her hair. Her color was natural again. Nothing obvious told of the events that had befallen her several months ago. How she'd been out running an errand when, in a heartbeat, she was staring down the barrel of a gun. Ann had been

73

trapped in an armed robbery where a police officer was murdered before her eyes. She was terrorized by his killers. The scar of her experience was not visible. But Tom saw it in her face. Heard it in her voice. She'd changed. Fear now nested in her heart and he did all he could to assure her she was safe.

"It's going to be okay," he said.

"I know."

But Tom saw the concern rising in her eyes.

"Covering crime, getting close to horrible things, it's my job. It's what I do."

"I know. It's fine. I'm okay. Really."

Ann no longer wanted him to quit. She didn't want him to stop being what he was. Her therapy sessions had helped her accept that.

"Ready, Mom." Zach slung his pack over his shoulder, hugged his dad, and thudded to the door.

"Give my love to Molly." She kissed Tom good-bye.

He switched off the set, then made one futile sweep of the house for the card before leaving.

On his way to the *Star*, he decided to swing by Hooper's neighborhood and knock on a few doors.

A retired lawyer was convinced he'd seen a

man leaving the apartment just before Molly found him. "A white man with a dark shirt," he told Tom. But he was unsure of the time. A few doors down a mother with two small children thought she'd seen a white man in a light-colored shirt near Hooper's place.

Tom wasn't sure what to make of it when he got to his desk and began prospecting through his notebooks, newspapers, press statements, and cassette tapes for the card that had accompanied Molly's flowers. He was rifling through it all when Simon Lepp appeared holding a file.

"What've you got there?" Tom asked.

"I was in the news library, going through some of Hooper's cases, then I tried calling around to see if there was any bad blood. It's something worth checking."

"Sure."

"Tell me, do you know if they're going to release what they found at the scene?"

"What do you mean?"

"Trace evidence, anything from the forensic or ballistics report. I know this stuff from the science beat."

"Depends. Usually they hold back on that kind of thing."

"I'm just wondering what motivated this homicide."

"Maybe the guy who killed Hooper is a nut job."

"Could be psychotic. Maybe," Lepp said.

"Maybe not. Could be Hooper's death is related to something entirely different."

"Such as?"

"A message, a lesson? Maybe it was to settle a score."

"A score with who?" Tom said.

"Maybe it's related to one of his old cases." Lepp shrugged.

"Maybe." Tom gave up searching for the card and went to the newsroom kitchen for a coffee. Hank Kruner, a weathered old copy editor who'd worked under Pepper on the national desk, pulled him aside to offer some free advice.

"Heard what happened the other day with you and Pepper and the scanners."

"Did you?"

"Irene hates to be challenged. And you not only challenged her," Kruner said, "you averted a disaster that was her doing. Violet was not pleased about us being so late on that cop murder. You proved Irene wrong. Again. Like you did with your undercover story when she was on national."

Tom nodded.

"Watch your back with her," Kruner said. "Watch it good."

Back at his desk, Tom's line rang. It was Irene Pepper, demanding he come to her office. When he arrived she swiveled in her high-backed chair, tapping her pencil against her nails.

"I'd like to change our approach to the Hooper murder," she said.

"Change it how?"

"You agree this story is huge."

"Absolutely."

"I want you to lead a reporting team on it."

Tom said nothing. Her pencil tapping stopped as she assessed him. "I've recently discovered something about you," she said. He noticed a personnel department folder on her desk. "You're one of the highest paid reporters in the newsroom."

She let the fact hang in the air.

"Well, there's my Pulitzer nomination, the fact that I break national exclusives, and, oh yeah, Violet Stewart gave me a raise so I wouldn't take offers from other papers."

"Ancient history. What've you done lately?"

"I don't know what you're getting at," he said. "Just let me do what I'm paid to do. Let me chase the leads I'm developing on Hooper."

"You have leads? What leads?"

"I've got some calls out. Just let me do what I do best rather than babysit a team. You be the manager. I'll be the reporter."

"All right. Tell you what. I'll cut you loose to chase exclusives, on one condition."

"Which is?"

"Press Molly about that first-person piece. I'm not giving up on that."

Tom eyed her briefly, reining in his distaste before returning to his desk, where he called Molly's apartment.

Della answered.

"How's Molly doing?" he asked.

"She's a bit shaky but functioning."

"Can I talk to her?"

"She's out with Cliff's sister and Ray Beamon picking out a casket."

Tom said nothing.

"You sound funny," Della said. "Is Irene getting to you?"

"Just a little tired of all the BS."

"Aren't we all?"

"Tell me something. Remember when you took the flowers from Molly's desk to her place last night? She ever guess who sent them?"

"Naw. She's been getting so many she can't keep track — you know the D.A., the tactical team, newsroom people, fans. Why do you ask?"

"Something you said got me thinking. The first flowers came so early, like almost instantly."

"Right."

"Who would send her flowers so fast after she'd found Hooper?"

"I agree, they were fast, but someone's got to be first. Besides, who's to say they were about Cliff? Maybe they were for something else. You know, a story. We get that sometimes. Her show with Vince Vincent or something else in her life. I mean, without the card it's hard to say who sent them and for what reason."

"I found the card last night under her desk, but I lost it before I could read it."

"Then it's a mystery. Listen, I'll tell Molly you called. I have to go."

Tom tried to sort out his frustrations. First with Pepper, then over the fact that he'd lost the card. Well, if he was going to work this story, he should track down Sydowski. Standing to leave, he bumped his keyboard and an envelope appeared.

The card.

There it was. A blank envelope. Unsealed. He turned it over in his hand thinking there was no harm in looking. He opened it. The flat, square card inside had an embossed frame and a flowered corner. Written in longhand with a blue pen was the message *I'm thinking of you.*

No signature.

11

A nocturne by Chopin floated through the Chev's six speakers as Linda Turgeon drove them back to Hooper's neighborhood in the rain. Sydowski's gut twisted as he stared at the latest ballistics reports, because the only thing he could see was Beamon's scraped knuckles.

Ray was his suspect.

But Sydowski wasn't prepared to reveal his suspicion to anyone. If Turgeon hadn't come to it already, she would soon enough. Their sworn duty was to gather the evidence for a solid case. And that was what they would do. Problem was, he didn't have a single shred of anything he could use to challenge Ray.

Not yet.

As the car's wipers flapped, Sydowski grinded on a Tums and went back to the reports. They knew Hooper's gun hadn't been fired. And they hadn't found the murder weapon. The bullet pried from Cliff's apartment wall and the bullet recovered from his *hemorrhaged brain* were confirmed as being .40-cal Winchester SXT Talons. The standard issued to all SFPD officers. It was

80

also available to the public.

"What about the lands, grooves, and twists? Were the bullets fired from a .40-cal Beretta?" Turgeon asked.

It was the weapon issued forcewide.

"One of the rounds was badly damaged," Sydowski said. "Ballistics still has more work to do, then there's imaging and the databases to check against other unsolveds. Other pistols besides a Beretta can also fire this kind of bullet."

"Still, your thinking on this is that Cliff knew the shooter."

"He was punched. That's an intimate type of assault."

"Right."

"If he didn't fight back, it fits with the possibility of it being someone he knew. Maybe he tried to talk his way out of it."

"So it's personal."

"And it could be something else entirely."

"Like what?"

"I don't know."

Sydowski said the fact that OCC and Management Control were quick to pounce on Hooper's case troubled him. What did they know about Hooper? Maybe everything. Maybe nothing. If it was an execution, then Hooper had been a threat to someone. Hoop had been a cop long enough to make a lot of people unhappy. But who would be stupid enough to kill him and think they'd get away with it?

Molly had given them the names of old boyfriends, guys she'd dated for a significant time. None of them held any grudges or were the jealous type, she said. Sydowski and Turgeon had confirmed their whereabouts and quickly cleared them.

They retreated into their own thoughts, listening to Chopin, until they arrived in Upper Market. The rain had stopped. Blankets of thick silvery clouds cast a pall over the neighborhood.

The criminalists had called them to the scene.

They headed along the wet sidewalk to Hooper's building and Sydowski pulled together what he knew to walk himself through Hooper's final moments. Hooper had gone home after his day at the detail. He was to meet Molly Wilson later. Neighbors saw his car out front, indicating he was home. They also saw a male, or males, visit. A white man was seen leaving. Fairly linear, so far, Sydowski thought as they passed through the gate and made their way to the rear and up the stairs.

He was waiting for him.

Sydowski climbed the stairs thinking the killer knew Hooper and was waiting for him at the top of the landing. If he didn't know him, would he still go up? Maybe he wasn't threatening? Maybe he pulled a gun and demanded Hooper unlock the door?

No forced entry. No struggle. Hooper let him in, and once inside, the killer disarmed him, then fired a round. It was a warning round, judging from the angle and height, fired at chest-level into the wall, to compel Hooper to do as he was told. Hoop would obey, but he would be cool, thinking, *I can talk my way out of this, or get to my off-duty gun.*

"Hey, Walt." Phibbs with Crime Scene met Sydowski and Turgeon in the kitchen. "The place is clear. We're done with it."

"You've got something?"

"Yes, Finn's got it in the bedroom."

Maybe Hooper was ordered into his bedroom, then onto his bed. The killer was enraged, he could barely wait. Talk was useless. It was quick, he smashed his fist into Hooper's head, or he did it to subdue or confuse him. Then he drew his gun close and fired, causing the star-patterned contact wound on Hooper's temple. Then he set Hooper's weapon and ID on his back.

Mission accomplished.

"Walt?" Turgeon repeated. "You with me?"

"In here," Finn called.

"Sorry." Sydowski followed Turgeon to Finn, who was in a white jumpsuit, into the darkened bedroom where Hooper died.

"All right," Finn began. "I'll bring you up to speed. We're done here, but we followed up on the wall here where you thought there

83

was an attempt to clean up some blood."

"Yeah," Sydowski said.

"There was. We got samples of Hooper's blood, his type is A-positive. Then once everything else in the room was processed, and you were done, we went to work on the wall."

Finn had prepared a jug of water, sodium perborate, sodium carbonate, and Luminol. He'd attached a small sprayer, then applied the solution to the bedroom's ceiling, floor, and wall, including the wall that had drawn Sydowski's attention after he'd spotted blood droplets. The process, known as chemical luminescence, would detect any blood a suspect may have wiped clean, or made invisible, to the naked eye. Once the solution contacted blood, it reacted to ultraviolet light.

Finn asked Turgeon to close the door and Sydowski to draw the curtains. It was still overcast outside. The room went black when Finn killed the lights. He switched on a purplish blue foot-long wand of ultraviolet light and held it to the wall.

"See, it looks like your suspect dipped a gloved finger in Hooper's blood to do this."

Sydowski slipped on his glasses and an eerie glow reflected on his face.

Scrawled in Hooper's blood, the killer had written one word in ten-inch letters: *Why?*

12

The towers of St. Ignatius Church jutted from a hilltop some two miles south of the bay and the Golden Gate Bridge. Near Golden Gate Park, next to the University of San Francisco.

Its classical baroque architecture was lost on the news crews, who kept a respectable distance, and the unseen police surveillance teams, who recorded everybody attending Cliff Hooper's funeral.

Molly Wilson and Hooper's sister, Andrea, clasped hands as they entered the church after his casket was removed from the hearse and wheeled inside.

It was placed in the sanctuary and bathed in the sunlight descending through the Holy Spirit depicted in the stained-glass dome. The low soothing hum of the organ and the smells of incense, candles, and fresh flowers wafted over the gathering.

Molly sat next to Andrea and her husband. Next to Molly sat Hooper's partner, Ray Beamon.

Given that Hooper had not died on duty, the service did not entail a full police color guard. Several hundred mourners were there. Scores of dignitaries. Among them: the chief of police, the mayor, the commissioner, justice VIPs from Sacramento, Sydowski, Turgeon, everyone from the homicide detail, along with police officers from across the bay, the state, and the country.

Tom and Ann Reed sat with Della Thompson, Acker, Violet Stewart, Simon Lepp, and other friends from the *San Francisco Star* who'd come to pay their respects. Irene Pepper sat at the back along with scores of other reporters and editors from Bay Area newsrooms who knew Molly.

She wore pearl earrings and a matching necklace. A gift from Hooper. Running her fingers tenderly over the single gem on her gold chain, Molly remembered when he gave it to her. They'd gone to Golden Gate Park for an afternoon. He'd joked about wanting to give a lasting gift, like carving her initials into a tree, he kidded. But he was too law-abiding. Besides, he wanted her to have something she could keep with her at all times. So he teased her by scrounging in his pockets. "Let's see." He grinned at possible tokens of affection: a paper clip, gum, change, then a small jewelry box. "What's in here?" Cliff was so sweet. Molly thought of his smile as the music trailed away. The congregation shuffled their funeral cards and the officiating priest went to the microphone at the small podium to commence the service.

"Everyone who knew Hoop loved him," he began, summarizing the life of Clifford James Hooper, a fifteen-year veteran of the department who died at age forty-one.

"He was born and raised in Lodi, California, where he'd worked relentlessly at realizing his dream of becoming a detective. When he was a boy, he'd written in his journal: 'I want to be a police officer so I can catch bad guys by using my brains, like Sherlock Holmes.' "

Some chuckled softly. The priest smiled and went on. "After earning a degree in criminology, he joined the San Francisco Police Department, graduating with third-highest average scores. His first detail was in Ingleside where after one year on the street he was decorated with the Medal of Valor for disarming a mentally disturbed, knife-wielding man who was holding his twelve-year-old daughter hostage. Both are alive and well and living good lives thanks to Cliff."

The priest continued highlighting Hooper's rise within the department, ending with Homicide. Then he listed the others at the service who were going to pay tribute. Molly touched her eyes with a tissue and fidgeted with her sheet of paper on which she'd written what she was going to say. It was folded neatly into quarters. She would speak near the end. The mayor was up first and began by honoring the entire department.

"We know that every day you start your tour, you put it on the line for us, and for that, this city is deeply grateful," the mayor said. "We can only pray that whoever did this to a fine son of the city is brought to justice."

Molly gazed at the beautiful stained glass, the Corinthian columns, and wished this were all a bad dream, a horrible dream as the police chaplain followed the mayor.

"Something evil brought us all together today," the chaplain said. "Something wicked has pierced our hearts. But it will never defeat us. For no such act of cruelty, no attempt by darkness, shall ever succeed. We will prevail."

Hooper's sister was next. Andrea squeezed Molly's hand, then her husband's before going to the podium where she reflected on how all of her life she'd looked up to her big brother. How after their parents passed away she became closer to him, her rock during the storms of her life. "Cliffie," she said, staring at his casket, "you'll always be my hero."

Molly began to quiver, wondering if she could go through with this as the chief of police went next, barely containing his anger.

"Not many of you are aware, but I knew Hooper when I was a captain and he worked for me a few years back. He went undercover on some dangerous operations and he got the job done. And done well. He was one of the finest officers I've ever had the pleasure of working with." The chief took his time so the weight of his words could be felt.

"What happened to Hoop is an insult and an outrage to our police family," the chief said, letting seconds pass. A few people coughed, some sniffled. "Yes, we're all hurting, and that's understandable. But make no mistake. This will not weaken us. Find solace and draw strength from our maxim. '*Oro en paz, fierro en guerra.* Gold in Peace. Iron in War.' We don't just wear it. We don't just carry it around. *We swear by it. We live by it. And we die by it.*"

Molly watched Beamon rub his knees. He was next. She patted his hand. He went to the podium, gripping its sides as if struggling not to fall.

A few rows back Sydowski raised his chin, tightened his arms across his chest, and absorbed every iota of Beamon's demeanor.

"My family moved around a lot when I was a kid. As an only child, I never knew the feeling of a large family until I joined the SFPD," he began. "I was in Robbery before I went to Homicide a few years ago. That's where I met Cliff." Beamon paused.

"He'd already put in quite a few years in Homicide when he got me for a partner. But he was cool with that. He was patient. He was my mentor and maybe sometimes we didn't see eye to eye —" He stopped to rub his right hand across his lip, and Sydowski tightened his focus on Beamon's scraped knuckles. "But he taught me, watched over me. He was my brother and I loved him."

Turgeon touched the corners of her eyes. Sydowski shifted in his seat, thinking long and hard, reassured by the fact the police surveillance team was capturing video and audio of everyone inside and outside the church.

Molly took a deep breath, squeezed her piece of folded paper, then patted Beamon's shoulder as she rose to take her place at the podium.

She unfolded her sheet, its crisp crackling echoing. Then she cleared her throat to assure herself that she'd have the strength to push words through her mouth. "Just read your words. Read aloud, slowly and clearly," the priest had advised her before the service on how to get through it.

"Cliff was a kind, gentle man who always worried about the children who got caught up in some of his cases. He wanted to have his own family one day and I know he would have made a terrific dad."

Molly kept her eyes on her sheet because she was too nervous to raise them and look into all of the faces before her. She could feel their anguish, their suffering, their loss, and their rage.

"I know Cliff loved police work and thought the world of all of you." Molly lifted her head to the congregation, cast a sweeping gaze over them, before seeing something that made her heart stop.

A man who had been standing at the rear of the church, listening as the others eulogized Hooper, was now taking slow steps up the aisle toward her, his face coming into view until Molly recognized him. She was stunned. He found a pew with an empty seat. He settled into it and looked at her.

Oh my God! This can't be!

Transfixed for a moment, Molly struggled with her composure before she finished reading her words. Afterward, the priest gestured to Beamon to assist her back to her seat. Everyone at the service had assumed she'd been overwhelmed by grief. No one knew the truth.

Molly had just been visited by a ghost.

13

Warm breezes fingered along the waterways that laced the heart of the San Joaquin Valley to the small country cemetery near Lodi where San Francisco Police Homicide Inspector Clifford Hooper was buried.

There was no marker. His headstone was not yet finished. Dying flowers blanketed the dark earth of his grave. It had been a few days since mourners stood to watch his casket being lowered into the ground. Then returned to their lives and private fears.

Only Bleeder was here today. Alone in the silence, broken by the panicked chirp of a small bird in high-speed flight, as if fleeing the fact that a murderer stood among the dead.

Bleeder had come to pay his final respects. And as the sun dropped beyond the Pacific, casting twilight over the valley and the Sierra Nevadas, one question burned in his mind.

Why hadn't Molly acknowledged what he'd done?

Hidden in the shadows at the edge of the cherry orchard bordering the burial ground, he reached down for a long stalk of grass, placed it in his mouth, and chewed on his situation.

Molly must know. Deep in her heart she had to know. So why hadn't she signaled to him that he was getting through to her? It'd been days since he'd removed Hooper. Why was she ignoring him? He repeated the question during the drive back to San Francisco.

The road rushed under him, time blurred, and memory pulled him back through his life. His father was a career officer in the military, a job that pinballed his family across the country. As an only child, Bleeder grew up associating the smell of cardboard moving boxes with the sting of being the new kid at school, the perpetual target of humiliation by hometown boys.

He grew accustomed to his loneliness.

When he reached his teens, he found the adventurous girls were drawn to the mystique of *the new guy*. Their boredom led to the occasional sweaty embrace at slow dances on Friday nights in the gym. But nothing beyond that. That is, until he met Amy Tucker, a goddess from another world.

She was a local beauty, a contender for homecoming queen who shocked him at one dance when she appeared before him, her eyes hinting at danger, like embers that had swirled from a distant fire.

"You're real cute," Amy had said, taking his hand, peeling him from the wall for a few

dances. The Police's "Every Breath You Take" floated in the air and he held her so close he could feel her heart beating against his chest. They were bathed in light streaking from the mirror ball. She smiled, then kissed his cheek, then his mouth. Her lips tasted like cherry candy. She parted them and her tongue found his. Later that night they made love under the empty stadium bleachers. Amy was his first. She blew away his loneliness and his soul came to life.

He bought her flowers. They held hands between classes. But he missed the warning signs, the stares and stifled giggles in their wake at school, until the afternoon he walked home alone through the field by the train tracks. Then it all became crystalline.

Kyle Chambers and his friend Rowley Deet were waiting. They were big farm boys who were defensive tackles on the football team. Kyle and Amy had been going steady for two years . . .

". . . before you showed up." Kyle jabbed his forefinger in Bleeder's chest. "What the hell do you think you're doing with Amy, huh?" The insides of Kyle's forearms were scarred from a late summer of hoisting hay bales onto a conveyor. "She's my girl, shit-head."

"No, she's with me."

"She *used* you and you know it."

Used? Jesus. He didn't want to hear that.

But the giggles. The stares. The way Amy always grabbed his hand on cue when Kyle was near. No. She wouldn't *use* him like that. It couldn't be true.

"Stay the hell away from her." Kyle's forefinger jabbed him again.

"Don't do that," Bleeder said.

"Oh yeah?" Kyle stepped closer. His breath smelled of beer.

"You heard him," Rowley said, his muscles stretching the tanned skin of his upper arms. "Stay away from Amy."

"Go to hell."

"Say that again?" Kyle laughed. Rowley, too.

Bleeder didn't care. *Used. Jesus. Why?* He just didn't care.

"Go to hell, Kyle, and take dick-brain with you."

Bleeder blocked Kyle's first punch, slowed his second, but Rowley doubled him with a pile driver to his gut, so powerful it winded him and he puked. Then Kyle dropped him with a direct hit to the head. Bleeder fell to his knees in a starry stupor, unsure whose boot plowed into his kidney, not feeling the flurry of head blows that sent him to the rock-hard earth of the worn path. He writhed in liquidy islands of undigested ham, lettuce, Swiss cheese, and peanut butter cookies from the lunch his mother had made him. His face was wet with blood, snot, and drool.

"Got it now, shit-head?" Kyle stood over him. "She used you to piss me off."

"Look at him. He sure is a bleeder," Rowley said.

Kyle chuckled. "Hey, bleeder, you learned your lesson?"

Bleeder.

He didn't speak. He didn't cry. He rolled onto his back and through the bloody web of his humiliation blinked at the sky, staying that way long after Kyle and Rowley walked away, long after the echoes of their laughter faded. He drifted in and out of consciousness as the stars emerged.

"She used you to piss me off."

Lying there, he heard a distant hammering against the sky, then felt the earth tremor. *She used you.* An approaching maelstrom of steel-on-steel grew with a trumpet that emerged into the scream of the sixty-car freight train that thundered by him, pounding into the night, leaving him in silence with nothing. Except the truth.

She used you.

He heard it over and over as his ears rang. His brain throbbed. He smelled something electric in the air. His head pounded. He tasted copper on his tongue. Something bad was happening. His skull hummed and he gripped his head until a surreal calmness fell over him. Then Bleeder spoke to him for the first time in a voice as clear as if a new

96

person were standing before him. But he was inside. In his head.

Don't worry, sport. It's not over. I'll take care of it.

Who was that?

He prodded his head before scrambling to his feet, navigating the dark to his house, where he crawled into bed and scared his mother to death. They said he fell into a coma state, or something, that lasted for just over three days. After he got out of the hospital, he'd refused to tell his mother, his father, the doctors, the school people, not even the sheriff's deputy with the squeaky leather holster, what had happened.

"I don't know what happened. I never saw them."

Amy never called him. None of the kids called him. When he went back to school the chess club boys said the white bandage on his head made him look like a Civil War soldier home from battle. Amy ignored him. Acted like she didn't even know him as she walked to classes with Kyle, his big farm boy arm around her. Once Kyle made a show of snarling over his shoulder, "You following us, Bleeder?"

"Bleeder?" Amy giggled.

"Yeah, that's his new name. Bleeder. Take a hike, Bleeder."

"Don't worry, *Blee-Dur.*" Amy giggled. "You're still cute." Then she whispered something in Kyle's ear, making both of them laugh as they walked away.

Alone at night in his room, he would stare at the cracks in his ceiling, wiping his tears. His head would throb as if a spike were being hammered into his brain, and the pain hummed in a dark corner of his mind, until it became a strong voice, an *entity* within.

Is that you, Bleeder?

It's me, sport.

Will you help me?

You bet. I'll take care of it.

He never breathed a word about Bleeder to anyone. Bleeder was a powerful and dangerous new friend. No one else would understand how it worked between him and Bleeder. That's why he had to keep him locked away, hidden.

Not long after the incident his father got transferred and they moved away. Another state, another town, another high school. That move lasted about nine months, then they moved again. More cardboard, more humiliation.

But now he had Bleeder.

And from that point on, he lived his life as most people do, functioning normally. But under times of stress, he sought comfort in the secret he possessed while grappling with the fear that maybe his secret possessed him.

Such thoughts, brought on by his visit to Hooper's grave near Lodi, were making his head hurt. He tried to shrug it off, reaching in the seat next to him for his bottle of headache pills, downing ten tablets.

As night descended he thought, *It's funny how everyone wears a mask. To hide who we really are. So we can bear our little buckets of pain.* Over time, he had perfected his mask. No one knew that Bleeder was behind it, studying them. His mask allowed him to get close to Molly Wilson. Like Amy, she had stirred his desires. But he needed to get closer still to reveal the truth, reveal what he'd come to know. That he possessed a deeper understanding of her. More than anyone could know. That they shared something more profound than any two souls could ever experience.

Soon she would see.

The Bay Area and San Francisco's skyline glittered as he crossed the Bay Bridge into the city. Bleeder needed to work harder to make certain she would know the truth.

They belonged together.

It was a shame about Hooper. But she'd been getting too close to him. Bleeder couldn't accept that. It was dangerous. It wasn't right. Action was unavoidable. At first Bleeder fought off his urge to act, hoping she would choose the right course. But she didn't. So Bleeder took charge.

What was done was done. And he was stronger for it. His mask could barely conceal what was seething beneath the surface of his skin. He was supercharged. Forget the past. Forget everything. All that had happened up until this point. Bleeder was alive. Bleeder was in control.

In San Francisco, he wheeled through the hilly streets to the edge of Russian Hill, then North Beach where he resumed his vigil of her neighborhood and building.

God, how he loved to watch her and dream of when they would be together forever.

14

Molly tried to shove Frank Yarrow from her mind.

Why did he have to show up at Cliff's funeral?

Molly's apartment came into view as she turned the corner on the last leg of her morning jog. Anger had fueled her run.

Of all the places and times to appear. He emerged like a specter. Molly was paralyzed. His appearance had left her speechless. She hadn't told a soul about him. Grief had overtaken her at the service, she'd explained later.

She dropped her keys and the morning paper on the kitchen table, then collected fruit from the refrigerator and counter. She sliced bananas, oranges, and strawberries into small heaps, dumping them with low-fat milk into the blender. The whine of the mixing blades suited her rage. She had ignored Frank at the service and was relieved not to see him afterward.

In the gathering following the funeral, Molly had made it clear to her friends and coworkers that she wanted to be alone for a while. God, would this hurting ever stop? she wondered, just as her phone rang. She'd let the machine get it. But the caller didn't leave a message. After a few moments, it rang again.

Molly stared at the ceiling. It was likely a reporter. The calls followed the same pattern. Then a third call came. Unable to stand it, she seized the phone.

"What is it?"

"Hello, Molly, it's me, Frank."

Ice shot up her spine and her scalp tingled. She didn't know what to say. *Hang up now,* she told herself.

"Are you there?" he asked.

Her emotions swirled and she sat down.

"I'd really like to talk. Please."

"This is a horrible time," she said.

"I'm sorry. If you'd just give me a moment."

"I've got nothing to say to you. What you did, showing up the way you did at the funeral, was stupid. What's wrong with you?"

"I read about it all in the papers. I tried calling you but couldn't get through. I had to be there."

"You didn't have to be there. Your timing stinks. Let me make myself clear. I am not interested. *Leave me alone.*"

"Molly, please. I have to talk to you. I've changed."

"Stop it."

"So much has changed."

"It was a long time ago."

"I'm leaving town soon and I'd really like to see you before I go."

She slammed the phone down. She didn't need this. Not him. Not now.

It rang again.

Damn it. She seized the receiver.

"I thought I told you —"

"Molly, are you all right?" Her father said.

"Dad. Oh, I'm sorry."

"Is everything okay?"

His strong voice pulled her back to Texas, to his strong arms and his plaid shirts that smelled of fresh soap and his pipe.

"No. Not really."

"You said you didn't need me to fly out there before. How about now?"

"No. Thanks, Dad."

"You're sure? I know you. You keep a lot bottled up, like me."

"I know."

"It's okay to lean on someone every now and then. Hell knows I should've done that when your mother passed on."

"I've got a lot of friends here, Dad. I'll be okay."

"How you been getting on, really? A lot of people here have been asking after you. And a lot of reporters been calling me, asking about you."

"What did you tell them?"

"I told them all what I could. I saw no

harm. I figure it's like a professional courtesy, seeing how you're in the business. Our family has nothing to hide."

"Right." God, her father was so naive when it came to the media!

"Well, I'll let you go. Now you call me if you change your mind about me coming out, and I'll be on the next plane."

"I will, Dad. Thanks."

Molly was exhausted.

She took a hot shower.

Steam clouds rose around her, carrying her back through her life to when she was seventeen and so scared. She remembered the smell of diesel, the rush of air brakes when the Greyhound stopped in Houston. The clinic wasn't far from the depot. A crumbling stone building without windows. It smelled bad. Like strong medicine. Like the vet's office when they put down Jangles, her cat. The soulful cries of sick puppies in their wire cages now harmonized with the gentle sobbing of young girls *in trouble*.

No one knew Molly had come to this place.

A consultation, the nurse called it. You're not too far along. You have options. Read the material. But does it hurt? Molly didn't know if she could do this. Damn it, it was Frank Yarrow's fault. No, it was her fault. How could she be so stupid? She had dreams.

Damn it, Frank.

Stop thinking about it, Molly ordered herself as she scoured her scalp.

That part of your life ended in Texas.

A lifetime ago.

So why did he have to show up in San Francisco *now?* She supposed her name in the news had drawn him, but God, she just couldn't take it. An absolute nightmare from her past on top of a nightmare in her present.

15

In the *Star* newsroom Tom pushed the story.

He dialed the number of a very well placed police source.

Come on. Be there. He checked the time. Less than an hour to deadline. His call was answered after the second ring.

"Hey, it's me, I need help," Tom said.

"Give me one minute, I'll call you back from another phone."

He looked around the newsroom. Della Thompson was at a news conference. Nothing big expected. Simon Lepp had been dispatched to the Ingleside police district office to pursue some angle for Pepper. No one around to overhear him. He was clear to talk. His line rang and he took the call from his source.

"What's up, Reed?"

"I need to know what's going on inside the Hooper investigation."

His source said nothing for a long time.

"It's not good. Emotions are running high. Hell, Hooper was well liked and there's a bad smell to this one."

"What do you mean?"

"The brass wants this thing blitzed. Green-lighted the overtime, you know the drill."

"Sure."

"And on big cases like this, Homicide's pretty good at sharing with the other bodies brought in. I'm talking on a need-to-know basis, but they're usually open, right?"

"Right."

"But on this one it seems they ain't sharing the time of day. It's got everyone pissed off. Grief and anger are entangling everybody."

"Do you know why that's happening?"

"I have an idea."

"Care to share it?"

"If I give you anything, it could come back on me."

"Come on. I'm kinda jammed here."

"Look, it's hot right now. Dangerous for anyone to leak anything."

"I'm really jammed. I'd owe you."

There was a long heavy silence. A promising silence.

"All right, but you have to confirm this with other sources. You got this on the wind, understand?"

"On the wind."

"We heard that Management Control and OCC paid Homicide a visit very early in the case. It got them all freaked out."

"Why? Isn't that procedure, administratively speaking?"

"Read it any way you like. But sparks flew. Hooper hadn't even been autopsied and there they are ready to second-guess the investigation before it even started."

"But why? Was Hooper dirty? Or were they just playing politics?"

"It suggests a toilet full of ugly things."

"Like what?"

"Anything from an internal suspect to internal corruption. Who knows? It's pissing people off and raises a lot of dark questions."

"Jesus."

"You *did not* get it from me."

Tom hung up and punched the number for the Office of Citizens' Complaints, eyeing the clock as it rang. He requested an official comment for a story saying that within hours of Inspector Hooper's murder OCC visited the homicide detail to talk specifically about Hooper's case.

"I'll have to get someone to call you back, Mr. Reed."

"I need to talk to someone now."

"Yes, someone will call you right away."

Tom then called the Office of Management Control for the SFPD and was put through to Lieutenant Dan Taylor. After listening, Taylor said, "You know that we never comment on any ongoing investigation, whether we're interested or not."

"Is that a denial?"

"We never comment."

Tom tried a bluff.

"I understand you were present at the meeting, Lieutenant?"

The phone slammed down in Tom's ear.

Whoa. Tom grinned. He wrote down Taylor's response, created a new file on his computer screen, and began drafting a new story. Then Nan Willoughby, spokeswoman for OCC, returned his call.

Tom said, "I understand officials from OCC *and* Management Control visited the homicide detail after Inspector Hooper's death."

"That's correct." Now he had confirmation.

"And the nature of the visit was, I understand, to talk about the case?"

"I'm afraid I cannot discuss the nature of the visit."

"Why were they there?"

"I can't discuss that."

"All right, Nan, let me try this: When OCC presented its most recent *public* report to the commission, it discussed the need to improve relations with the department."

"That's public, yes."

"So, did the visit, which you've confirmed, have anything to do with the concerns the office raised in its recent public report?"

"In part."

That stopped Tom cold.

"What's the other part?"

"I can't comment."

"Nan, OCC visited Homicide to improve relations *and* . . . ?"

Her silence screamed volumes.

"I'm afraid I cannot discuss that, *at this time*."

Man, something's going on.

"Fine. Thanks." Tom then flipped through his file cards for the cell phone number of a senior rep of the Police Officers Association and asked him to comment on what he had.

"What do you think this means?" Tom asked.

"I think it's terrible for a million reasons."

"Give me one."

"It creates an impression that political agendas are attempting to push this case in the wrong direction. Rather than pursue a killer, they want to pursue a victim. A decorated officer. They're suggesting Cliff Hooper deserved what he got. It *appears* they're tainting him before the facts are known."

Using the new information, background on the homicide, OCC, MC, and the police commission, Tom pulled together a new story. It was political rhetoric, but it was chilling.

"This is dynamite," Acker said after reading it on his monitor.

Pepper held her tongue. Earlier in the day she'd dropped the *Chronicle* on Tom's desk. It had lined a story saying police had video-taped Hooper's funeral service, hoping to capture his killer. Tom told her it wasn't news. It was procedure and that if she would be patient he would deliver an exclusive to eclipse anything the competition had.

"Just dynamite," Acker repeated, adding, "We should sell it to front."

Tom nodded, then started for home. He slipped on his jacket, cut across the newsroom.

He never saw the messenger step off the elevator to the newsroom, carrying fresh roses for Molly Wilson. Exactly like the previous bouquet. There was a card, only this time it was in plain sight and read:

Please, Molly, I'm still thinking of you.

16

The staff of the *Star*'s night shift worked with calm, quiet intensity against the deadline for getting the next day's paper off the floor.

No one was aware Simon Lepp was in the newsroom. Out of sight in his corner alcove hidden behind the fronds of spider plants and ferns, he was on the trail of a killer.

And he loved it.

In the soft light his glasses mirrored articles about old homicides investigated by Inspector Cliff Hooper. Gang shootings, sadistic sex-torture slayings, domestics, robbery-homicides, deadly drug deals, and hooker murders flowed across his screen. He absorbed every word, made note of every player, any unusual details.

It was late but he was energized, jacked up on caffeine and the rush of being on the big story. Reporting on a cop murder was a far cry from writing the staid science beat. This was the story everybody in the Bay Area was talking about.

The other day while in line at a coffee shop, Lepp overheard two office workers discussing it. And then he saw a taxi driver reading *his story* in the *Star*. It was wild. So dramatic. So much at stake. He was getting serious play and working with the paper's top guns. Like Tom Reed.

He was a genius.

Tom's idea to go to OCC at the outset of this case was brilliant. It worked beautifully. Lepp glanced at a copy of Tom's article confirming that Internal Affairs people were studying Hooper's murder, which raised questions about internal corruption.

Now Lepp was doing his part, examining every case Hooper had handled to find the link. Earlier he'd chased a hunch from his research that it had originated out of Ingleside. Nothing. But it had to be here. The case that would fit with what OCC should be looking for. He wanted to break something on this story like Tom. He wanted to put investigators on the track of a killer. It had to be here. He could just feel it. One of these cases would point everyone to a killer.

Lepp nudged his glasses, then cast a sad look at Molly's empty desk. His heart went out to her. He remembered the few times she'd gone out with him. A movie. A Billy Crystal comedy. They'd gone out for a few dinners. One glorious night they walked along the Golden Gate Bridge. Neither of them had done that in a while. He told her little-known facts about its construction. She seemed to be fascinated. It was good. She was so different from any other woman he'd known.

Then she told him she wasn't ready for a relationship, that she was still dating other guys. "Let's just be friends, okay?" She kissed his cheek. And that was that.

It hurt a bit but he got over it. Better to have loved and lost. A few months later, Molly started dating Hooper. Lepp was wondering if Cliff ever realized how lucky he was to have someone like her when his screen saver activated, distracting him from his thoughts.

He clicked back to his archived stories and resumed searching for a while longer without much success. He hadn't found the link yet. He looked at his watch. He'd been here long enough and he slipped on his jacket. As he passed Molly's empty desk, he thought of her.

He wished there was something he could do to ease her pain.

Something to assure her that she had friends and there would be better days ahead.

17

Molly placed a frozen chicken pasta dish in her microwave and set the timer. The oven droned as she sat alone at her kitchen table struggling with Cliff's murder.

As her entree revolved on the carousel, Molly's head began to ache. Pressing her fingers to her temples, she tried kneading the pain from her brain. It was futile. The timer bell chimed.

She picked at her food. Tension had turned her neck and shoulders to stone. She needed to clear her mind. She tossed her chicken pasta in the trash and changed into her running gear.

The sun had dipped below the horizon. Faint light painted the sky.

She would run until dark.

She wanted to run forever. A distant cable car clanged. A siren wailed. She'd traveled several blocks. In the dying light she thought she saw a man in a car. Following her. Maybe not. Molly kicked up her speed, turned a corner, and charged uphill.

The guy vanished and she ran hard for

another twenty minutes.

It was dark by the time she got back to her building. She stopped out front to cool down. It had been a fierce run. Breathing hard, she fished into her pocket for her key, keeping her head down as she approached her front steps, never seeing the man on the porch until he stepped from the shadows.

"Hello, Molly."

She froze. The familiar voice pulled her back, rocketing across the fields of her memory, to a time when she lived in her parents' home, a time of textbooks, chaotic hallways, the clang of steel lockers, of sweat-soaked passionate Texas nights in the cab of her boyfriend's pickup. To the day her life had changed forever.

"Frank? Frank Yarrow?"

"It's so good to see you. It's been so, so long."

She swallowed, glanced around.

"I already told you over the phone that this is a bad time for me."

"Please, hear what I've got to say, then I'll go." When Molly hesitated he added: "It won't take long, I have to catch a plane."

Inside her apartment he sat on her living room sofa while she disappeared to her bedroom and pulled on a sweatshirt. She emerged, patting her face with a towel. She got a bottle of water, then sat in her sofa chair a good distance from him. He was dressed in a sport coat, denim shirt, faded jeans. His body looked as lean and firm as it did when they'd first met. A few tiny wrinkles near his blue eyes, tanned face, strong voice.

"I know this is probably the worst time to talk about us."

"It's not good," she said. "I don't know why you do this. Over the years, you've written to me, called me, always tried to stake this nonexistent claim to me."

"I know but please just hear me out."

"I wish you would stop this and go back to Texas, or Kansas."

"Kansas City. I'm working as a corporate security consultant."

"Fine. Great. But you've got to stop this, okay? Stop writing, stop calling. Just stop it."

"We had something."

"We were kids, Frank. It was a long time ago."

"But that's just it, don't you see? We were kids, but since then our lives have taken so many turns in so many ways. I need you to know that I realize how wrong I was back then. Wrong about the way I reacted toward you. And the more I recognized that, the more I got thinking about second chances in life, thinking about you."

"Stop thinking about me."

"The way things have gone for me, how could I not think about you?"

"You're not listening."

"I had to see you. When I learned that you weren't married I took that to mean there was hope. I had to see you. I was in San Francisco on business when I heard about the murder on the news. I'm so sorry for you. That's why I showed up at the service. I wanted to be there for you. I'm trying to let you know that I think our time has come. There are so many signs —"

"Please stop this. I've heard this before, and you should leave now."

"In my whole life you were the only girl who ever cared about me. The only woman I ever truly loved."

Her eyes stung.

"Then you left me. Left for college, your career. It nearly killed me."

"You went on with your life. You got married."

"It didn't work. She wasn't you. We just got divorced. I thought my life was coming to an end. *Again.* And when something like that happens, it forces you to think back on your mistakes, you know?"

She looked away.

"Listen. You're hurting from your divorce. I'm not the answer. You may think I am because you're hurting. But I'm not. You just have to go through this alone. Ride it out. We can't go back in time. We can't live in the past. Listen to me. I'm not going to

118

change my mind and I'm not interested. Please understand that."

His fingers trembled ever so slightly as he rubbed his lips.

"All I'm asking for is a little understanding here. I'm asking you to open your mind to the possibility of us giving things a second chance."

"No."

"Hold on," he said. "Don't answer now. Take some time. Think it over. I'm leaving town tonight. I'll be back in a few weeks. I'll see you then."

"No. Don't. I've listened. Now leave and don't come back. I won't change my mind."

He didn't move. He stared at her for a long moment.

"All I'm asking for is for you to think things over."

She went to the door and opened it.

He stood, ran a hand through his hair, then came to her and stopped within inches.

"Just think things over. That's all I'm asking."

He looked at her for several more seconds before he left.

She closed the door, locked it, leaned against it, then slid to her floor. She pulled her knees to her chest, thrust her face into her towel, and sobbed.

18

Sydowski took in the headline of Tom Reed's front-page story in the morning edition of the *Star*. He unbuttoned his collar as he read at his desk in the homicide detail.

"Who would betray us?"

Turgeon was still reading over his shoulder, holding two mugs of fresh coffee.

"Anybody could've leaked it."

"Why do a thing like this and why now?"

Turgeon set the mugs down and sat on a corner of Sydowski's desk.

"Maybe it was someone who wanted to make OCC and the internal people look like they're obstructing us by getting in our faces."

"Then they've failed. This creates the impression that these guys swooped in on us because Hooper was dirty and the department was moving to cover it up." Sydowski took a hit of coffee. "We don't need this dumped on us. Not now."

Sydowski spotted Gonzales. "You read this?" he asked.

"First call came to my home at five-thirty. The chief's an early riser."

"Somebody's messing with us," Sydowski said.

"Well, shove this crap aside. We've got a case status meeting," Gonzales said. "Everybody, let's go."

The detectives made their way to room 400, the larger meeting room, where they were joined by other investigators and brass who dropped in from their offices on higher floors. They revisited the autopsy and latest ballistic reports during a meeting that was short and tense because of the leak to the *Star*. Immediately afterward, Turgeon and Sydowski headed for Diamond Heights.

"I hate where this case is going," Turgeon said. "But I think we need to test guns, and you know what I'm talking about."

Sydowski and Turgeon knew that whatever was said in their car stayed in their car.

"No, we don't have to test guns."

"We don't?"

"Not yet."

"Why don't you just come out and say it?"

"Ray's our suspect."

Turgeon let out a long hard breath. "Do you think he did it?"

"I don't know. I've got a lot of questions. But you have to understand, we need hard evidence. Something to challenge him with."

"I know."

"If I go at him now and he gets a lawyer, it's over. I've got to build my case against him. So far, I've got nothing but a gut feeling telling me Ray's hiding something and it looks real bad for him."

"So test Ray's Beretta against the recovered rounds. If the rounds came from his weapon, end of story."

"They didn't come from his service gun."

"How do you know?"

Sydowski held up a thin file folder.

"What's that?"

"Ballistics report from six months ago. Ray fired two shots at an armed drug-dealing 187 suspect who drew down on him and Hooper when they went to question him, remember?"

"Oh yeah. The Financial District. Two rounds into the wall. The guy gave it up."

"I just got the report on that. Ballistics comparison shows Beamon's Beretta did not fire the .40-cal round that killed Hooper. So we don't have to test his service weapon."

"What about his off-duty gun?"

"It's a .32 Smith and Wesson," Sydowski said.

"A .32, which means Ray's guns weren't involved."

"Which means nothing. Ray could've used another gun. A throw-down."

"So that's all we have."

"No. Ray's right knuckles had fresh bruises the morning after the murder. The M.E. said Cliff was punched by someone using their right hand."

Turgeon glanced at Sydowski.

"I thought Ray scraped his knuckles working on his Barracuda the night Hoop was murdered."

"That's what he said. He also said he never left his house that night."

"And?"

"I think he's lying and I'm going to prove it."

19

Sitting on his rear balcony, Ray Beamon took another sip of beer and looked at the city lights winking below his bungalow perched on a northern slope of Bernal Heights.

On the table beside him there was a thick brown envelope with the words *For Ray* handwritten by Hooper's sister, Andrea. It had arrived by courier. Beamon put off opening it because he'd been thinking of Molly. Ever since they'd buried Hoop next to the cherry orchard near Lodi, he couldn't stop thinking about her.

Finishing his beer, he drew the back of his hand across his mouth, then went to the refrigerator for another. His house was small, but it came with a view and a garage where he could work on his Barracuda. His neighbors, the two lesbians who lived across the street, had shown up with a tower of prepared meals for him after reading about Hooper's murder. Nice people, Beamon thought, grabbing a cold beer and returning to the balcony.

He touched the sweating bottle to his forehead, twisted off the cap, glanced at the envelope as the distant scream of sirens rose from the Outer Mission. He felt as if something were closing in on him.

Funny.

After the 1906 earthquake, people moved here to feel safe in the wake of disaster. Now here he was, feeling the world descending on him. All right. He opened the envelope. Inside, a handwritten note said:

Ray, I think Cliff would want you to have these. Love, Andrea.

It was folded around a dozen color snapshots taken about a year ago at an FBI party. There they were, the three of them. Molly between Beamon and his partner. Hooper had only been dating Molly for two or three months. He shuffled through the pictures to a nice shot of Hooper with his arm around Molly among a few of the feebies goofing around with the guys from Homicide. Here was one of Beamon and Molly smiling at each other. Just friends. Right. He pulled one picture closer and stared into Hoop's eyes.

It had all started at this party.

Sure, he knew Molly from crime scenes. And he agreed with every other cop in San Francisco, she was easy to look at. She was always all business at scenes. Always. Until that night, at that party. It was the first time he had gotten close to her without a corpse nearby.

She came to him like a dream, taking his

hand, pulling him up to slow-dance with Hooper pushing him. "Go on, she doesn't bite, Ray." Hooper loved it. Just friends. Having a good time. Until Beamon slid his arms around her and pulled her tight. Felt her hands on his shoulders, drank in her fragrance. Looked into her eyes. Feeling something electric, feeling his heart stop as if a trigger had been pulled.

He'd never meant for this to happen.

But it did happen. Fate had set it all in motion that weekend when Molly had called his place looking for Hoop.

"He went fishing in Nevada with two ATF guys."

"I thought he was working on your car with you," Molly said. "We were going to drive down the peninsula this afternoon. I wanted to pick up some antiques."

In the silence that followed, Ray offered to take her.

And Molly accepted.

The afternoon stretched into the evening. They took a moonlight stroll along the Pacific. Stopped for dinner at a little place, had some wine, walked on the beach, things got warm. They got a room and nearly broke the bed.

God, in all of his life, he'd never known anything like this could happen.

Hooper never knew.

Beamon couldn't think straight. Christ. She

became an obsession. He wanted to see her again. Needed to see her. He knew she was going with Hoop but Beamon yearned to date her. It was exciting. It scared the hell out of him.

Then it got worse.

A short time ago he and Hooper were working on a fresh homicide. Walking between doors on a canvass somewhere in the Sunset when Hooper dropped his bombshell.

"I know I've only been with her a few months but I feel Molly's the one. I'm going to ask her to marry me. I'd like you to be my best man."

Beamon was speechless. He didn't know what to do. What to say.

"Did I surprise you?" Hooper asked.

"Sure did, partner. Congratulations."

"So will you do it, buddy?"

"I'd be honored to be your best man."

A grin lit up Hooper's face as he shook his hand. But Beamon knew at that point that he was going to have to do something. He didn't know what. And before he could decide, things went crazy. Went to hell on Hooper's last day. Beyond Beamon's control. God, it wasn't supposed to end like this. Not with Hooper murdered. OCC, Management Control, Sydowski.

Oh, Jesus, Beamon never thought it would end like this.

He had to tell Molly what really happened.

She had a stake in this, too. There were degrees of guilt, he thought, rubbing his knuckles and feeling the soreness, the scrapes against his skin.

20

Surrounded by candlelight, Molly Wilson was floating, adrift in the fragrant water of an herbal bath, when the apartment buzzer shattered her calm. She ignored it but the visitor kept buzzing, forcing her to towel off quickly, slip on her robe, and pad to her intercom.

"It's me. I need to see you," Beamon's voice crackled.

"It's late, Ray," she said after letting him in. She smelled alcohol. "I'm making you coffee. I hope you didn't drive."

He followed her to the kitchen.

"I'm not drunk." Beamon saw the snapshots fanned out on Molly's counter. Copies of what Hooper's sister had sent him. He met her gaze. She was waiting for his reaction. No words were needed. The pictures took care of that.

"Molly, I wanted to see you."

"I want to know why," she said. "Why would someone kill him?"

Beamon took her shoulders.

"You've got to hang on. We'll get through this."

The kettle hit the boiling point and whistled. She poured two cups.

"Do you think Sydowski will find the person who did it?"

He peered into his black coffee.

"I don't know. They've pushed me off the case."

"Sydowski and Gonzales said it wasn't right to have you helping. Procedurally. It'd be a conflict, or something." Molly said.

"Yeah, well, Sydowski's coming after me. I could feel his eyes on us at the funeral."

"You? Why? That makes no sense. He'll just want you to go over old cases, search for threats or vendettas to build his suspect pool. That's basic. That's what the *Star*'s been doing."

He looked at her for several moments.

"You never told me how it was for you, being the one who found him."

"I get nightmares."

"You never told me exactly how you found him."

"No," she said. "Only Sydowski and Turgeon. I never told Tom, or my friends."

"You can tell me."

"I can't."

"I'm his partner, I've a right to know."

"Talk to Sydowski."

"Molly, please. It might help me find out what happened. Understand what happened. Maybe it'll help the case."

"Don't do this."

She turned her back to him. Beamon waited several long moments before he asked: "Did you tell Sydowski about us?"

"God, no."

"Reed?"

"No. No one."

"Guess you have a lot of secrets to keep." Molly turned around.

"What's that supposed to mean?"

"I'm sorry. I'm not thinking clearly," he said.

"Why do you think Sydowski's coming after you?"

"Molly. Come on. A victim's murdered in his home. You track down everyone in his circle. Nearest and dearest. You know that," Beamon rubbed his tired eyes. "I haven't been able to sleep. I've been thinking about all of our old cases and I come up empty. It's driving me crazy. I want so bad to get to the truth."

Molly studied his hands, his pained face.

"Is there something more you want to tell me?"

"No." He turned away, blinking. "Yes." He turned back. "What happened with you at the church, at the service?"

"What do you mean?"

"When you were speaking, you stopped as if you were afraid."

She closed her eyes as if to make the subject vanish.

"I saw an old friend. A guy I'd just as soon forget. He's gone out of my life. Look, it's really late."

Beamon placed his hand over hers and she felt a warm current course through her. "You're so beautiful."

"Don't do this."

Strands of hair slipped from behind her ear and curtained wildly over her face. Their eyes met. He reached up and tucked her hair back, she touched her cheek to his warm palm. Her robe had loosened, exposing the top of her cleavage. She didn't move to cover it. Instead she pulled away from him and stood by the sink to look at the lights of the Golden Gate glittering in the distance.

"You have to go," she said to his reflection in the window.

He placed his large hands on her shoulders and kissed her neck softly, causing her skin to tingle. He turned her around and they kissed, long and deep, her lips parted. His hands opened her robe, landing on her naked skin, exploring her, caressing her, making her pulse quicken. She released a moan.

"We have to stop. I can't do this. It's not right."

Beamon's eyes narrowed and he stared hard at her.

"Are you having second thoughts about us?"

"No. It's just that we shouldn't be thinking

of ourselves now. We should be helping find Cliff's killer."

"I took risks for you."

"What? What risks? What are you talking about?"

"It doesn't matter now."

"What risks did you take for me?"

She ran after him as he headed for the door. He stopped and turned.

"He knew."

"What?"

"Cliff knew about us."

"How could he? I never told him. I never told anyone. How could he know unless —" She looked at Beamon, unsure of what she was seeing. God, no. Her hands flew to her face.

"Good-bye."

"Tell me what's going on. Ray!"

He left and Molly steadied herself against the wall. What was happening? The ghosts of her life swirled around her, like a gathering storm. She slid to the floor.

She sat alone in silence for the longest time, understanding nothing. What was Beamon talking about? She had to know. She had to force him to explain. She deserved to know. Sitting there, Molly lost track of time until she was exhausted. She collected the cups and began rinsing them in the sink.

She looked out the window, down to the street, and froze. She clutched the neck of her robe. A man was standing on the sidewalk in the shadow of a tree.

Staring directly up at her.

Molly's skin prickled with anger.

She couldn't see him clearly. Couldn't get a good look at him. Had no idea who it was, but damn it, she'd find out. She'd find out right now.

She'd had enough of his crap.

Molly yanked on her jeans and a sweater. She grabbed her pepper spray, personal alarm, and cell phone. Furious, she flew down the stairs and out the front door.

But when she got to the tree, no one was there.

21

Bleeder's heart pounded as he strode down the street away from Molly's building. By the time he got to his car, his ears were ringing and his head was throbbing. He drove across the Bay Bridge to seek sanctuary, somewhere out of the way where he could think.

The Dead Horse Bar.

It was a squat building on a forgotten corner near the edge of Berkeley, a few blocks inside of Oakland. It had cracked weatherworn bricks and windows painted over and barred. Inside, large TVs glowed over the sweeping horseshoe-shaped bar. Except for a couple of sad cases shooting pool, the place was empty. Bleeder took a stool and ordered a beer.

Relax, she didn't see you. If she did, so what? She knows you, knows the mask you wear. How could she suspect anything more than a friend watching over her? That's right. Relax, she didn't see you.

But it wasn't working out the way he'd planned. Hooper was gone, yet Molly was taking too long to grasp the truth. How much longer would he have to wait before she realized the magnificent thing he'd done for her?

Give her a little more time.

How much? He yearned to reveal himself to her. He'd been so careful. He'd earned his right to her. *Earned* it. *Be patient.*

Remember how it started with Kyle? Remember?

Far from perfect.

In the weeks after Kyle and Rowley had beaten him into a coma, Bleeder had kept his word to take care of *everything*. By day at school, Bleeder endured the taunts and teasing, which eventually faded with his bruises. As expected, he vanished back into being less than nothing. Invisible again. Only this time he was roiling under the surface. This time Bleeder took control, honing his anguish, meticulously sharpening it into his sword of vengeance.

At night Bleeder put Kyle under surveillance, as if he were an insect in his personal lab. He studied Kyle's life away from school, analyzed every move he made. His routine, his habits, his chores, where he gassed his car, where he went for burgers and shakes with Amy. Bleeder probed for points of vulnerability.

But it didn't go well at first. In fact, the whole thing almost blew up in his face.

On the nights he could get his father's car, Bleeder would track Kyle, study him, and anticipate where he was likely to go with Amy on a given night, at a given time. Like on Friday nights, around nine-thirty. It was Big Duke's Diner. They'd sit in their booth by the big front window. Amy usually got a shake and Kyle got the works, a cheese-burger, fries, and cherry cola.

Bleeder would park where the lot lights barely got through the branches of the stand of creaking trees. But he could see them. One night Bleeder watched Kyle leave the booth to go to the restroom. But he'd lost sight of him and he grew anxious.

Kyle's face appeared at his door.

"Bleeder, what're you doing sitting here all alone in the dark?"

"Finishing my rings." Bleeder nodded to the dash. He always arrived early and ordered something to eat while he watched them.

Kyle placed his hands on the car's frame and leaned in to Bleeder.

"Amy saw you."

"So?"

"Says you're being creepy. Spying on us. She doesn't like it."

"It's a small town and I'm just sitting here minding my own business."

Kyle's hands moved lower. Bleeder saw Kyle's big football ring.

"Yeah, well, get over her. She was just fooling around with you to get at me. Got it?"

"I got it. She never meant it when she told me you were an asshole?"

Kyle laughed.

"That's a good one. A real good one. I sure had it coming. And, man, I'm sorry if me and Rowley were a little rough on you," Kyle slipped his hands in his jeans. Laughed some more. "You know, I like you. See, it's good we can joke. Let bygones be bygones. Be men about this, right?"

"Right."

Kyle's big right hand shot into the car for Bleeder to accept as a peace offering. "No hard feelings. We understand each other?" Kyle was all charm.

Bleeder looked at Kyle's hand, debating whether to shake it. Deciding to take it, he shifted his body to raise his hand. Kyle's arm vanished to return in a blur, his fist and ring smashing like a steel piston against Bleeder's left temple.

Lightning flashed before Bleeder's eyes and a million volts charged through his brain. He nearly passed out, the punch resurrecting every measure of pain from his previous beating. Kyle grabbed Bleeder by the hair, then leaned into his ear and hissed, "Stay away from us, shit-head. Got it?"

Kyle took Bleeder's onion rings, then rejoined Amy.

Bleeder gripped the steering wheel. Breathing evenly, he held on with both hands

138

until his vision cleared. As he sat blinking at the night, everything moved in slow motion. Kyle's Camaro rumbled by him. Kyle was eating and raising Bleeder's rings like the victor's trophy. Amy was grinning pitifully at Bleeder, then gave him a mocking finger-wiggling wave.

Alone that night in his room, Bleeder put his bandage back on to hide the fresh bruise, telling his mother the next morning that his head had started to hurt again.

Now, a lifetime later, as he sat in the bar rubbing his temples at those painful memories, Bleeder assured himself that he had learned from his mistakes.

"Hey, pal," the bartender said.

Bleeder shook himself from his thoughts. He'd been staring blankly at the basketball game on TV.

"I'd like to switch it to the news, if you don't mind," the bartender said.

"Go ahead."

"Closing time in fifteen, you good with your beer? Hardly touched it."

"Yeah, thanks."

"Need a cab?"

"I'm fine."

"Sure?"

"Put the news on."

A five-car pileup with a tour bus near the San Mateo Bridge was the top local story, followed by a building contract scandal at

City Hall, then the next story was an update on Hooper's case.

"The murder of San Francisco Homicide Detective Clifford Hooper remains steeped in mystery, but according to a report in the *San Francisco Star*, the SFPD Management Control Squad, which investigates internal police affairs, has indicated an interest in the case, along with the Office of Citizens' Complaints. . . ."

Bleeder smiled.

Almost immediately after Hooper's death, he'd arranged for certain dangerous information about Hooper to make its way to Citizens' Complaints. Didn't need to be true. Bleeder knew it would cause a stink for the zealots in OCC and MC to go to the homicide detail and mess with them. He knew it would raise the flag of alleged corruption, turn up the heat on the investigation.

And now it was paying off, bringing him closer to his prize.

Molly Wilson.

22

Driving downtown to meet sources the next morning, Tom used his cell phone at every red light to try to contact Sydowski. No luck. He tried Molly Wilson's home, then her cell. Nothing. He tried a few cop sources knowing they'd go mute because of his story. He was right.

Damn.

He sensed something was brewing, something happening on this story. There had to be a way to bust it wide open. Tom had learned long ago from Sydowski that Internal Affairs and OCC's intelligence usually flowed from two streams: pissed-off cops and the street. He jabbed in a number he kept in his head. It took seven rings before a man's rasping voice answered.

"Yes."

"This is Tom. Is Lois around?"

"Hello, Tom. I've seen her around, yes."

"Is she well?"

"I don't think so. Not at the moment."

"When she feels better, would you please contact me? I've been trying to reach her."

"Yes. I will do that."

"Thank you. It's very important."

Tom took advantage of the next red light to try another call. Man, it was obvious. Why didn't he think of it earlier? He'd call Ray Beamon. No one had gone after Hooper's partner for data, or an interview. Maybe he'd react to his OCC story.

Before he could call, his phone rang.

It was Tammy, the newsroom receptionist, and she was whispering.

"It's happened just like you said. Irene's called a meeting on the cop murder but she told Acker not to tell you."

"Of course, she's trying to bushwhack me. When is it?"

"Thirty minutes."

"Thanks. I owe you."

The instant Tammy spotted Tom in the newsroom she directed him to the boardroom. Acker, Lepp, and Della were just seating themselves when he arrived. Pepper had her back to them while pouring coffee at the credenza. When she turned to see Tom, crimson rose on her cheeks.

"Oh, I'm glad someone reached you," she lied.

Acker's attention pinballed between them. Whatever thoughts he had, he kept to himself.

"All right," she said. "This will be a very short meeting on the Hooper case to see how we can advance the story."

"Hey," Acker said to Tom, "great piece on the OCC."

Ignoring the compliment, Pepper plowed ahead.

"Della, you're mining the neighborhood and Hooper's friends," she said.

"Yes, I'm close to putting together a long take on Hooper's last twenty-four hours," Thompson said. "From the moment he rose, until Molly found him. I just need to talk to a few more friends."

"And, Simon, how are you doing?"

"I've been going through Hooper's old cases, see if anyone threatened him, gauge his enemies. By the way, looks like you reported on the majority of Hooper's cases." Lepp turned to Tom.

"You find anything?" he asked.

"A few things but I'm going to need more time."

Tom noticed that Pepper was focused on her doodling when she asked him, "And what are *you* working on?"

"I'm still pushing the investigation angle. And following my OCC story and I'm working on street sources."

Pepper said nothing about Tom's exclusive story. She'd been drawing circles on her pad, keeping her attention on her doodling. "Where's Molly? What's she doing?" she asked Tom.

"I don't know."

143

"So you have no idea if she's working on that first-person account of the night she found Hooper?"

"No, I don't think she's up to it. But I don't speak for her."

Pepper's eyes went to Tom.

"Okay, thank you, everybody. We're done for now." She stood and opened the door but she closed it before Tom could leave. "I'd like a private word with you."

He sat and sighed.

"What else are you chasing?"

"I just told you."

"You've got a direct link in the chair beside you into the heart of San Francisco's top crime story and you've gotten nowhere on it."

"What're you talking about? I'm breaking stories."

"Not the stories I want."

"What is it? What do you want from me?"

"I want you to break news on the Hooper murder. I want blistering exclusives that will rock this town."

"I'm doing that."

"Not fast enough for me."

23

Everyone had overlooked it except Sydowski.

It was one of those things he'd filed away.
A note he'd scrawled on a canvass report.

The timing was good.

Sydowski was alone when he wheeled into
Upper Market to a well-kept stucco bungalow bordered by a thick stone wall and the
requisite security system. It was three doors
from Hooper's building.

The residents, a Drug Enforcement Admin-
istration Agent and his son, had left for a
trip to San Diego the morning after the
murder.

They were back now and expecting
Sydowski, who'd called ahead.

The night Hooper was murdered, the
agent's son was on the street talking about
cars with a friend. Neighbors said the son
was a "car nut."

His name was Ryan. He was in his twenties, well built, and had a small broken heart
tattooed on his forearm. He also had a firm
handshake, Sydowski noticed when Ryan answered the door.

"Thanks for agreeing to see me right away," Sydowski said.

"Sure."

Ryan's father, a thick-necked man with a brush cut, set fresh coffee on the living room table. Sydowski pulled out his notebook and got straight to business.

"Before you left, you and your friend were in the street near her house in front of Clifford Hooper's."

"Sounds right."

"Did you see anybody, hear anything out of the ordinary?"

Ryan shook his head. "Like what?"

"The whole time you guys were out there, did you talk to anybody, see anybody?"

"Just the Barracuda guy."

Without any reaction, Sydowski asked him to elaborate.

"He comes walking down the stairs from the second floor of the building."

"He was on the property?"

"Definitely. He comes walking out, crosses the road, right by me. I'm leaning against my pickup talking to my friend Nathan and this guy's walking right by me to his car across the street. A Barracuda."

"Did you talk to him?" Sydowski asked.

"I followed him and asked him about his Barracuda. I have a friend who wants to buy one and this thing was in mint condition. A

'66 Plymouth Barracuda Fastback. That ride purred."

"Tell me about the guy," Sydowski said. "Describe him."

"White guy, mid-thirties. Trim build. I'd say he was uptight, the way someone is when they've got something serious going on. It was like I shouldn't have bothered him."

"What did you talk about?"

"I just asked him if he would ever consider selling because I had a buddy who might want to buy it. I think I asked what he had under the hood. He said it was a V-8, 273 cubic inch, but he didn't want to sell."

"Okay, Ryan." Sydowski reached into his jacket pocket. "I'm going to show you some photographs. I want you to tell me if you see the man you talked to, the Barracuda guy, among them, all right?"

"Sure."

Sydowski began setting down on the coffee table six color head and shoulder shots of different white males in their mid-thirties. Ryan leaned forward. Sydowski never needed all six. When he snapped down photo number three, Ryan jabbed it with his finger.

"Him. Definitely him. He's the guy."

"Are you certain?"

"Absolutely."

Sydowski slid the picture into his shirt pocket.

"And . . ." Ryan went to the kitchen,

talking from there. "I just remembered something else." He returned with a slip of paper with a California license plate number. "Took that down for my buddy, to let him know I found a classic Barracuda for him. You can have it."

Sydowski copied the number in his notebook, then tucked the slip of paper into the pocket holding the suspect photo. In the car, Sydowski ran his hand over his face and looked to the distance.

Ray Beamon's picture was in his breast pocket and it felt as if it were burning a hole through his heart.

24

That same morning Molly Wilson was in a taxi bound for the Hall of Justice.

She'd called Ray Beamon at the homicide detail and was told he was in court. After passing through the security check she searched among the lawyers, prosecutors, and cops for someone she knew to point her to the trial he was on.

"That would be in Judge Ortiz's courtroom, the Jennings case," a tall man with a baritone voice said.

"Thank you, Judge Larredy."

Molly studied the docket. Jennings was on the next floor. It was thick with police, D.A. people, public defenders, bleary-eyed relatives of victims, and suspects looking confused, dazed. Shrader from Homicide, who was sitting on a bench, looked up from the sports section he was reading.

"Hey, Molly. How you holding up?"

"Doing the best I can. Is Beamon in there?"

"Yeah. He should be coming out now."

Two other detectives, Fred Keeler from Robbery and Donna Beckwith from Vice, approached her as the courtroom doors opened. Gonzales stepped out with Beamon. Both men nearly halted when they saw Molly.

"Ray, do you have a second?" she asked.

"Sure." He put his hand on her shoulder, then turned to his colleagues. "I'll see everyone later."

"Take care, Ray," Beckwith said.

Beamon led Molly far down the hall to a bench out of hearing range of the other detectives. "Is everything all right?"

"We have to talk."

"Listen." Glancing around, he kept his voice low. "There's nothing to talk about. You made it clear there's nothing for us. I apologize for last night. I was in bad shape. I have to get going."

"No, wait." She yanked hard on his wrist, taking stock of the detectives down the hall. "I want you to give me some answers." She was not going to back down.

"Fine."

At first she wanted to ask him if he'd hung around her place last night. But in the sober light of the Hall, it now seemed less important than what Beamon had said to her last night.

"You told me Cliff knew about us. How did he know?"

"Molly, this isn't the place for this."

"I deserve an answer and I want it now."

He stared hard at her, his eyes narrowing

like they did the other night. Beamon considered her question for a long tense moment.

"I told him."

"You told him."

Letting it sink in, Beamon looked down the hall, knowing the others were watching.

"But why? I don't understand. Why would you tell him?"

"I had to. Trust me. I had to."

"Why?"

"On that day, Hooper's last day, he bumped into Arnold Desfor, a retired San Jose cop here at the Hall. Desfor told Hooper that a few weeks earlier he'd seen me with you at the hotel restaurant along the peninsula. You know, the weekend Cliff was out of town. Desfor said that he'd come over to our table but we'd taken the elevator to the rooms. He told Hooper about everything."

Molly's mind spun.

"If this happened on Cliff's last day — and you talked to him about us — it had to be just before —" She turned to him as a horrible question swirled in her stomach.

"Cliff took Desfor's news real bad."

"I told him I wasn't ready for a serious relationship."

"But he was. That's why he took Desfor's news so hard, because it was you and me."

"When did you tell him?"

Beamon grew uneasy.

151

"I have to go. I've got to sort things out."

"But when *exactly* did you tell him?"

Beamon rubbed the back of his neck and blinked at the ceiling.

"I can't talk about this now. I have to decide things."

"What things? What happened when you told Cliff about us?"

"Jesus, don't do this. Don't do this here."

"The other night you said, 'Sydowski's going to come after me.' Ray, what does that mean?"

"I was upset, I was drinking. I'm sorry."

"Tell me what happened when you told Cliff about us. You told me you took risks. What risks? Tell me."

"For chrissake. We're in this together. So just stop and think. Don't do this here, goddammit."

"Jesus, what did you do?"

Beamon didn't answer. He walked to the elevator, leaving her alone. Molly looked down the hall at the detectives and considered telling them everything.

Now.

25

Ray Beamon's socket wrench clicked as he tightened his Barracuda's spark plugs.

"Excuse me, Inspector?"

The clicking stopped.

Beamon adjusted his head around the car's raised hood. Tom Reed stood at the entrance of his garage. Beamon eyed him. He didn't like this.

"Sorry for showing up unannounced, but you've been hard to reach lately. You didn't return my calls."

"I really don't have anything to tell you." Beamon went back to working under the hood. The clicking resumed.

"Just a few minutes for a short interview, Inspector, please?"

The chinking of metal against metal underscored Beamon's silence.

"You must have some theories. A story might yield a critical tip."

Beamon weighed everything. Tom could've been sent by Molly. Even Sydowski. He didn't know what Tom knew. Beamon thought maybe he could turn things around. Use an interview to put a few small things right, maybe make a slight *alignment*. It might be okay, if he kept his guard up, kept things natural. He tapped his wrench in his palm.

"I don't know much," he said, "and what I might know, I might have to hold back for the case, understand?"

"I understand."

"Okay, a few questions."

Tom pulled out his minicassette recorder. After testing it, the two men leaned against Beamon's Barracuda.

"Tell me about that last day. Walk me through it."

Beamon's summary of the day got him talking, but when he indicated he wanted to wrap things up, Tom brought out his most important questions.

"So who do you think wanted your partner dead?"

Beamon's head snapped up.

"I sure as hell wish I knew, because if I ever caught the guy who did it, I'd put one in his head. I'd kill him. No question."

Beamon read the surprise on Tom's face.

"Those are pretty strong words. Do you stand by them?"

Beamon let a long moment pass, then looked at the cassette, seeing the tiny reels on the recorder rotating, knowing that he couldn't take back what he'd said.

"I do," Beamon said. "I want to know who did this. I've thought about it over and over.

Who would want to kill Cliff? Why? It makes no sense."

"What do you make of the fact OCC and Management Control showed up in the detail shortly after Hooper's homicide? Isn't that odd?"

"Yes." Beamon was careful. "It puts a cloud over things."

"There's the impression, or suspicion, that Hooper was involved in something corrupt and that his murder arose from that."

Beamon shook his head.

"No way. Cliff was a decorated, decent, honest police officer."

"What about a vendetta from an old case?"

Beamon doubted it. Tom pressed him to reflect on some of their worst cases, including ones he and Beamon had worked on while in other details like Robbery and Narcotics.

"There've been threats but those who make a lot of noise never come after you. If someone's serious, you'll never hear them coming."

Beamon said he knew of no one specifically who'd try anything. Then after letting several moments pass, Tom changed the subject.

"And what about the relationship with Molly Wilson?"

Beamon didn't move. He looked at Tom as if he'd cocked a gun.

"What about her? What did she tell you?"

155

"How did you get along with her, her being Cliff's girlfriend and a reporter?"

"Fine. We all got along fine. Like I said, I know her, like I know a lot of the other reporters who are on the police beat. I also know her because of Hooper. We sometimes went to parties together."

"Like friends?"

"Yes, like friends," he said, ending the interview.

Long after Tom drove off and long after the sun had set, Beamon felt as empty as he did when they lowered Hooper's coffin into the ground. He sat alone on his balcony contemplating his life and the city lights.

Things were closing in on him.

He drank some beer, then went back to looking at the pictures Hooper's sister, Andrea, had sent him. Beamon stared at one of Molly, tracing her smiling face, recalling their time together, never dreaming where that moment would lead him.

Again he thought of Hoop, out in Lodi by the cherry orchard, then he thought of Molly. His hand shook slightly as he raised his bottle to his mouth.

God, help me.

26

Sydowski opened the small fridge in the far
end of the homicide detail, selected a bottled
water for Molly, then led her to an interview
room and opened the door.

"We'll talk in here. It's private. Make yourself comfortable, I'll get Linda. She's finishing up in the lieutenant's office."

Molly sat down, twisted off the cap. She
knew all about this small, barren room made
of white cinder block. It had hard-back
chairs on either side of a table with a wood
veneer finish. The room was wired to record
conversations. Taking deep breaths, she
glanced around. She'd felt empty since
Hooper's murder. Now that she feared
Beamon was responsible, she was afraid.

Could she do this?

These bare white walls. This was where detectives questioned murder suspects and witnesses. Where the truth was pursued with
righteous fervor. Not much larger than a
prison cell, designed so you could feel the
walls closing in on you.

Molly rolled the water bottle in her hands.

Sydowski had called her a short time ago

requesting she come in. "A few follow-up questions," he'd said. "Routine stuff." It had to have arisen from her accosting Beamon at court in full view of the others, she thought, as Sydowski and Turgeon entered. They were carrying ceramic mugs. Files were tucked under their arms. Chairs scraped as they seated themselves.

"Thanks for coming by." Sydowski leaned forward to study her for a moment. "Anything we can do?"

Half smiling, Molly shook her head. He slipped on his bifocals and opened his manila file folder, then wet his forefinger and took his time going through pages. Molly forced herself to focus on mundane things: the bottle cap, Sydowski's watch, his bifocals, the flash of his gold crowns when he spoke.

"It's been a while since we took your statement of what happened that night. We'd just like to go over a few areas. Make sure we have a clear picture of everything."

She nodded.

"You've said the last you heard from Cliff was when he called you near the end of his shift that night."

She nodded.

"How did that conversation go?"

"Brief, something like, we're still on for tonight, right? I'll see you later at Jake's. Like that."

"How was his tone, his demeanor? Any-thing unusual?"

"No. He was upbeat. Nothing unusual."

"I want to go over something again. It's very important."

"Okay."

"When we talked right after you'd found Hooper, I asked you about your ex-boyfriends and the chances any of them would have been jealous enough to go after him. You gave us some names. We checked them out. Then there is this." He lifted a page in the file, stared at it for a long time. "You said a lot of jerks contact you because they see you on Vince Vincent's show, *Crime Scene*."

"That's true. They write or call."

"But nothing stands out?"

"No."

"Let's go back to ex-boyfriends. Of all the guys you've known, not one would've had any reason to have a run-in with Cliff?"

Molly said nothing.

Without taking his eyes from his file, Sydowski said: "And what about Ray Beamon?" Then he peered over his glasses. "Ever go out with him?"

Her breathing quickened. *Tell him. Now is the time. Tell him everything.* She began but the words died on her tongue and Sydowski leaned forward.

"Don't hold back on me, Molly."

She blinked.

"This is the time to get it off your shoulders."

She felt something deep inside weaken and fracture.

"Is there anything you want to tell us?"

Molly could no longer look into Sydowski's eyes. Tears fell as she nodded her head slowly, feeling the hard white walls closing in on her.

"Yes, I dated Ray. Recently." Molly cleared her throat. "Cliff found out the day he was murdered. I think Ray told him and something happened. Something went wrong."

27

The creamy morning fog smothering the coastline haunted Sydowski as he drove the unmarked Impala south of San Francisco on Highway 1.

The Chev had been tuned up recently and was running quiet. He had opened the windows a quarter of the way, picking up the occasional crash of waves, the screams of gulls, the sounds of things *unseen* out there in the thick clouds, wrapped in mystery.

Like the truth about Hooper's murder.

He rolled up the windows and finished the last of his coffee as they drew closer to Half Moon Bay. It was cradled between the breathtaking coastline and rolling green hills. It offered everything you'd expect of a small seaside town: art galleries, restaurants, crafts, quaint bed-and-breakfasts, golf courses, motels, hotels, spas, and new resorts, like the Moonlight Vista Hotel.

Molly Wilson had told them they'd find evidence there.

The Moonlight Vista was a new two-story Mediterranean-style complex, with two hundred rooms on a cliffside overlooking the ocean.

Tall palms bowed over the entrance canopy, their fronds hissing in the breeze as Sydowski and Turgeon entered the darkened lobby. Within minutes a man wearing a blue suit appeared.

"Eduard Sanchez," he said after Sydowski and Turgeon showed him their identification. "We spoke. This way, please."

Sanchez's office was dark. There was a state-of-the-art flat-screen computer on one side of his large mahogany desk.

"You have the warrant?"

Turgeon opened her valise, unfolded the papers, and passed them to Sanchez. He read carefully, thoughtfully. He turned in his chair to his computer keyboard and began typing, stopping from time to time to consult the information on the warrant.

Sanchez studied the screen as his printer kicked to life. He retrieved the printed documents, handed them to Sydowski.

"These are all the charges to Beamon's room for this date. Room service charges indicate a meal for two people. Breakfasts," Sydowski said.

"Yes. Two guests. As you are aware, most hotels don't require identification of additional guests. Please follow me for the other matter."

Sanchez led them to a room behind the main desk that was jammed with monitors, computers, and control panels. Nick Miller, the man in the swivel chair, shook hands with Sydowski and Turgeon. "I've got what you want here. Watch number 12." Tape was rolling at high speed.

"We watch the lots for car thefts, accidents, you name it. The pool. All entrances, exits, lobbies, common areas. Elevators and hallways. We archive the footage for one year. We get all kinds of claims, 'I slipped in the hall, I'm suing,' or, 'Our kids never destroyed the paintings in your hotel hallway, prove it.' It's in the fine print that we monitor all public common areas for security. Most places do."

The tape on monitor 12 stopped blurring.

"The hallway where your subject was a guest at the time of check-in."

Sydowski and Turgeon watched a clear color recording of Ray Beamon, dressed in jeans and a T-shirt, entering the room with Molly. She was in shorts and a T-shirt. No luggage. Several hours after that, Beamon and Molly exited. Sydowski checked the restaurant receipt. The time fit with credit card records.

The tape raced. Miller stopped to show them returning to their room. The tape raced again. Time blurred. Miller slowed it to show a staff member dropping copies of newspapers at doors. A few hours later Beamon's door opened and Molly wearing only a loose-fitting white robe emerged. As she bent down, her

163

breast spilled out and she pulled the robe tight, laughing. Behind her, bare-chested and wearing only a towel around his waist, Ray Beamon playfully pulled Molly back into the room.

"Stop it right there," Sydowski said.

There it was. The image of Molly bent down, the robe barely covering her. Her attractive smile, her tousled hair, and behind her Beamon, his broad chest with forests of hair, wearing only a towel, his hands gripping Molly's hips. It burned into Sydowski's gut. He saw disgust on Turgeon's face as he popped a fresh Tums into his mouth and grinded on it.

"All right," Sydowski said.

After they'd finished viewing all the tapes they seized them, thanked Sanchez and Miller, then left.

Outside, they didn't go to the car but went to the beach, stopping to lean on a large rock warmed by the sun. They looked out at the ocean as the surf rolled in and gulls cried.

"You know, I thought I knew Ray," Turgeon said. "I thought we were family. I got to like Molly, too."

Sydowski's face hid his overwhelming sadness.

"That tape of them in the doorway." She stopped. "Why? Was this all about jealousy? Sex?"

"We've seen people do worse for less." Sydowski shook his head, unconsciously detecting other birdsongs, terns, and whimbrels, sounding like a requiem over the rush of the sea.

"You know they sat together at his funeral. They dropped roses on his casket," he said.

Looking out at the Pacific Ocean, Sydowski saw that the fog had lifted. The unseen things that haunted him in this life were visible.

Time to talk to the district attorney.

He was ready to go at Ray.

28

Tom slipped off his jacket and searched the newsroom for someone he could trust.

He sat at his desk, opened his cassette recorder, and removed the tape of his interview with Ray Beamon. He popped the plastic tabs at the back to ensure that he couldn't accidentally record over it. Then he rattled through his desk for a felt-tipped pen and wrote *Ray: I'd kill him* on the tape.

A shadow fell over him, distracting his attention.

"What's that?" asked Simon Lepp, unable to see what Tom had scrawled.

"An interview with a cop. It might be useful." Tom slipped it in his pocket. "How're you doing?"

"Not so well. That's what I wanted to talk to you about. Have you got a minute?"

"A quick one."

"I haven't found much going through Hooper's old murder cases that would point to a vendetta or threat."

"I know, it's not like it's going to be obvious."

"And I went to the Ingleside district office

and talked to some guys there. They suggested that I not only look back at any beefs during Hooper's time in Homicide, but look at his entire career track."

"Like Narcotics, Vice, the tac team."

"Yes. That's a lot of looking. Any suggestions?"

"Well, I'd drop Tac. They don't really interact with people. Narcotics would be a good start. Excuse me." Tom spotted Acker. "Go back on stories about drug busts when Hooper was in Narcotics. I recall a lot of sparks during that time. Sorry, I have to go."

As Tom went across the metro section he noticed Acker was holding a coffee and a clipboard and looking mournful.

"You won't believe what I've got," Tom said. "We have to talk."

Acker glanced at his watch.

"Is it something for tomorrow's paper? Because I don't have much time."

"No. I want to hold this for a bit and make it stronger. Let's go here."

Tom pulled Acker into the office of a columnist who was on a three-month leave of absence. Tom snapped his Beamon tape into his cassette. It was cued to the quote he wanted Acker to hear.

Tom noticed Acker seemed to be grappling with some kind of personal problem and was more interested in the full-color poster of Fiji on the wall until the tape clicked on.

"Listen to this. 'I sure as hell wish I knew, because if I ever caught the guy who did it, I'd put one in his head. I'd kill him. No question.' "

Acker stared at Tom.

"That's Beamon. And it's our exclusive."

"That is dynamite, Tom. Fantastic. You're hot on this story."

"I want to hold it."

"Why?"

"I've got a strong feeling that something's happening on the case. Something huge."

"How long do you want to hold this?"

"I'll go through it all tonight. Then I need to go to Molly to see if she can help me with anything else."

"What do you want me to do?"

"You're the only one I've told. Don't tell Irene. Run interference for me for just a bit."

"I'll do my best but these aren't the best of times to be pulling things like this."

"What do you mean?"

"We'll talk about it later. Good story. A partner's revenge. Hell."

29

Emma Highgate of the D.A.'s office clicked her expensive pen over and over as Sydowski first rolled the police surveillance videotape of the mourners who'd attended Cliff Hooper's funeral.

The techs had highlighted footage of Ray Beamon, enlarging frames showing his scraped knuckles. Then Sydowski played the security tape seized under warrant from the Moonlight Vista Hotel in Half Moon Bay.

When it ended, Highgate listened carefully to Sydowski's summary of the investigation. She jotted notes on her yellow legal pad, then regarded the officers at the meeting. Along with Sydowski and Turgeon were Bill Kennedy, deputy chief of investigations, Captain Michelle Stroh, and Lieutenant Leo Gonzales.

"Short answer," Highgate told them, "you don't have enough to take this case to a grand jury."

"The tapes are strong, they've got impact," Stroh said.

"Maybe if you wanted to prove infidelity." Highgate shook her head. "You've got two consenting adults having a romantic fling in Half Moon Bay. It's not enough."

"Wilson dated Hooper. Cheated on him with his partner," Kennedy said. "Beamon betrayed Hooper and Hooper found out on the day he was murdered. That's a powerful motive."

"I agree. It's a morality thing. But you can't indict him on that alone. The rest is all circumstantial."

"What about Beamon's contradictions?" Gonzales said.

"What about them?"

"Beamon says he stayed home, worked on his car, and scraped his knuckles. We can prove he lied. Put him at Hooper's building with scraped knuckles. His injury is consistent with the autopsy," Stroh said.

"Circumstantial. No one witnessed Beamon strike Hooper."

"We got witnesses who saw him exit Hooper's building the night of the murder," Gonzales said.

"You have no physical evidence to put him *in* the unit. He could have called on Hooper, rung the bell. Left. He could've dropped by. Naturally he would have been seen by witnesses," Highgate said. "He's a friend. It's natural he'd be seen."

"What about those scraped knuckles?" Gonzales said.

"Weak. Beamon's account of that night can

be expected to be shaky."

"We can put him there and prove him lying about it."

Highgate underlined some points in her file.

"Guys." She flipped through the report. "You've got witnesses saying he was wearing a black T-shirt and witnesses saying it was a white T-shirt. A defense team would feast on that. I could just hear it, 'It's black, it's white, it's black, it's white. Ladies and gentleman of the jury, *clearly it is not black and white.*' "

"But we've got a license number of his Barracuda, a unique car we can put at the scene the night of the murder."

"But Ray was Hooper's partner. Again it's not unusual for him to be there. Heck, he and Molly Wilson would have plenty of trace evidence there. You've left plenty of opportunity for the defense to raise a lot of reasonable doubt." She flipped through her pages. "So far, your physical evidence is all but nonexistent. No match to a suspect on the bullets, no fingerprints, no DNA. Not much. No blood, hair, fibers."

Highgate began flipping through some of the scene photos, reports.

"What about the blood message on the wall? The placement of Hooper's gun and police ID? Did you exhaust all other avenues?"

"Writing analysis gave us nothing on the

blood. We chased down all the other aspects," Gonzales said.

"And?"

"We think Beamon, being an expert on homicide scenes, threw that stuff down as a distraction."

"In other words, nothing. All right," Highgate said. "There are reports alleging Hooper had made enemies with criminals who may have had motive. You got OCC and Management Control watching you. Has all of that been ruled out?"

"Cliff wasn't dirty."

"And you can prove this beyond any doubt?"

Turgeon stared at her, holding her words.

"Look," Highgate said, "I have to play devil's advocate here. You need a linchpin to hold it all together solidly. It's just not there yet."

Hating every moment of it, Sydowski slid a Tums in his mouth. Thinking back on the night Turgeon came to the hospital to tell him, Sydowski feared the sick feeling that bubbled in his gut would never leave him. This case took them into hell. In all his years on the job, he never thought he'd face something like this. Hooper and Beamon were like his younger brothers, or his sons. Now it was his job, his sworn duty, to build the case to prove one had murdered the other.

Sydowski swallowed the remains of his

tablet. His gold crowns glinted as he gritted his teeth. He knew what awaited him, for he had been performing some mental sleight of hand to make the inevitable disappear. To avoid the unavoidable. But his fear had materialized. It was sitting there before him, a psychological Hydra, ready to do battle.

"Emma," Sydowski said. "I know what we have to do."

"What's that?"

"I've got to challenge Ray with what we know."

"You think you can get him to confess?"

Kennedy shook his head.

"You're new to the D.A.'s office," Kennedy said. "Walt's got the highest clearance rate of any homicide investigator in California."

Highgate's eyes met Sydowski's.

"Given the emotional mine field here, the question I have to ask is, are you up to it?"

He couldn't answer.

Highgate was smart to exercise respect as she gathered her material into folders, indicating the meeting had ended.

"I hope you are, because a confession would seal it, Inspector."

When they were alone in the elevator, heading back to the homicide detail, Gonzales turned to Sydowski.

"What do you have to challenge him on?"

"His statement and my first notes."

"Your first notes?"

173

"I took notes after talking with him the morning after. Took down everything Ray told me in conversations about his whereabouts, his knuckles."

"That enough for you?"

Sydowski nodded.

"Where's Ray now?" Turgeon asked.

"Out with Harry Lance and Shrader, helping on their case," Gonzales said. Unease rose in his face. "This is going to tear up our squad once this gets out. I want you to go at him as soon as you can. Get it over with."

Back in the detail, Gonzales saw Lance on the phone. Shrader was getting coffee. No sign of Beamon.

"Where's Ray, Harry?"

"He took off."

"Took off where?"

"Just said he had something to do."

30

Hot coffee flooded over Ray Beamon's cup, scalding his hand. He winced as he wiped the puddle on the counter of the homicide detail, feeling the heat of someone's stare. He turned.

Sydowski was watching him.

"I'll get out of your way," Beamon said.

"You seem to be having a hard time there. Need some help?"

"Thanks, I can manage."

Gonzales had reached Beamon on his cell phone and asked him to come in to go over some files. The lieutenant and Sydowski wanted to ease into an interview with Beamon casually, apply the challenge slowly or see their case collapse like a house of cards.

Sydowski inventoried Beamon. His hair could stand a few more strokes with a comb. His jacket was wrinkled, as if he'd slept in it. His tie was loosened, his collar unbuttoned. Strain in his eyes. Lines cut into his face around the small patch of lower chin stubble his razor had missed.

He's living in torment, Sydowski thought.

"You getting enough sleep, Ray?"

"Barely."

Turgeon arrived and reached for her cup.

"Hi, Ray, where've you been? Card and Shrader and the guys you were helping lost track of you. Are you all right?"

"Getting by."

"Where'd you go?" Sydowski asked.

A moment passed.

"Drove up to Tamalpais. By myself."

"What'd you go out there for?"

"Stared at the sea and tried to figure out who did this to Cliff."

"Any leads for us?"

"No." Beamon took a hit of coffee. "I just want to step back from it all. It's hard. It feels like half of me is gone."

Beamon contemplated the black ripples in his cup while Sydowski and Turgeon helped themselves to coffee, exchanging virtually imperceptible glances, saying little, waiting for the right moment. For their chance to go at him. The squad room was empty. Dead silent, except for Lieutenant Gonzales. He was in his office, the door open, talking softly on the phone. Sydowski and Turgeon waited, until finally Beamon raised his head from his cup. "Would you guys bring me up to speed on where you're at?"

There it was.

Sydowski and Turgeon made a point of having Beamon see them exchange glances,

176

intentionally letting his request hang in the air.

"I mean, if it's all right?" Beamon added.

Sydowski rubbed his chin, looked around the empty room.

"I suppose we could give you a little update, if that's what you'd like. We'll get our stuff and go in one of the interview rooms."

"Interview room?"

"Sure."

"Can't you just brief me here?"

Beamon eyeballed Sydowski, cognizant of the ramifications, the implications, the psychological tactics at play. Going into the interview room would take it all to another level, raise the stakes. *Oh Christ,* he thought, running his hand through his hair. He knew this was coming.

"Ray, take it easy," Sydowski said. "It's a good place to update you. No one will interrupt us there."

Beamon thought for a moment before he said, "Fine."

Unlocking his wooden cabinet drawer for his files, Sydowski glanced at Gonzales, telegraphing the message that this was it.

The shot.

In the small white room, Beamon intentionally, or maybe by habit, took the chair he'd always occupied whenever he and Hooper worked on a witness, or a suspect. Turgeon sat across from him, Sydowski beside him, in Hooper's spot.

Chairs squeaked, papers were shuffled, throats cleared as they began with a general update, harmless publicly known stuff and the speculation from the press arising from OCC and Management Control, alleging that Hooper's murder was linked to corruption on the street.

"We don't know where that's coming from, Ray, any thoughts?"

"Cliff wasn't dirty, you know that."

"I know. But the way I see it, this was not a stranger thing."

"Really?"

"No sign of struggle."

"A burglar?"

"Not likely. No forced entry. Nothing missing."

"But what about —" Beamon halted.

"What about what?"

"Physical evidence. You released that he was shot. What about casings, the round — ballistics? Must be something from imaging?"

"There's not a heck of a lot we can tell you."

"So that's it? That's where you're at?"

"Pretty much," Sydowski said. "Can you help us?"

"Help you how?"

Sydowski opened his file. So did Turgeon. Sydowski slipped on his bifocals; Beamon felt the air tighten.

"We're still piecing together his last movements. I want to go over some things again. Once more, when was the last time you saw him?"

Beamon stared at Sydowski. Turgeon's pen was poised over her notepad. They probably were recording this interview, Beamon figured.

"Sure, but I already told you everything."

"When was the last time you saw Cliff?"

"Here at the detail. I asked him if he wanted to go for a beer."

"And?"

"He didn't have time."

"What was his demeanor?"

"Fine. Happy. Like I already told you, he said he was going to see Molly, like a date. So we never went for a beer."

"What did you do?"

"Went home. Had dinner, worked on my Barracuda."

"Did Cliff call you or did you call him?"

Beamon shook his head.

"So after seeing him here, you never saw him again?"

"Right."

Sydowski studied Beamon's body language.

"You're sure?"

Beamon nodded.

"Did he indicate if he was maybe going to meet someone else before his date with Molly Wilson?"

"No. Not to me."

Sydowski noted that the scrapes on the knuckles of Beamon's right hand had faded.

"You got those scrapes from working on your car, right?"

"I don't remember."

"I do."

A chill descended on them.

Sydowski flipped though his notes. "I wrote it down after talking with you the morning after Hooper was found. You told me you scraped your knuckles working on your car."

"You wrote it down? What is this?"

"We've got people who can put your Barracuda at Cliff's place the night he was killed."

"Well, I may have driven over to see him. He liked looking at the car."

"But you said you never left your place. Stayed in all night."

"I think I told someone I may have gone for a little ride. Christ, I can't remember every word of a conversation with you."

"That's right. I'm just trying to clarify things as to who may have been seen near Hooper's place. I want to be clear on what you told me."

Beamon licked his lips and said nothing. Sydowski went back to his file.

"How would you describe Cliff's relationship with Molly Wilson?"

"Good."

"Did Cliff ever discuss her with you?"

"What do you mean?"

"His plans, dreams, the future. How serious was he?"

"He really liked her, talked about settling down with her."

"And how was she with that?"

"Ask her."

"Did you ever date Wilson?"

"Sure, I mean, with Cliff we doubled, or sometimes just all visited. We were all friends."

"I see. But you never dated her like just the two of you?"

"She and Cliff were an item. Come on."

"So if you were at Cliff's house that night, did you go inside?"

Beamon said nothing.

Sydowski eyed him for a long time over his bifocals, taking stock of Beamon's face, his eyes, his hands. His breathing. His brow was beginning to moisten. "I know you're working me here, Walt."

"This is a simple thing we need to clarify. Were you there and did you go inside?"

Beamon dropped his head, stared at his hands, the remnants of bruises on his right knuckles, the veneer tabletop, Sydowski's and Turgeon's files. He noticed how in Turgeon's folder, pages of the scene report were exposed. He could see one clearly and began reading upside down until Sydowski noticed, reached over, and slowly tilted Turgeon's file. Turgeon reacted by pulling the file closer to herself. Sydowski let his question go unanswered and went to another.

"The night before Hooper was killed, I saw you with him. In the detail, remember?" Sydowski said.

Beamon didn't remember.

"You'd followed him outside our office to the elevator. I'd just stepped off. You'd said something to him that appeared to deflate him, take the good humor from his face. What did you tell him?"

Staring at his hands, Beamon grinned the grin of a man who realized he was trapped. He began shaking his head.

"It appears to me that Hooper's murder was personal. His killer had some connection, or link, to him. Maybe a direct link."

Beamon shrugged.

"Maybe it was a robbery. Or payback from some 800 we nailed in an old beef, some nutcase."

"I know but we're sure we can rule that out. It just doesn't look like it went that way to me. You see, my thinking is that Hooper knew his killer. This was personal."

Sydowski reached into his jacket pocket and produced a small videocassette tape. He set it on the table. Sydowski's fingertips caressed the tape as if it possessed a powerful force.

"Now I want you to think carefully how

you're going to answer, because I'm going to ask you this one more time: Did you ever date Molly Wilson?"

Sydowski turned the tape slowly. Beamon's eyes locked on to the label identifying it as security footage from the Moonlight Vista Hotel in Half Moon Bay, dated one week before Hooper's murder. A rivulet of sweat trickled down his back, as if it were a terrified living thing attempting to flee. All the spit dried in his mouth.

"Did you ever date Molly Wilson behind Cliff's back?"

Beamon stared at the tape. Stared as if it were his life, slipping from him.

"Make it easy on yourself. You owe it to yourself. To Cliff."

Beamon's eyes glistened. He blinked.

"Here's what I think happened," Sydowski said. "Cliff found out you and Molly Wilson, the woman he loved, were cheating on him behind his back. You tried to talk to him about that night. That's what was going on when I saw you at the elevator. He was supposed to see Molly at Jake's, but once he'd learned the truth about you and Molly he was devastated. In no shape to see anyone. So you went to see him. You drove over to try to talk it out. Smooth it over. But it was worse than you'd expected. Hooper was out of his mind. On the day he wanted to ask for her hand, he learns *this*. Can you imagine?

Maybe he suddenly lost it, or things got out of hand real fast. Maybe he came at you, you had to do what you had to do, right? Maybe it was an accident, or self-defense. Anyone in your shoes would do the same thing. But, God Almighty, you didn't want to kill him, he was your partner. Your *brother.* You didn't mean to do it. You got scared. You fixed the scene to send us off helter-skelter. Maybe tipped OCC to some bullshit corruption line from the street."

Beamon covered his face with his hands. Tears filled his eyes. He stared at the white cinder-block walls. Time ticked by. He blinked at Turgeon, at Sydowski.

"Ray," Sydowski said, "you spoke at his funeral. Placed a rose on his casket. Now's the time to unburden yourself. Ease your conscience. Be a man. Do the right thing. For you. For Cliff, for everyone."

Beamon stared at the walls for the longest time before he cleared his throat.

"Walt." His voice was a whisper. "You haven't Mirandized me."

"You're not in custody."

"Am I under arrest?"

"No."

"You going to charge me?"

Sydowski waited a beat before he said, "I'd like you to take a polygraph first. Then we can help you to help yourself. We can talk to the district attorney, explain how it was self-

184

defense, no special circumstances. No death penalty."

Death penalty.

Beamon's head snapped up.

"I want a lawyer and I want my rep." Beamon's voice grew louder as he stared at the mirrored observation window, knowing he was being watched. "Hear that, Leo? I want my lawyer and I want my rep."

"We understand."

"Nobody knows what happened. I'm not telling you another thing until I have my lawyer and my rep beside me," Beamon said.

"I understand. We want to help you do this right."

Beamon left. Turgeon shook her head as she finished taking notes. Gonzales stepped into the room.

"You did good. I know it was rough, but you did good."

Sydowski shoved a Tums into his mouth, nodded while chewing on it. Then he headed for the elevator.

31

Tom was at his home near Golden Gate Park studying his options and frustrating his son.

"There's nothing you can do, Dad. You're trapped."

He didn't respond.

Staring blankly at the chessboard, he'd lost sight of the game, for he was ruminating upon another battlefield. It was getting late and Molly had not returned his call. His cell phone was on. Fully charged and waiting for calls among Zach's throng of captured pieces.

"Dad, it's been five minutes. Come on. It's your move."

"Mmm."

He wanted to listen to his tape of Ray Beamon again. He had a bad, bad feeling about this. Beamon sounded as if he was hiding something. And why hadn't Molly called, or answered the messages he'd left?

Tom looked over to Ann curled up on the sofa reading a book. It struck him to ask her about the meaning of roses when their home phone rang with a call for her.

"Time for bed, Zach," she said after cupping her hand on the phone. "Let's go."

Zach pulled himself to his feet and kissed his mother.

"Good night, champ. We'll do more work on the battleship tomorrow." Tom rubbed Zach's hair, reached for his cell phone, then headed to his study.

After closing the door he sat in his chair, slipped on headphones, and played his interview with Beamon. Through his home system he could enhance the sound and adjust the speed so he could concentrate on every word and the tone.

He was convinced there was a better story than Beamon's emotional vow to kill his partner's murderer. While Tom was no expert on stress and voice analysis, he'd conducted enough interviews in his career to develop strong instincts about what people told him. And Beamon sounded as if he was under extraordinary stress. Not grief or mourning, but as if he was facing some overwhelming crisis.

It was during the segment where Tom had asked him about Molly. He'd missed it the first few times. It was quick, subtle, almost lost when Tom had started the next question.

"And what about the relationship with Molly Wilson?"

"What about her? What did she tell you?"

That was it. Tom replayed it.

"What about her? What did she tell you?"

What did she tell you?

187

Beamon's tone was guarded to the point of deception, as if he was trying to hide something about Molly and himself.

Tom needed her to hear this tape.

He reached for his phone and tried her number one more time.

32

Beamon could run to Canada, or Mexico, he thought. But he didn't like his odds. It was time to face the truth. He owed it to Hoop.

After Sydowski had taken a run at him, Beamon had left the Hall of Justice. He got in his Barracuda and just drove, south along the Pacific Coastal Highway. He was north of Los Angeles when he realized it was futile. Deep in his heart he knew he couldn't run. It was just that Sydowski had gotten to him.

In a roadside diner near the ocean Beamon nursed a black coffee, admitting that Sydowski had the key pieces. And he'd put most of them in the correct place. The only thing he didn't possess was the truth. Beamon held on to that card, reluctant to play it because no one would believe it. Not Turgeon. Not Sydowski. Nobody, except one person.

Maybe.

Molly would believe him. What choice did she have? She was the spark that ignited this inferno, he thought, returning to his car, heading it to San Francisco and his chance at redemption.

★ ★ ★

Night was falling when he rang her bell.

"Ray, where've you been?" Molly said, opening the door. "I went to your house. You weren't home. I've been trying to reach you. What the hell's going on with you?"

"Sit down. I'm going to tell you everything."

She was wearing sweatpants, a T-shirt. Her hair was pulled back into a ponytail, worry lines pressed into her face. She wore no makeup. Her eyes searched his with anger and fear.

"Sydowski's probably working on getting warrants to search my house, my cars, probably yours, too. He's coming at me hard. He knows that I went to Cliff's apartment that night."

"Did you kill him?"

"Just listen to me. This is going to be hard, but I'm going to tell you everything."

Molly's phone rang. She let her machine get it.

"A few weeks back, before he died, Cliff told me he was serious about you. He was going to propose to you. He was talking about getting a ring, had asked me to be his best man. He wanted to marry you."

"I never knew this. I told him all along I didn't want a long-term relationship."

"I know. He was in love with you and thought he could win you over to wanting to be with him."

190

"No. No, I never felt like that, I —"

"On that day, his last day, he told me how he was going to pop the question to you that night. How you were the best thing that'd ever happened to him, he wanted children, he worshiped you."

Molly groaned.

"He started going on how he had it all planned, was going to pick you up at Jake's in a rented limo, take you across the Golden Gate to some special restaurant near the bay in Sausalito, then pop the question."

"Oh no."

"Then he bumped into Arnold Desfor from San Jose, who told him he'd seen us at the hotel in Half Moon Bay. It destroyed him. It happened at the end of our shift and he barely left the Hall without taking me apart."

Molly stared at the floor.

"So I go home and work on my Barracuda. But this thing's just killing me. So I drive over to his place to see him."

Molly's head snapped up. Beamon swallowed. His throat tightened, his eyes stung, and his voice weakened. He stared off and traveled back in time, back to Hooper's apartment.

"I told him that Desfor was right. I told him the truth. I tried to couch it. I said, yes, it was a one-time thing. And he should talk to you because maybe it showed you weren't ready to settle down. But I'm making a bad thing worse and I'm just babbling and he's, he's —"

"What — what did he say?"

"He was devastated. I'd never seen a guy free-fall so fast. He started saying things that didn't make sense. Then he calmed down, said he'd be okay, just needed to think, and that I should go. We heard the phone ring, that must've been you. It set him off. He disappeared into his bedroom, I followed him, then boom, he's got his Beretta aimed at me."

Beamon shook his head.

"I put up my palms, walked toward him, and talked him down. He starts crying, acts like he's going to surrender his weapon to me, but then whips the gun to his temple and scares me to death. I don't know what's going to happen. I yell and jump him. I grab at the muzzle with my left hand, punching his head with my right. To jolt him out of it, you know. We fall on the bed. It takes every bit of strength to get the Beretta from him, but I do."

Beamon inhaled, then exhaled.

"I manage to coax Cliff to his sofa, where we talk. I clean up the place, try to be cool. Talk to him. I tell him I'm so sorry. That I thought you'd made it clear to him that you weren't committed to him. But he's such a sensitive guy. He was crazy about you."

Molly said nothing.

"Then we hear his cell phone going, it must've been you again. He doesn't answer but we talk for a long time. At one point he says he'd suspected maybe something was up with us but had dismissed it. He collected himself. I know he's got an off-duty gun somewhere, but he won't tell me where. We keep talking. He assures me he won't shoot me or himself and holds out his hand for his weapon. He's my partner. He's calmed down, his breathing's fine. So I give it to him, knowing he's got another gun somewhere in his place anyway Then he asks me to leave. Again, I'm wondering if I should go. I'm still a little jumpy. But Cliff starts insisting I leave. And to be honest, I'm so torn up I can't bear to see his pain. By this time he seems rational, like the worst has passed. So I leave."

Beamon looked into his empty hands.

"I get halfway to my house and I think, I've made a huge mistake. I should go back. I should take charge. I shouldn't have left him like that. I get home and spend the rest of the night torturing myself about leaving him. Was it right? I wasn't thinking clearly. Maybe part of me wanted desperately to get away from the ugliness of the situation, maybe that's why I left him. At home I couldn't sleep. I was tossing and turning until I got the call that you'd found him."

"Who was it?"

"Turgeon. When she told me over the

193

phone, the first thing I thought was that Cliff had committed suicide and it was my fault. I was overcome with guilt. That's why I kept everything inside. I felt it was my fault."

A long moment passed with Molly hugging herself.

"Tell me, Ray. Did you kill Cliff, even by accident?"

"No, Molly, I swear to God."

Absorbing his words, she paced about the room, then said, "All right, we have to tell Sydowski. Fill in the blanks for him."

"I know."

"We have to lay it out for Sydowski that Cliff's killer is out there. We'll tell him the truth."

"Sydowski will think I've come to you to back up my line."

"No. He's wasting too much time pursuing you when you didn't do it. We should call him right now and tell him, tell him everything. You said he knows most of it. This way, Sydowski can eliminate you and focus on finding the real killer."

"All right. I swear to God, I thought Cliff had taken his own life after the blowup with me, but when you found him on his bed with his gun on his back, his ID and star displayed, then obviously someone had organized the scene."

Molly's breath froze in her throat. Her eyes widened. She stared at Beamon.

"*How did you know those details, Ray?* That's Sydowski's hold-back."

"I'm not sure. I think you must've told me."

"No, I didn't. I haven't told anyone, Ray."

Beamon said nothing.

"The only people who know are Sydowski and Turgeon. Ray, how did you know I found Hooper on the bed with his gun and ID displayed?" Molly went to Beamon, pressing him. "Sydowski wouldn't tell you. No one knows, Ray, so how did you know?"

He stood, passed his hand through his hair, stared at the floor. Maybe he'd seen it in a file. He was unsure. Over the last few days, he'd been overwhelmed, unsure of anything. He started shaking his head. He didn't know how to answer her.

"Molly, I must've picked it up somewhere."

"Ray? Answer me, goddammit. Where did you get that?"

Ray stared coldly into her eyes, then left.

Molly screamed after him, racing down the stairs to the street, trotting after him, pounding on the window of his car as he drove off.

"Ray! Ray!"

Molly stood helplessly on the street watching his taillights disappear into the San Francisco night. She made her way back into her apartment, closed the door, leaned back against it, and slid to the floor, sobbing.

33

Come on, girl, be strong.

The tear tracks had stiffened on her cheeks by the time Molly drove down Mission Street to Bernal Heights.

It was late. She'd spent the last few hours calling Beamon. It was futile. She adjusted her grip. She'd find him if it took all night. She needed to convince him that he had to go to Sydowski and tell him everything about that night.

Everything.

Waiting at a red light, Molly felt faint. Had to be stress. She had no time to worry about that, she told herself, as she continued south.

Turning east off Mission, she grabbed her cell phone and tried Beamon's home number again. It rang and rang. *Come on.* She squeezed her phone, cursing when his machine answered. Again, she tried his cell phone. Again, no answer. Damn. She tossed her phone into her passenger seat and accelerated up the hill to Beamon's street before skidding to a stop in front of his bungalow.

The living room curtains were drawn. The bungalow waited for her in darkness. She

196

went up the walk, pressed the doorbell, and heard it echo through the small house.

Nothing.

Aside from the distant din of traffic drifting up from the 101, it was quiet. She went to the garage, looked through the security bars of a side window. She saw the glint of the Barracuda's chrome.

No Beamon.

She went around the house to the rear. A galaxy of city lights stretched below to the skyline glittering in the distance. No sign of Beamon. Molly's head felt light again. She steadied herself against the house. Blinking, she took a few deep breaths.

Okay.

She returned to the front. *He's got to come home sometime.* She'd sleep on his doorstep if that's what she had to do to make him face the inevitable.

At the door, she jabbed the bell again.

Nothing. It was silent. Damn it. In frustration she tightened her hand into a fist and pounded on his door. She hit it once and gasped.

It swung open.

"Ray?"

What's going on? She tried to think. Go in? Or call somebody? Her head was throbbing. She couldn't think.

"Ray?"

No answer. This was so stupid. He'd probably forgotten to lock it coming in or going out, she reasoned, then prayed as she stepped inside. Her fingers found the lights and she turned on as many as she could find.

"Ray?"

Molly detected something in the air, a trace of a burning smell. Maybe from cooking, or from working on the car. It was familiar, she thought, walking through the house, switching on lights as she progressed. Nothing seemed out of place. Beamon's cell phone was on the kitchen counter. It was on, working. In the living room, the red light of the answering machine was flashing.

Molly swallowed.

"Ray?"

It was so quiet, so still. Her stomach was beginning to knot as she moved down the hall, coming to his spare room, which had his barbells, bench, and stationary bike. She moved on to the bathroom. Hit the lights. Nothing. She turned to leave, then stopped.

A yellow towel dampened with brownish stains was left on the vanity. The sink was filled with water. It was pink. Molly's hand went to her mouth. Her stomach tightened.

"Ray!"

She backed from the bathroom and inched toward Beamon's bedroom, an avalanche of dread thundering behind her.

The door was open.

Molly found the light switch.

In that first microsecond of realization, the first thought that registered in her brain was: *Ray, get up, we have to talk.* Then she saw the firework splatter pattern on the wall behind Beamon's head. He was half seated staring wide-eyed at her like a macabre puppet with a black hole centered above his eyebrows. He was covered in goose down from the pillow used to muffle the blast. Feathers had adhered to his blood. His Beretta and police identification rested on his stomach.

Molly did not remember if she started screaming before or after seeing the message in blood pleading from the wall behind her.

Why, Molly?

34

Startled by screams, Ray Beamon's neighbors peered from their windows.

Molly had emerged from Beamon's bungalow to the front doorstep, trembling and sobbing. Vivian Masters and Gertrude Lorimer abandoned their card game and hurried across the street to comfort her.

"Ray's dead. Ray's dead," Molly whispered over and over.

Masters and Lorimer were stunned. Their attention went beyond Beamon's open door but neither entered his house. Lorimer stayed with Molly while Masters ran home and called 911.

Two of the district's closest SFPD units and an ambulance responded with lights and sirens. The first officers secured the primary scene, escorting paramedics to Beamon's body. They found no signs of life, thus setting in motion an investigation into the death of another homicide inspector.

The first responding uniformed officer had two years on the job. A stickler for procedure, he and his partner protected the scene, took quick careful notes, collected initial statements and information, then told dispatch to alert the homicide detail.

At the Hall of Justice, Inspector Jay Tipton and his partner, Jeff Vidor, were on duty. Tipton took the call.

"What? Repeat that address? Repeat the name? Who made the find? Right. Okay."

Vidor's jaw dropped and he cast a glance at Beamon's desk when Tipton told him. Then Vidor jabbed the cell phone number for their boss. Lieutenant Leo Gonzales. He was at home watching John Wayne in *The Searchers*. Gonzales was sorting out their strategy to charge Beamon with Hooper's murder when his phone chimed softly in his chest pocket.

"Leo, this is Vidor. Ray Beamon's dead. At home."

Vidor heard nothing but a static hiss at the other end.

"Leo?"

"Christ Almighty. Are you sure?"

"Just came in from the unit on-scene."

"Goddammit. Did he off himself?"

"I don't know. We'll take it. We're on our way."

"No, I want Sydowski and Turgeon. You go, but you assist them."

"But we caught it —"

"I want Sydowski on it." Gonzales hung up. With fumbling between his glasses and his cell phone, he accidentally activated

201

Turgeon's number on his speed-dial menu. Hers was next to Sydowski's.

She was at home struggling to take her worried mind from Hooper's case. It had been keeping her up nights. She was trying to reread *Crime and Punishment* when Gonzales broke the news.

"Oh God. No. I can't believe this," she said.

"You call Walt. I'll meet you there. I've got to alert the brass."

Sydowski and Turgeon arrived together, parking amid the district black-and-whites. Their radios crackled and emergency lights strobed, making the entire neighborhood pulsate in red. Residents gathered at the yellow tape the uniforms had stretched around Beamon's yard, concern drawn on their faces. Beamon's house stood alone against the twinkling lights of the city he'd served.

Sydowski and Turgeon talked with the responding officers, started their own notes, tugged on latex gloves and shoe covers, then ducked under the tape at the entrance to the house and went to work. They barely spoke, proceeding methodically, clinically, for at times it was as if they were underwater struggling in slow motion against a current of horror. For a deafening moment, all Sydowski could do was pray that Beamon had committed suicide. But it was evident by the scene that such prayers were in vain.

Someone was killing San Francisco's homicide detectives. Killing his friends. Rage and pain swirled in Sydowski's heart, pushing him to the edge.

It was as if he'd stepped into the deepest darkness. Hours ago he'd braced himself to charge Ray with Hooper's murder. And now Ray was dead. The same way as Hooper. They were partners in death. It nearly brought Sydowski to his knees. He reached deep into his gut, scrambling for anything he could cling to, clawing for the strength he needed to see this through.

He took several deep breaths.

Righteous investigation was his only weapon.

He would break this case down into the tiniest parts and analyze each one until he found the truth. God, he had to.

He *had* to.

In Beamon's bedroom, Turgeon turned to Sydowski as she inspected the scrawled message to Molly on the wall.

"She's the obvious link."

"Or the obvious suspect."

Turgeon waited for Sydowski to elaborate.

"We've got a whole new case now," he said.

After they were done in the murder room, Sydowski talked to the medical examiner's people and the criminalists at the scene about recovering a range of evidence, cell phone, answering machine, phone records, e-mails, the fatal round to compare with the rounds in Hooper's case. He wanted them to test Beamon's gun, scour the house and neighborhood for any other evidence. Go through his cars, his garage. None of them took offense that Sydowski was telling them to do what they were trained to do. None of them were insulted. They knew he was raging against the violation. They understood. They were hurting too.

Sydowski had requested a residue test whereby an investigator would rub a cotton swab with a nitric acid solution on a person's hands. Analysis could detect gunshot residue that stuck to hands that fired a weapon, or were close to one that was fired. Sydowski approached one of the crime scene technicians.

"Did you swab Molly Wilson like I asked?"

"I did. It's going to Hunter's Point along with much of everything else we'll pick up here."

Turgeon pulled him aside, dropping her voice. "You don't seriously think it's her?"

"I don't know what to think. Maybe we should have swabbed her from the get-go in Hooper's case. Get a warrant for her apartment and car."

"In Hooper's case she was alibied solid from the cabbie, the calls, the witness. Hell, Ray practically put himself at Hooper's apartment. We had a lock on him. He was our suspect."

"And now he's dead," Sydowski said. "Wilson's the person who found both of them. Wilson's the person who screwed both of them."

"What about the blood messages, the gun placement, the IDs?"

Sydowski shook his head as Gonzales had arrived and signaled them to join him outside in a private corner of the yard where they were out of earshot. "This is bullshit," Gonzales said. "Did Ray do himself because we were fixing to go at him?"

"No. It doesn't look that way at all," Sydowski said.

"Christ, what then?"

"Looks like he got the same deal Hooper got. Same pattern with his gun and ID set out on the body."

Gonzales removed his unlit cigar and spat on the ground.

"And we got a similar blood message on the wall," Sydowski said. "Only with this one, there was no attempt to wash it away. It was for Molly Wilson and telegraphed for our benefit."

"What's it say?"

"Two words: *'Why, Molly?'* We should keep all that stuff as hold-back."

Gonzales glanced at the crowd growing on the street. "I got Vidor, Tipton, Shrader, and Card canvassing now. The district's given us every uniform and auxiliary they can spare to search the neighborhood."

Sydowski nodded.

"The chief and the commissioner want an early morning news conference to assure the city that the Hooper-Beamon deaths don't put the citizens in danger," Gonzales said.

"Always have their eye on the big picture, don't they?" Sydowski said.

"The chief has given us a blank check to assign more bodies to the investigation. Robbery, Narcotics, and General Works — just tell me who you think you need."

"I need to talk to Molly," Sydowski said. He ran a hand over his face, ignoring the TV news crews and the glare and flash of the news cameras. He and Turgeon blew off the reporters who were shouting questions to them as they strode along the crime scene tape to find Molly.

Sydowski felt someone tug his arm and he protested. Turning, he saw Tom Reed from the *San Francisco Star.* He'd elbowed his way to the front of the press pack where he'd strained the tape to reach Sydowski, who was glaring at him. Tom was making a phone call gesture to his ear. Sydowski shook his head. Tom vanished. Seconds later, Sydowski's cell phone rang.

"Walt," Tom said.

"I can't talk now."

35

Molly sat in the ambulance staring blankly into the night as emergency lights streaked across her face. A paramedic and a uniformed female officer were with her while the investigators were inside Beamon's house, working the scene.

The officer was praying for Sydowski to hurry up and take over. She'd been sitting here watching Molly for an eternity. She wanted to know what had happened inside Beamon's home. But she didn't dare ask. Sydowski had warned her only to listen and take detailed notes of anything Molly said. Relief washed over the officer when he tapped on the vehicle.

"How is she?" he asked.

"Some psychological trauma," the paramedic said.

"Can she go with us to the Hall?"

"She should be fine."

"Let's go. We'll talk at the Hall," Sydowski said.

Molly had been shivering and was wearing the female officer's patrol jacket. Brilliant light flashes rained on Turgeon and Sydowski as they helped Molly from the ambulance to their car. The imagery of the *San Francisco Star* crime reporter wearing a cop's jacket at the scene of another dead detective would attract national interest. Newspaper photographers using long lenses banged off frame after frame.

At the Hall of Justice Sydowski and Turgeon escorted Molly through the homicide detail, passing by the empty desks belonging to Cliff Hooper and Ray Beamon. All activity ceased. Several detectives pulling duty on the case turned to stare.

She did not make eye contact with any of them. She was not handcuffed. She was not under arrest. And despite Sydowski's anger, she was not *yet* a suspect. She was their number-one witness. The shuffling of Sydowski's shoes and the whisk of Turgeon's and Molly's soft soles were the only sounds in the detail as they walked her to an interview room where they left her alone.

In the squad room, Sydowski removed his jacket, poured coffee, and got ready to take her statement as Gonzales approached him.

"Robbery and Narcotics are helping canvass around Wilson's place. Neighbors say there were some sparks there earlier tonight, which is unusual. It's a quiet community."

"What kind of sparks?" Sydowski asked.

"Wilson took some kind of beef with a white male to the street."

"Any description or details?"

"Just the sketchy kind. Maybe you can use that."

When Sydowski and Turgeon entered the interview room he slapped his files down and rolled up his sleeves without removing his eyes from Molly. His face was cold.

"I'm going to need your help now. Understand?"

She nodded.

"You're going to walk me through everything that's happened tonight. And you're going to tell me everything. Every personal, intimate detail. Everything I ask, do you understand?"

Molly's red-rimmed eyes met his as she nodded, then began telling Sydowski all she knew.

"A short time before I found Ray, he'd come to my apartment. He told me you suspected him of killing Cliff. He said that on the night Cliff was killed he'd gone to his apartment to talk to him after Cliff had found out Ray and I had been together. They fought. Ray punched him. But Ray said that Cliff was alive when he left. Heartbroken, but alive."

"What did they really fight about?"

"I told you, it was about Cliff learning that Ray and I had gone to Half Moon Bay. He'd learned it on the night he was going to propose to me."

"Did you take your little talk with Ray to the street in front of your place?"

"Yes."

"Why? What did you fight about?"

"Like I said, I feared Ray was involved in Cliff's death. It didn't go away tonight when he came to me. I wanted him to come to you. To give it up."

Sydowski looked at her for a long icy moment.

Early indications from the scene suggested Ray's gun was not fired. The murder weapon was missing. And it would take a long time yet to analyze the swab tests of Molly's hands to indicate if she fired a gun. Moreover, the results could be challenged in court. But Sydowski tried pressing a few quick buttons.

"You know we took a residue test of your hands."

Disbelief spread over her face as she awakened to the implication and swallowed hard.

"I didn't kill him."

"The evidence will tell me if you did or didn't."

"I didn't kill him." Her voice broke.

"Who killed him then?"

"I don't know."

"You don't know!" Sydowski's chair shot across the floor as he stood. "The guy's leaving you personal love notes and you don't know who it is!"

She covered her face with her hands.

"Oh God, I'm so sorry. I don't know. Maybe it's an ex-boyfriend, maybe some nut through the paper, or from the TV show. But I swear, I just don't know who's doing this. I swear to God. I don't know!"

Sydowski stood over Molly, letting her words hang in the small room for a long desperate time before he picked up his chair.

"You're not going home tonight."

Molly looked at him, then Turgeon, before coming back to Sydowski.

"You're arresting me?"

"We're taking you someplace right now. For your own safety."

Molly stared helplessly at the veneer top of the table.

"Where?"

"You'll find out when we get there. And then you're going to help me go back and work on those names we got from you before. Everyone's a suspect. Every old boyfriend and every whack job that's ever contacted you, fantasized about you, or tried. Do you understand?"

Molly nodded.

Downstairs a handful of reporters were in the lobby waiting for another shot at Molly. Tom Reed was among them. But he knew Sydowski would call the security desk to check the presence of the press so he could bypass them. Tom slipped from the pack unnoticed to the fourth floor. He came upon

Molly, Turgeon, and Sydowski as they were leaving by the stairs.

"Not now, Reed," Sydowski said. "Go away."

"Are you okay?" Tom called after Molly.

"I don't know," she said.

"Who do you think did it?"

"Everyone's a suspect," Sydowski said before they went through the door.

Tom stood there, writing down Sydowski's quote, then called it in to the *Star*'s night desk in time for the final edition. As sirens wailed in the distance he walked to his car, wondering, *Who is preying on the detectives of San Francisco's homicide detail?*

36

Just after 11:00 a.m. pacific standard time, reporters from every newsroom and bureau based in the Bay Area jammed the Police Commission Hearing Room in the Hall of Justice for the first press conference on the death of San Francisco Homicide Inspector Ray Beamon.

Pictures of Beamon and Cliff Hooper stared from a corkboard on the far right.

All morning, running updates from the news wires intensified interest by hammering on the dramatic elements in the case. The victims: two detectives, partners, murdered in their homes within two weeks. No suspect had surfaced. The twist, according to unconfirmed leaks, was that the two dead cops were romantically linked to *San Francisco Star* crime reporter Molly Wilson. By the time the conference started, the story had rocketed near the top of national news lineups across the country.

Local stations and twenty-four-hour news networks went live when San Francisco's police chief, flanked by grim-faced commanders and detectives, entered. All talk in the room ceased, still cameras flashed, notebooks were flipped open, tape recorders clicked on as the chief took his seat behind the microphones heaped on the table before him.

Although he was now more politician than street cop, his eyes gleamed with the fury burning in the pit of his stomach. Two of his best were taken on his watch. And their killer was still out there. The chief glanced at the press group, then read a brief statement. His voice was as strong as it had been for Hooper's eulogy.

"The San Francisco Police Department is asking the public's assistance for any information related to the murder of Ray Beamon, an inspector with the department's homicide detail. Inspector Beamon was found deceased in his residence last night. We strongly suspect his death is directly related to that of Cliff Hooper, also an inspector with the department's homicide detail, who was found deceased in his residence on the evening of the tenth. We're asking anyone with any information on any aspect of these cases to immediately contact law enforcement authorities. That is all we can say at this time. I will not speculate or discuss case details. I will take only a few questions. Starting with you, waving your hand."

Several reporters starting talking at once.

"Yes," the chief said, "the woman from *KTW*."

The woman stood. "Sir, recent reports indicate Molly Wilson, a reporter for the *San Francisco Star*, was known to Beamon and Hooper. Can you confirm that?"

"Yes."

"Can you elaborate on Wilson's relationship with them and how it connects her to this case?"

"No. Next question."

Again the room surged.

"You. You in the blue shirt," the chief said.

"John Miller, Associated Press. Has Molly Wilson been ruled out as a suspect?"

"She's cooperating with the investigation. That's all I'm prepared to say. Last question."

Last question? Reporters complained. Ignoring them, the chief pointed to a reporter among those standing at the side of the room.

"Tom Reed, *San Francisco Star*," he said. "Chief, do you have anything that points you to a suspect or a motive?"

"We're working on all avenues of investigation."

The chief stood to leave amid a barrage of questions, but Tom's demand drowned out all of the others.

"Hold it one minute, sir!" Tom said. The chief halted, then turned to him. The room fell silent. A few TV cameras swung to Tom as still cameras shot picture after picture.

"With all due respect, Chief, I think the people of the city deserve better answers than you've been providing this morning."

As a veteran of many battles, the chief was aware of the emotional ties between his dead detectives and the *Star* newsroom. He bowed his head slightly. "I'll take one last question, Tom."

"Do you have a suspect in this case?"

"I'll make it clear. We have some leads. And we urge anyone with information on these cases to contact us. Thank you all."

First Hooper. Now Beamon. What the hell was happening?

Returning to the *Star* building, Tom struggled to make sense of the last few hours. In the elevator, his body tremored as he ascended to the newsroom. He hadn't had any sleep.

Coffee.

He craved coffee and got some from the newsroom kitchen before heading to his desk. On the way he saw Irene Pepper sitting in his chair, tapping a cassette tape against her nails. The one of his interview with Beamon.

"Good little conversation you've got here," she said.

He tried to guess how she'd found out.

"I can't help but think you were hiding it from me. Not good." She grinned.

"I was not hiding it from you. I wasn't

done with that story."

"And when were you going to tell me about this?"

"When I was finished checking things out on it."

"Well, I've listened to it and I want you to write this up today."

"I think we should wait," he said.

Seeing what was transpiring, Acker came over.

"And you knew about this Beamon interview too?"

"Yes," Acker said. "It wasn't finished. Tom needed to check a few things out."

"There's nothing to check out. We go with it today."

"I think we should wait," Tom said.

Acker nodded.

"Why?" Pepper asked.

"Beamon's murder is *the* story today. Our exclusive would be lost," Tom said. "Besides, I can leverage it with Homicide."

Pepper touched the tape to her chin and swiveled in the chair.

"No, we go today for tomorrow's paper."

"It'll just get lost," Acker said.

"It'll have little impact," Tom added. "If we wait a few days the story will cool and this interview will be hot. By then I'll have had time to leverage Homicide for more. It'll demonstrate that we own this story, Irene."

Pepper stood.

"No. We go today."

"That's a mistake," Tom said. "No one can possibly beat us on this interview now. We should wait a few days and get the best bang out of it. Going now would be a big mistake."

Pepper eyed both men.

"I'm not the one who made a big mistake." She put the tape in Tom's pocket. "You did. We go today."

37

By the time the news conference had started that morning, Sydowski and Turgeon were driving back to the location where they'd taken Molly the night before.

Listening to Mozart as they left San Francisco, they headed south, then east over the bay. Sydowski had not slept at all in the night. He lay in bed for ninety minutes flipping through the Old Testament searching for answers. Finding none, he'd forced himself to think of his birds, the weather, ordinary thoughts. Anything to keep ahead of the horror.

Now, as the Chev's tires click-clicked rhythmically along the San Mateo Bridge, Sydowski took stock of the case. The autopsy found that Beamon had died of a single gunshot wound to the head. The recovered round was a .40-caliber SXT Talon. The residue tests on Molly were negative. Canvass reports had two neighbors hearing a pop coming from Beamon's bungalow in advance of Molly's arrival. In Sydowski's mind, Molly was no longer a suspect, but rather the single thread running through the bleeding wound inflicted on the homicide squad. He needed her to lead him to the killer.

They exited the bridge. Destination: Union City.

The San Francisco police and the California Justice Department used a small house on a quiet street in the Old Alvarado area to park witnesses safely when things heated up. It's where they'd taken Molly. Today, Union City was sitting on it in an unmarked vehicle. Inside, two San Francisco detectives and a nurse were with her watching TV news reports on the case. Molly was on the sofa bed, knees drawn under her chin. She glanced up at Sydowski and Turgeon.

"Why don't you guys take a break at the coffee shop down the street while Linda and I talk to Molly?" Sydowski said to the others.

"Would you like us to get you anything?" the nurse asked.

Molly smiled and shook her head, thanking her watchers as they left.

Turgeon switched off the set.

Sydowski sat on the sofa chair nearest Molly, produced his notebook. He got to work, asking her to review the list of all the men she'd dated for at least a month or longer over the last few years. The same list they'd drawn up after Hooper was killed.

Before he pursued Beamon.

His murder meant a realignment of the case. Hell, it was a new case. It meant going back on everything hard. Scrutinizing Molly's boyfriend list. She took Sydowski's pen and looked at the names. She took a few moments to think about it, made notes, then passed it back to him.

"Murdoch, Glazer, and Yarrow, you never gave us these guys after Hooper," Sydowski said.

"They don't live in the Bay Area. And I don't think they were even around at the time Cliff and Ray were killed."

"Tell us about them and we'll determine if that's true."

"Steve Murdoch's a movie technician who lives in Los Angeles. Travels a lot. I dated him when they shot Pitt's last movie in Golden Gate Park. He works mostly on big-budget films. Rob Glazer, the airline pilot, lives in San Diego. I met him on a flight. Frank Yarrow's an old boyfriend who was in town on business, then left."

"What does Yarrow do?"

"A security consultant, or something. I think he lives in Kansas City, I think, or Colorado before that. He's recently divorced and shaken by it. He wanted to see me. Oh, and Glazer, it turns out, was cheating with me on his wife. I didn't know at the time. I told him I hated what he did to me and to her. He was a creep."

Molly went through her bag for her address book and gave Sydowski every iota of contact information she'd had on all of the men.

"Some of this might be outdated," she said.

"What about the message on the wall?" Sydowski passed Molly a color picture from the crime scene:

Why, Molly?

"Does that scrawl or script look familiar? Anyone you know use that phrase, or term, a lot? Any idea of its significance?"

Blinking quickly, she shook her head.

"What about the crazies, the idiots who contact you through the paper and Vince Vincent's TV show?"

"I never really see them or have any contact with them. We have security at the paper. I might get a strange letter or pervy e-mail at the paper."

"And Vincent's show."

Molly shook her head.

"The station blocks or intercepts everything. The producer has told me how some of the stuff addressed to me is revolting and disgusting. Guys send videos of themselves doing things, or call, or write to graphically discuss their fantasies. You'd have to check with the show."

Sydowski studied a page in his notes.

"The last time we talked, you said you had

this weird feeling someone was watching you. You said you felt it that night at Jake's bar just before you found Hooper."

"At times it was like I was being watched or followed. Even now, I'm not sure."

"What do you mean?"

"I mean, I could've been just hyperparanoid after finding Cliff. I mean, I thought I saw a guy. But it could've been a reporter or photographer. Could've been a cop."

"You have a description, a vehicle, a plate? Anything?"

"No. White guy maybe. A late-model sedan."

"Nothing more than that?"

Molly shook her head. "It could've been my imagination."

"Why do you think that?"

"Because I haven't gotten a full night's sleep since Cliff was killed. I've been ex-hausted and an emotional basket case." Her chin crumpled and she covered her face with her hands. "And now this."

Turgeon passed her a tissue and rubbed her arm until Molly regained a measure of composure.

"How long will I have to stay here?"

"This is not protective custody but we think it's best if you keep a low profile for a few days," Sydowski said.

"I want to go back to my apartment. I

need to start putting my life back together."

"Just a little while longer until we get on top of this," Sydowski said.

"Well, can you take me to my place so I can get a few things, clothes and stuff?" Molly asked. "This was all so sudden."

"I'll take care of it for you later today," Turgeon said. "Just write down what you want and where I can find it."

Molly pulled a reporter's notepad from her bag and started to list items. When Sydowski and Turgeon drove back to San Francisco, the afternoon sun was brilliant over the bay. The waves sparkled like diamonds as a bitter-sweet Italian opera wafted through the car's speakers. It seemed a fitting piece of music for a nightmare, Sydowski thought, as he reviewed Molly's amended list of former boy-friends.

The suspect list.

He slid a Tums in his mouth and cracked it between his teeth.

38

After Tom finished his story on Ray Beamon's final interview he sent it through the computer system to the night desk for editing.

It was early evening.

Exhausted, he loosened his tie and bit into a chocolate bar. The questions troubled him. Who was hunting the city's homicide detectives? And why? How did Molly figure into it? Who knows?

Tom leaned back, dreading Sydowski's reaction to the story tomorrow. He was the one forever pushing Sydowski to swap data. But now that Irene Pepper had forced him to go with Beamon's last words before Sydowski was even aware the tape existed, any chance of using it as leverage for a story from him was dead. *Brilliant news judgment, Pepper,* he thought.

Tom crumpled his wrapper and brushed his hands just as she materialized at his desk, holding a bunch of white roses.

"Just read your Beamon story. Not bad."

He looked at the flowers. They were wrapped in blue pin-striped paper.

"I saw these arrive for Molly early this morning long before the other flowers." Pepper nodded to several bouquets on Molly's desk. "Someone put these in the fridge and must've forgotten."

He said nothing.

"Would you please give them to Molly tonight?" Pepper smiled. "Pass along my condolences and let her know I'm extremely interested in a first-person story from her. It would be fantastic and we could syndicate it nationally. I'm not talking about her writing right away, of course. But very soon. Especially given that she figures so prominently in the murders of two detectives and the killer's still out there."

Tom said nothing.

"I'm assuming you're going to see her."

"Police have taken her someplace. No one knows where."

"My word. They must fear for her safety." Pepper saw others approaching. "Think about what I said, Tom. Maybe Della or Simon can help you get these to Molly."

Della Thompson and Simon Lepp watched Pepper return to her office. Thompson picked up the new roses she'd left on Tom's desk.

"More flowers. Who're these from?" She read the card affixed in plain sight. " 'Molly, leave the past in the past and look to the future.' "

She passed the card to Tom.

"What do you think?"

After reading it he said, "Another strange note for the collection. And as I recall, the same wrapping as the bunch she got right after Hooper's murder. And these came early just like the other bunch did with Hooper's murder."

Tom fished around in his drawer for the earlier card.

"It had a strange note of condolence, too. Listen. 'Please think of me. I'm thinking of you.' And I think another bunch wrapped in blue pin-striped paper arrived after the first bunch. She got three strange ones. You're shaking your head."

"You're thinking it's the guy?" Thompson asked.

He shrugged.

"Well, I doubt it," she said. "First of all, it looks to me like a woman's handwriting on both cards."

"Sometimes the flower shop people write the cards for you," he said. "So you couldn't assume anything from the handwriting."

"All right. I just don't see anything that strange about them. She's received quite a few flowers since this all began," she said.

"But where are these from?" Tom asked, examining the other flower bunches on Molly's desk. "See, these all have logos, or names of the stores somewhere, on the card or wrapping. But not these. Just blue pin-striping, which is distinct from the others."

Thompson kept shaking her head.

"Molly received a lot of flowers from everybody," she said. "They've come here, or her apartment, from cop friends. Some went to Hooper's place and now Beamon's too. I heard quite a few went to Vince Vincent's show. A lot of folks out there send flowers with cards."

"You know," Lepp said, "it's been getting out how she knew both guys. Maybe some crazy out there is jealous and is trying to woo her now."

"Maybe." Thompson half smiled. "This is San Francisco. No shortage of wackos. But I think the theories you guys have aren't that solid."

Lepp changed the subject. "So, how do you think the investigation will go now?" he asked Tom.

"I think they'll follow two basic tracks. Again, they'll go back on Beamon's and Hooper's old cases looking for beefs, any link, and they'll go back on Molly's networks, disgruntled ex-boyfriends, and anyone who had the potential to be pissed off at her for any significant reason."

"I'll keep doing what I'm doing," Lepp said. "I'll search old stories. Beamon was in Robbery. I'll talk to the guys there about old beefs. And Hooper worked in Taraval and

Mission, which I haven't checked yet."

"And I'll press my sources." Tom watched Thompson stifle a yawn. "As for the flowers, all I'm thinking is maybe we should check this out when we have the time. I'm just curious to know who's been sending them."

Thompson collected them. "I'll take them home and keep them for her. I'm wiped."

"Hold up, I'll walk out with you," Tom said.

At home Ann had left him a plate of burritos, refried beans, and rice warming in the oven. It was good. After eating he had a hot shower, which melted away enough fatigue for him to spend time with Zach before the evening ended.

They worked together on his model of the U.S.S. *New Jersey*, passing the time talking quietly about the battleship. But Tom sensed Zach had something more troubling than World War Two history on his mind.

"Is there anything else you want to talk about, son?"

"Well, there's something I wanted to ask you but it's not about the ship."

"Go ahead. Shoot."

"It's about the murders you're writing about."

"The murders." Tom hesitated. "Okay . . . what about them?"

"The guy's just killing cops, right? I mean,

I'm sad for them and their families, but he's not going to be mad at you for writing about him, right?"

Tom looked into Zach's face. This was the toll. The price exacted on his family from his job. He swallowed, then brushed Zach's hair.

"No. He's a sick person who seems to have it in for detectives. Maybe he's a bad guy from their past. I don't think we have to worry about it."

"But Molly Wilson's your friend and she's kind of part of it."

"Yes, and she was friends with the detectives. So was I, a little bit. It's good that you're sympathetic. But don't worry, okay?"

Zach nodded.

Afterward when Ann was getting Zach off to bed, Tom crouched by the shelf holding her library of books on flowers, plants, and gardening. He inventoried the spines of her books. He was searching for one he hoped would be the key, one to the door that would bring him closer to the truth behind the murders.

The flower angle gnawed at him. He refused to give up on it. Where was that reference book? Despite the challenges of San Francisco's climate, Ann had been working hard on creating a rose garden at their house. And after her recent ordeal she'd followed through on her intention to join a local rose society. She'd also devoted more time to studying the history and language of flowers. She'd become an amateur expert.

"What are you looking for?"

"I need to know something about roses. Like what does it signify when you give someone white roses? You know, the deeper meaning, that kind of thing."

"You're talking about the language and symbolism of flowers."

"That's it."

"That's easy. First off, giving someone white roses can mean a lot of different things, but generally it means silence, secrecy. Or that you want to share a secret with someone."

"Really?"

"I wouldn't get too worked up over it."

"Why?"

"Most people have no idea about the significance."

Most people don't go around killing homicide detectives, Tom thought later that night as he tried to sleep. The meaning of white roses gnawed at him.

Secrecy.

It fit with the fact that the cards were unsigned. There could be something here.

39

Molly's pain was his pain.

Like everyone, Bleeder saw the news pictures of her being escorted by the detectives from Ray Beamon's house in Bernal Heights. Absorbing the images filled his heart with expectation. He was getting closer.

And closer.

Bleeder yearned to see her. Ached to see her. As dangerous as it was, he'd promised himself a glimpse as his reward for taking care of another obstacle. It was inspiration to keep going. He'd been so exceedingly careful, so exceedingly patient. Something would happen.

He'd earned it.

Bleeder snapped to attention. *Here we go.*

An unmarked Chev Impala braked to a stop in front of Molly's building. Inspector Linda Turgeon got out to talk to the uniform keeping vigil. The rookie officer had barely kept awake after polishing off his submarine sandwich, then working his way through the sports pages of *USA Today*.

Bleeder was invisible to him.

He was in a rented car with dark windows

parked two streets over where he had a perfect line of sight on Molly's building. He was near a small park next to a vacant lot. He drew no suspicion from any neighborhood busybodies. He had a small parabolic microphone aimed at the cop. It boosted sound some seventy-five times. Bleeder heard every bite and crunch it took the officer to down his sandwich. He heard every radio dispatch. And he had a high-powered night-vision scope.

He saw and heard everything.

"I'm just going in to pick up a few things for her," Turgeon told the officer before she entered Molly's upper apartment. A few moments later she trotted out with a shoulder bag.

"Inspector?" the officer called to her. "How much longer we going to sit on her house?"

"Likely until after the funeral when things cool down. Hang in there."

Turgeon wheeled her car from the edge of Telegraph Hill, making her way to the freeway south out of the city. Bleeder came alive. His fingers squeezed the wheel as he followed her. Along the drive, he thought of Molly as the most important question ate at him.

Why?

Why haven't you realized who I am and what I've done for you? It's dangerous for you to wait too long. What's it going to take for you to understand that we belong together? Bleeder tried to relax. *Be patient. It's going to happen. The press is doing its thing. The police are doing theirs. And you're doing your thing. Keeping vigil, waiting until she sees the light.*

And she will see the light.

He thought of Molly's soft skin against his, her scent, and the curves of her body.

In his mind, their souls had fused.

He was helping her to understand. Removing all obstacles. Hooper was an obstacle. Now he was gone. Beamon was an obstacle. Now he was gone. Bleeder wouldn't allow any more obstacles. *How long before you realize that you're mine?*

Just like Amy was mine.

Yes, well, that whole matter was unfortunate.

As they headed south on the 101 to the San Mateo Bridge, Bleeder thought of another bridge, one from his past, and he journeyed back. After the fiasco with Kyle at the diner, he'd changed his strategy. The town was too small for effective surveillance, so he'd decided to craft an in-country operation.

The answer was simple.

Amy's family lived at the edge of town, inside the county line, down a narrow one-mile stretch of blacktop, nicknamed Hangman's Lane. It was the site of the county's last execution in the 1800s, according to the local history in the library. Bleeder had looked it up.

One punishing winter, a mute, demented hermit named Lud Striker tore off his clothes, sharpened his ax, then chopped up his animals. His six cows, his horse, his pigs, his chickens, his dogs. Even his cats. Then he covered his body with their steaming bloody entrails and roamed his fields to the home of his neighbors, with whom he'd had a bitter and long-standing feud over property and water access. Striker murdered them all in their sleep. A farmer, his wife, their three children. They found him in the farmer's bed, asleep among the corpses. Striker was hanged from a tall oak tree.

A story of vengeance.

Bleeder loved it and he loved driving down Hangman's Lane alone at night, along the twisting road that cut through wooded and hilly dairy country. At one point, it curved sharply, then dropped into a valley to a railroad tie bridge that stretched across a creek thirty feet below.

Bleeder got to know that section of road intimately. He put his research to work. Every night after cruising around town with Amy in his Camaro, Kyle would drive her home down the lane. They'd make out on the front porch until the house lights flickered on and off around midnight, which meant Amy's parents were signaling her curfew.

Like clockwork, Kyle would fire up his Camaro, grind through his gears, squealing in each one, as he rumbled down Hangman's

Lane, rocketing through the tranquil rural night with Led Zeppelin cranked.

Bleeder discovered a slip of a cow path shrouded by a thicket, under a stand of chestnut and oak trees near the bridge. For several nights, he backed his dad's old Ford into it, vanishing into the darkness. Thinking of Lud Striker and waiting. He had a clear line of sight for Kyle's approach from Amy's house, the Camaro's lights growing bigger, its engine and music louder. Without fail, Kyle would crest the hill, rip down the creek valley, hugging the curve so fast the car's suspension would strain until the oil pan would nick the road surface on the approach to the bridge, emitting a comet's tail of sparks from the undercarriage.

Kyle never once slowed down before the bridge.

Like clockwork, the oil pan scraped, sparks would fly, and he would blast *clump-dum-clump* along the bridge over the creek.

Afterward, Bleeder walked to the spot, knelt, and examined the series of deep scrapes left by the oil pan. Scores of them. A clear indication that the farm boy was routinely hitting the bridge at high speed. *Tsk, tsk.* Bleeder shook his head, gazing at Kyle's disappearing Camaro, its lights shrinking under the endless night sky, until, poof, Kyle was gone.

Bleeder ran his fingertips over the scrapes,

feeling how they scarred the surface, just as Kyle and Rowley had scarred his face the day they beat him after school in the field by the train tracks.

Bleeder's wounds had healed, but the violation still burned.

My turn to give you a lesson . . .

Now as he followed Turgeon's tailights into Alvarado, Bleeder surfaced from his thoughts.

Alert, he kept a safe distance. He trailed the Chev through a sleepy residential area until the brake lights came on, then went off, when Turgeon stopped in front of a small bungalow sheltered by huge shade trees.

Bleeder identified the unmarked cars parked nearby. County guys and maybe an SFPD car. He rolled his rental car swiftly into a side street that allowed him cover and a safe line on the small house.

Only a moment. That's all he wanted.

Bleeder set up on the house, directing his night scope to a window with a crack between the curtains. The anticipation was excruciating as he adjusted the focus. He saw a curtain ripple. A blur. A glimpse of Turgeon. Then . . . Molly was trapped in his crosshairs.

His prize.

It won't be long now.

40

Stiff and sore, Sydowski dragged himself to his door before dawn for the morning edition of the *Star*. It was still dark. The case had kept him awake all night. As he studied the paper in his kitchen, Tom Reed's interview with Ray Beamon jerked him awake.

"What the hell is this bullshit, Reed?"

Sydowski devoured the story, then grimaced as he took a hit of black coffee. *Would've been interested in knowing about that interview, Tom. Might've been able to work something out.*

Too late now, sonny boy.

Sydowski scratched his whiskers, then went to his aviary with the full weight of the case on his shoulders. He listened to the soft chirping until it was time to go to his meeting with Gonazales and Turgeon at an admin room at the Hall.

It was just the three of them.

Gonzales dropped his worn leather briefcase on the table, deposited himself in a swivel chair.

"I've been getting calls. All last night and this morning. 'Friendly enquiries of support' from the mayor, the commissioner, and the chief. They want this thing cleared fast. They say it's like an open wound festering on the image of this city and its PD."

"There's a surprise," Sydowski said.

"Well, frankly, I don't give a damn about them. We owe it to Cliff and Ray, *and* we owe it to our detail, to clear this." Gonzales blinked back his emotion, then continued. "No one knows of our huddle here. I want you to put all your hold-back and theories on the table now. I want to get a feel for where we're at. *Exactly where we're at.* So whatever is said here, stays here. All right?"

"Fine," Sydowski said.

"Did we make much progress with Molly Wilson's first list right after Hooper's murder?"

"We checked out the names and cleared them initially. Then we went hard on Ray when it all pointed to him."

"We're back on those names. What do we have now?"

"We have a larger suspect pool in alpha order." Sydowski slid a page to Gonzales. "I did some checking this morning, talked to Molly, and amended things."

Gonzales stared at the list:

Duane Ford, SFPD Tac Team, San
   Francisco
Rob Glazer, technician for big films,
   Los Angeles

Manny Lewis, D.A.'s office, San Francisco
Cecil Lowe, ATF Agent, San Francisco
Pete Marlin, U.S. Marshal, San Francisco
Steve Murdoch, airline pilot, San Diego
Park Williams, FBI Agent, San Francisco
Frank Yarrow, corporate security,
    Kansas/Colorado

Sydowski opened his notes.

"Molly dated every guy on that list for at least a month. No one longer than six months, she figures."

"Any bad breaks, violence, grudges, threats?"

"None according to her."

"What about casual dates?"

"That's another list. It includes people at her newsroom, mostly friends. We pretty much cleared them already as to who was working when. That went fast."

"You say you amended the A-list?" Gonzales continued studying it.

"Yes, Glazer, Murdoch, and Yarrow were her add-ons because they don't live in the Bay Area. We'll run through all of them as fast as we can and pare it down."

"Most of the guys on this list would know about crime scene investigation and techniques." Gonzales shook his head. "We got nothing physical from either scene. No leads from the autopsy. Just SXT Talons. No casings. No weapon. No latents. No DNA. No fibers. Our balls are in a vise here. Christ."

"Look, this is a new investigation," Sydowski said. "Give us the bodies and we'll check these guys out. Eliminate whoever we can from this list. We should be able to knock it down pretty fast."

"It isn't going to be easy. If our guy is one of these eight, then he's going to expect you to run at him and he's going to be alibied solidly. He's going to cover his tracks. Be airtight on his story. He's not going to make it easy for you. So never let your guard down with any of them."

"We'll check, double- and triple-check their whereabouts."

"Let's go back on the physical stuff. What about the ritualistic nature, the placement of their guns, IDs, the blood message on the wall, the word *Why*. What do we make of that?" Gonzales asked.

"I did some work with Dee, the FBI VICAP coordinator at Golden Gate. We checked on serials, gangs, blood cults, ritual placement of items. Everything. Blood messages. Key word stuff. Murders of law enforcement officers," Turgeon said. "We also checked everything against other databanks, CLETS, LEADS, PIN, CABLE, CDC's systems, NCIC."

"Any hits?"

"Nothing." Turgeon shook her head, went through her notes.

241

"Could be that all that stuff with the blood message and ID could've been done to throw us off. A cop would know about things like that," Sydowski said.

"So would anybody who reads murder mysteries," Turgeon said.

"Maybe we ought to bring in a profiler," Gonzales said.

"To tell us what we already know?"

"To tell us what we don't know," Gonzales said. "Look, we also have the TV show, *Crime Scene*. I called over. The producer has volunteered everything sent to Molly from crazies. No warrants needed."

"They probably want to work it into their show," Sydowski said.

"Play along if it helps the case." Then Gonzales said, sliding Sydowski that day's *San Francisco Star* with Beamon's last interview, "It would be good for us to know everything Ray said about old cases, threats, and vendettas."

Sydowski's eyes raked across the front page.

"I'll be taking a hard look into that."

41

Silence and secrecy.

That was the age-old symbolism of giving white roses. But what the hell did it mean in Molly's case? Tom wanted to know.

Did they have anything to do with Hooper's and Beamon's murders? What did those cryptic notes mean? It rankled him. He had to find out.

He glanced at his watch as he headed across the Bay Bridge to Oakland. He didn't have time to pursue it. Not now. Late last night and earlier today he'd transcribed his interview with Beamon. Every word. The part where he'd asked Beamon about vendettas kept coming back at him . . .

". . . There've been threats, but those who make a lot of noise never come after you. If someone's serious, you'll never hear them coming."

That part.

"There've been threats . . ."

What threats? Who made them? When? Tom kicked himself for not pushing Beamon on that question. And he cursed Irene Pepper for making him rush the story before he'd

243

had the chance to go to Sydowski on what Beamon had said.

Hell, he was going to have to be smarter. A lot smarter with Pepper.

It was his own damned fault for leaving his tape out in plain sight knowing she was one of the *Star*'s worst desktop snoops. Anyone could've seen it near his keyboard. *Admit it. You were careless. Now you're paying the price.*

Sydowski hadn't returned his calls this morning, leaving Tom to try connecting with his best street sources. Angela across the bay was first. Word was she'd been around. He parked his car near a warehouse on the waterfront a few blocks from Jack London Square, then hit the street asking around.

Angela was white and in her mid-thirties. She had short bleached hair, was partial to big hoop earrings, jeans, and black leather waist-cut jackets. More important, she was his conduit to Donnie Ball.

Donnie was an East Bay County detective. Make that a *former* detective. The big red-haired Irish American was doing nine years after the FBI nailed him for robbing banks. Ball was a brilliant egomaniacal dumb-ass. But he was tuned in to a lot of data on the criminal and cop grapevine. Even from his Level-IV, maximum-security residence at Folsom's C-Yard. And he was good at bartering valuable intelligence via his girl on the outside, his angel, Angela.

After an hour or two, the blast of tugs and cries of shrieking gulls overhead were the only sounds Tom had picked up from the waterfront. No sign of Angela. He'd try again tonight, he reasoned, after crossing back over the bridge and heading for San Francisco's Mission District and another source, Lois Hirt.

He parked a few blocks from the Six-teenth-Street BART Station, began walking the streets while bracing for frustration. Lois was one of his best sources. In all the time he'd known her, she'd never once lied or misled him. Her information was dead on the money. Every time. But finding the college dropout was about as easy as reaching the summit of Everest.

Lois Hirt was a heroin addict.

And at times she was as elusive as the wind.

After nearly ninety minutes of checking the usual places, of asking and waiting around, he'd recognized that sinking feeling. He'd struck out. No way was he going to connect with her today. After packing it in and heading back to the car, his cell phone rang.

"Reed."

"Got your message," Sydowski said. "What do you want? I'm busy and grouchy."

"Sounds like two of the dwarves."

"Reed."

"I've got to talk to you."

"About what?"

"You know what."

"By the by, your story pissed me off."

"I just want to talk."

"I don't have much time for you, pal."

"It might be useful for you to meet me. We can trade things."

Sydowski emitted a long, tired sigh.

"Nick's. I'll be there in half an hour."

42

Nick's Diner was a short walk from the Hall of Justice and a hangout for crime fighters who favored greasy fried food and strong coffee. Tom found Sydowski alone in a corner and ordered a cup for himself.

"How's Molly doing?" Tom asked.

"Think of the circumstances and draw your own conclusions."

All right. Sydowski was pissed off.

"You know, I was planning to come to you with Ray's interview before we ran it."

"But . . . ?"

"An editor made me go with it as soon as she found out."

"Just following orders, huh?"

"Come on."

"Hey, what was it you said at the beginning of this thing? How we could 'cooperate' because of the *Star*'s connection here?" Sydowski grunted, then grabbed a well-read copy from the counter and spun it on their table. "This is you cooperating? You're the one always asking me to leak you stuff, give you stuff. Turns out it's a one-way street with you."

"My hands were tied."

"You couldn't even do me the courtesy of a call? A heads-up to say you had Ray's last interview and you were going to publish it? How many times have we tipped you to arrests, breaks, leads?"

"You said you wouldn't make any deals on this case."

Coffee arrived, diffusing the tension. Sydowski glanced at the street to let his blood pressure simmer. Then he reached for a toothpick.

"You got anything going, any strong leads?" Tom asked.

"We've got a couple of things going."

"Like what?"

Sydowski raised his eyebrows. "Let me reach into my pocket and give you my case notes." He shook his head and looked away.

"What's the deal with OCC and the internal guys? Is it political or is there something to this?"

"Jesus Christ, Reed."

"Well?"

"Look, you're wasting my time. You said you might have something to give me?"

Tom slid the tape of Beamon's interview to him.

"I made a copy for you."

"It's old news now, pal."

"Listen to it all. Ray said there'd been threats."

Sydowski put the tape in his pocket. His poker face gave nothing away.

"We're looking into Hooper's old cases," Tom said.

"Good for you. I've got to go."

"Wait, I gave you the tape."

"So what? You expect something in return?"

"Well, yeah."

Sydowski pursed his lips and glanced at his watch. He cooled off enough to give Tom a shot at a lead for a story. "Ask me questions," he said.

"What?"

"Ask me questions. You know how we investigate, so hurry up."

"You're looking at everything connected to Hooper and Beamon."

"Obviously."

"Old cases, threats, vendettas?"

"Sounds logical."

"But since I don't know all the physical evidence or scene stuff, it looks like there's a strong link to Molly."

"You think?"

"So you're going to scour her circles."

"There you go. You're smart. Keep going."

"All her boyfriends, they'd be your suspect pool, or people you want to talk to and clear."

"Keep going."

"Are you concentrating on anyone in particular?"

"You answer that one."

"No. Not yet. You'd cast a wide net and start tossing out those you could rule out immediately. You're not focusing on anyone. Am I right?"

Sydowski said nothing as Tom concentrated, then produced his notebook. "You'd start with ex-boyfriends she's dated for a time over the last little while," he said.

"Keep going."

"Tying them to physical evidence and whereabouts when the murders were committed."

"Hurry up. I've got to run."

"You've developed a list and will reduce it as you rule them out one by one. At the same time you're looking for the link to any evidence from the scene like a weapon, a print, and checking it against any threats arising from old cases, maybe any ritualistic pattern."

"Keep going."

"The boyfriends are only one aspect of your investigation. You'd be interested in guys she's dated for any period, say a month or two, long enough for feelings to develop. Long enough to stir the fires, as it were."

"Colorful reasoning. Not bad."

"And I'd likely know who most of them would be."

"Would you?"

"Let's see, Manny Lewis, then there was

Fordy, Duane Ford." Tom began making notes as Sydowski checked his watch. "Rob Glazer, the movie guy, then Park from Golden Gate Avenue. Cecil from ATF. The pilot, what was his name? Murray, Steve, Steve Murdoch, and the marshal. Marshal Marlin, I used to tease her, Pete Marlin. That's all of them."

Sydowski stood.

"You missed one."

"One? Who?"

"Frank Yarrow."

"Frank Yarrow?"

"That's all you get," Sydowski said. "You want to play detective, be my guest. Just don't get in my way and be careful with those names. I've confirmed nothing."

"Can I talk to Molly?"

"No. Not for a while."

"Can you have her call me?"

"No." Sydowski slipped on his jacket. "I'm so glad we had this time together. Give my best to Ann. She should get a medal for putting up with you."

The gold in Sydowski's crowns glinted as he placed a couple of dollars on the table and left.

43

Ray Beamon's funeral service was held at St. Mary's Cathedral.

Several hundred mourners attended. Dignitaries, ranking officers, and detectives, all in dress uniforms, their badges bearing a black diagonal stripe. One by one, speakers gripped the sides of the podium as they eulogized him.

" 'There is an evil which I have seen under the sun, and it is common among men,' " the San Francisco police chaplain said, quoting from Ecclesiastes. "Ray and his partner Cliff battled that evil every waking moment of their lives in their unyielding service to this city. Now that evil has taken them, leaving us to ask, *'Why?'* My friends, it's futile to ponder an eternal mystery. It's wiser for us to draw strength from their example. *These were fine, fine men.*"

Afterward, the pallbearers carried out their task. Sydowski headed the team, which had been selected from the homicide detail. Across the street behind the crowd-control barriers, dozens of news crews recorded them delivering the casket to the hearse.

Engines started and then police motorcycles, followed by police cars, led the procession, their lights flashing and chrome gleaming in the bright sun.

In the limousine behind the family car, Molly Wilson sat between Ann and Della Thompson, who squeezed her hands whenever a sob escaped. Tom Reed was with them in the car's opposite seat.

The soft strains of a harp whispered through the limo's hidden speakers. Molly's mind flitted between memories of her times with Cliff and with Ray as she wrestled with the horror that had befallen her. She feared she would scream whenever she remembered the moments when she'd come upon them.

Who did this? Why? Oh God, why?

Tom reflected on the toll their business had exacted on all of them, getting so close to stories. They coiled around you, squeezing you, crushing you. They had all paid dearly, he thought as they neared Colma, a place he had visited too many times to report on too many tragedies.

Located at San Francisco's southern edge, it had more than ten cemeteries side by side in a mile-wide expanse that stretched two miles. A rolling sea of crosses and headstones. Colma, the little town where the dead outnumbered the living, had earned many other names.

In his circle of cop and reporter friends,

253

Tom called it Silent City.

Hundreds of mourners arrived at the cemetery. Sydowski and the pallbearers received the casket. White-gloved uniformed officers of the color guard gave a hand salute until it was placed at the graveside where the officiating priest concluded the burial service. Beamon's family had agreed to a three-member rifle honor guard. Taps was played. When it ended, the pallbearers folded the flag. Sydowski gave it to the police chief, who presented it to Beamon's mother.

Her chin crumpled and her head dropped as she pressed it to her face. Beamon's father comforted her. News cameras captured the moment for the next day's front pages while above them, gulls screeched.

Their cries floated on a gentle wind that rolled over Colma.

44

A few days after Ray Beamon's casket was lowered into the ground, national news organizations were hammering hard on the story.

The *New York Times* ran a front-page feature that jumped to a quarter page inside. The *Washington Post* put one of its star color writers on it and *USA Today* said the case of San Francisco's murdered homicide detectives was shrouded in a bone-chilling mystery worthy of Hollywood.

Irene Pepper had left copies of the stories on Tom Reed's desk. He seized them, went to her office, and knocked on the door.

"Excuse me," he said.

She looked up from the file folder she was studying.

"Did you read those stories I gave you? The national press is going to take this away from us if we're not careful," she said.

"I read them. They're regurgitating what we've already reported. In fact, they're quoting the *Star.*"

"Your job is to keep us out front on this story."

Tom figured it would've been futile to

point out to her that *now* would've been the time to run the Beamon interview. And he sure as hell wasn't going to reveal that he'd come up with a list of possible suspects after some major fence-mending with Sydowski. Pepper would destroy his lead before he'd have a chance to develop it.

"I've broken stories on this. We're in front."

Pepper ignored him and chewed on her pen.

"Do you have any idea where Molly is? Because this would be a good time for a first-person story from her. It would blow everyone away and put us back in the game."

"I don't know where she is. And I don't think she's in any position to be writing something like that at this time."

"Really? I don't think you're in any position to be deciding that for her. Your job is to break exclusives for me and you're overdue. So get busy." Pepper returned to her file folder, dismissing him.

Heading to the kitchen, Tom recalled Hank Kruner's warning about Pepper. "Watch your back with her." Well, like so many others at the *Star*, Tom didn't trust Irene Pepper. Especially now. The way she'd kept him dancing on a tightrope, she had to be up to something.

"Hey, Tom." Simon Lepp was making fresh coffee. "I saw you go into Irene's office.

What'd she have to say?"

"Who knows? She never makes sense. She thinks the *New York Times* is going to steal our thunder in our own backyard."

"I don't think that's going to happen," Lepp said. "We're all over it. Closer to it than anybody."

Tom agreed, then asked: "Where're you at with your stuff?"

"I went to Taraval and Mission. Didn't get much, but one guy seemed to remember an old accusation, or something against Hooper that flared. Something to do with drugs."

"Sounds vaguely familiar."

"I'm going to try Narcotics again. And there was also a rumor that Beamon had some stink come up out of his days in Robbery."

"I don't remember that but the narcotics thing on Hooper is worth checking out."

Della Thompson returned to the newsroom and joined them.

"I just got off the phone with Turgeon in Homicide. She said Molly wants to go home and they're considering moving her soon."

Back at his desk, Tom opened his notebook to the page with the names of suspects. Or rather, "persons of interest," as investigators liked to say. He chuckled at all the slippery terminology they used. They'd stress that a person was in no way a "suspect."

He might be a "witness" or a "person of

interest." It was all cop code, which when translated said: "We think you could've done it. And we'll keep thinking it until you cooperate and prove otherwise."

He doubted Sydowski would soon go public with the names and he didn't think it wise for the *Star* to publish them without first doing some intensive digging.

But it was a hell of a list, he thought, sipping his coffee.

Pete Marlin, Park Williams, Duane Ford. Cecil Lowe. And Manny Lewis. *From the D.A.'s office.* Damn. Rob Glazer. Steve Murdoch and Frank Yarrow. Most of these guys were cops. Smart detective types. He'd do some quiet poking around.

At the very least he could put together a searing piece saying that the suspect pool reached into the D.A.'s office, the FBI, ATF, the U.S. Marshal's Service. It'd be a rattler of a story.

His line rang, startling him.

"Reed."

"Tom, I'm so sorry," Tammy said from the front desk. "I was watching like you asked. I just stepped away for a moment, so I missed him."

"What is it?"

"Another bunch came for Molly."

He hung up and rushed to the newsroom reception. Tammy was holding fresh white roses wrapped in blue pin-striped paper.

"How long ago?"

"A minute, tops."

He hurried down the stairs to the lobby and the security desk where a white-haired potbellied security guard sat behind a glass booth.

"What is it there, young Mr. Reed?"

"Weldon, did you get a look at the guy who just came in with flowers?"

"I look at everybody. What's the panic?"

"Did he sign in for you?"

Weldon spun the book around for him and pointed to a signature.

It was indecipherable.

Tom cursed.

45

Riding the elevator back up to the newsroom, Tom was struck with a way to find out who was behind the flowers and the notes for Molly.

The twelve white roses were still with Tammy at the reception desk. He removed the card affixed to them. It said: *Molly, hope you're now looking toward the future.* It was unsigned.

"Can I borrow your scissors?" he asked.

Tammy watched him cut a strip of the blue pin-striped wrapping paper. Then he glanced around and lowered his voice.

"I need you to help me fast and keep it between us."

"Sure, anything. I'm so sorry I missed the delivery."

"Get on the Web and get me a locator map with names and addresses of all the flower shops nearest us."

Tammy's keyboard began clicking as Tom went to the photocopier and made a duplicate of the card. Then he went to his desk, typed up the eight names on the suspect list, and printed off several copies before grabbing his jacket and heading out.

"Here you go," Tammy said. "There are four within a few blocks and three more beyond that."

The first on the map was a block away. Somewhere Over the Rainbow Florists. Tom showed the clerk the card and asked for help.

"All I really need to know is if you think the flowers came from this shop. It would've been a few minutes ago."

As the clerk studied the inscription, he glanced over her shoulder at the rolls of wrapping paper. Nothing that looked like blue pinstripes.

"Sorry," she said. "Not from us."

The second shop was Delights and Dreams. The two owners studied the card and writing, then shook their heads. Tom could see an assortment of wrapping paper at the arrangement table behind them. No blue pinstripes.

It was the same story at Cloud Nine Floral.

The next shop was five blocks away. The Pacific Dreams Flower Shop. It was slivered between a leather boutique and a currency exchange. He approached its frosted glass door thinking the key to this case might be on the other side.

The store's humid earthy air enveloped him. The shop was intimate. Pumps and fluorescent lights hummed, water gurgled over polished rocks in the fountain and goldfish pond. Palm fronds canopied over terraces of plants, vases, displays of all sorts.

Tom was the only customer. He browsed by the large glass coolers with colorful arrangements of lilies, carnations, and scores of flowers he couldn't identify. Most important, there was an abundance of roses, long-stemmed, sweetheart, and in all colors. A good supply of white ones.

"Can I help you?" said the young woman at the counter. She had an orchid in her hair. Her nameplate said Leeshann.

"I hope so. My office just received some flowers. Lovely white roses, Oh, like twenty minutes ago."

"Uh-huh."

"And, this may sound silly, but we're trying to find out if they came from here. It's part of a long running office detective game thing."

She smiled. "Like a friendly office joke?"

"Exactly. Yes. We send gifts to each other, then try to figure out who sent them and from where. The other team's always beating us. We're checking all the flower shops around us."

"That's not so silly. You wouldn't believe the stuff I hear about."

He passed her the card. As she examined it, he noticed that the card's tiny floral

262

border matched the blanks next to the register. His pulse quickened. Looking over her shoulder, he saw among the rolls of wrapping paper a style in blue pinstripes.

"When we find out where they came from," Tom said, "we're going to send him twice the flowers. It's part of the joke to let them know we figured it out. That we're on to them this time."

Leeshann nodded.

"Cool. Sounds like fun. Yup, it looks like one of ours."

"So the flowers came from here, really?"

"Looks like it. But I can't tell you who sent them. Against the rules."

"Of course. I wasn't really asking who sent them. We have a pretty good idea who sent them." He dropped his voice. "We just needed to know where Manny sent them from."

"Manny?"

"Or it could've been Duane?"

Leeshann shook her head.

"It was like twenty minutes ago? Wait," Tom said, pulling out a folded copy of the list. "Hang on. The gang at my office gave me the 'suspect' list."

He passed it to her. She read it and shook her head.

"None of these names are familiar," she said. "I bet Alice handled the order. Unfortunately she just left for a dentist appointment. Can I keep this and ask her?"

"Sure," he said. "Look, I'll be away from my desk, so I'll call her."

"And you are?"

"Tom. Thanks." He smiled. "Please let Alice know this is all part of an office joke kind of thing. But promise me you won't let these guys know we're on to them."

"You're secret's safe with us." Leeshann winked.

46

Molly's smile obliterated his darkness.

Perfect straight, white teeth. Full red lips. Bangs swept carefree to one side. Gracefully she raised her right hand to tuck some errant strands behind her ear while her eyebrow arched. Her eyes sparkled as she made her point.

That's it.

Bleeder froze Molly. Trapping her. Making her his virtual possession.

His skin tingled at the sight of her. He stared at her face, her throat, her plunging neckline. He had recorded some of her appearances on *Crime Scene,* the weekly television spot.

Understandably, she'd been unavailable for the most recent shows that dealt exclusively with Hooper's and Beamon's murders. Like tonight's show. Tonight, a reporter from the *Chronicle* and a columnist from the *Guardian* were filling in, trading theories with Vince Vincent.

The commercial had ended.

Bleeder surfaced from his thoughts and switched from his tape of Molly back to the evening's program. The panel jabbered on until Vincent said time was up.

"This suggestion of corruption and romantic links to Molly Wilson, a regular panelist on this show, has definitely cast a cloud of intrigue over this very disturbing case," he said in closing the show.

The lady from the *Guardian* nodded. "My sources tell me the pressure is causing fracturing within the SFPD's detective ranks and creating tension in the *Star* newsroom."

The *Chronicle* guy added, "At its core, this is a gripping whodunit. It could lead anywhere."

"Indeed. Thank you both. We'll keep our viewers posted here, on *Crime Scene*," Vincent said, wrapping it up.

Fractures within the SFPD?

Terrific. But how long would it last? Bleeder absorbed Molly's frozen face as his scissors clipped a photo of her in *Newsweek*. A beautiful shot, he thought, walking to his wall and using four map pins to hold the latest Molly captive on it. Bleeder smoothed his hand over it, then stepped back, enjoying it with the other pictures of his collection as his stomach twisted with yearning.

Molly was taking too long to realize that she was the sun in his galaxy. Too long to appreciate his vision, his desires, his needs. She was complicating things. *The way Amy had complicated things*. It made their situation

vulnerable to new obstacles. Vulnerable to ca-
tastrophe. What if Molly failed him, the way
Amy had failed him?

No.

Bleeder had worked too hard. He could
never allow that. Could *not* allow that. It was
long ago. Things were different now. Molly
must see that time was running out for her
to realize who Bleeder really was so he could
pull off his mask and help her know what he
knew. Help her to see what he saw.

You're not like Amy. You can't be like Amy.

Bleeder's head began aching. He sat down
in his sofa chair and held it between his
hands, letting it sink into the thick cushioned
back. He feared things would deteriorate like
they did with Amy. Pain trembled through
his body. He closed his eyes to let the darkness enshroud him as he journeyed back.

To Hangman's Lane . . .

For weeks Bleeder had kept a close watch
on Kyle, observing his weakest points, until
one warm, moonlit night when it all came to
pass. Kyle's Camaro had rumbled down the
deserted country road to Amy's house where
he'd gone to visit her for the evening.
Bleeder had followed him. He parked unseen
by a stand of chestnut and oak trees near the
bridge, a quarter mile away.

He walked through the pastures, the corn
and barley fields, coming up behind the out-
buildings and the house, finding cover in the

267

thickets and tall grass near the front porch. The family's dog yelped and whined, but Kyle and Amy were too involved to notice.

Bleeder watched them from the darkness. Watched them kissing, watched them hugging, watched Kyle, his bulging farm-boy arms and his hands all over Amy, touching her, seeing her silky hair tousled, watching her hands sliding to Kyle's jeans, glimpsing her bare shoulder. In the stillness, amid the crickets he heard them panting, moaning. Amy's sighs.

How could this be?

Amy should be with him. She'd told him *he* was her boyfriend. Kyle was too possessive. Too controlling. Bleeder had to rescue her from Kyle. That's what she wanted. That's what she'd said. Now, watching them, seeing them *like that*, Bleeder felt his stomach knotting and his heart shattering, launching wave after wave of rage.

He strode back through the tall grass, the fields and pastures, his face shiny with tears. He sat in his car and waited until he saw the lights at Amy's house flicker.

It was time.

Bleeder stepped from his car and set to work. He went to the bush and, one by one, hoisted out four basketball-sized boulders he'd collected from previous nights. Grunting under the strain, he set them down one by one a few feet apart, across the narrow breadth of Hangman's Lane. They formed a stone barrier at the approach to the railroad tie bridge that spanned the creek some thirty feet below.

Bleeder had positioned the last rock when in the distance he heard the Camaro. He went back to his car, saw Kyle's headlights progress down the road. He heard the engine growling. Heard Led Zeppelin. Heard Kyle grind through his gears, squealing in all of them as he rumbled nearer, rocketing through the night.

The Camaro's lights grew brighter, its engine and music louder as Kyle crested the hill, ripped down the creek valley, hugging the curve so fast the car's suspension strained.

As usual, Kyle never slowed down before the bridge.

The rocks awaited him like a firing squad. The instant he saw them at the bridge, it was too late. He never touched his brakes. He tried to swerve but the combination of speed, momentum, shifting weight of the car, the artillery impact of the rock against the undercarriage catapulted the Camaro skyward, the engine and Led Zeppelin screaming, metal screeching as it crashed in an arch through the guardrail, plunging through the darkness to the creek below.

Bleeder looked in all directions. No one around. He walked to the road and, one by one, heaved the stones back into the bush. In the moonlight he inspected the point of impact, tossing a few stone chips into the creek. Same set of scrapes and scars from Kyle's reckless driving habits. Nothing new.

"Help!"

Bleeder walked along the bridge and looked below. He heard muffled music, saw the Camaro's headlights. The car was almost perfectly overturned and submerged. The driver's door jutted from the black water.

"Somebody help, please!"

That would be Kyle.

Bleeder worked his way down the slopes to the bank of the narrow creek. By the light of the moon he saw Kyle clearly. Horror and pain written across his face, blood webbed down his temple and cheek. *The cheek Amy had kissed.* Kyle reached his arm out in vain. Bleeder saw Kyle's outstretched hand and his division title football ring. Remembered the fist that smashed against his head. Bleeder didn't move. He watched Kyle's eyes blinking in recognition of his schoolmate a dozen yards away.

"Bleeder! God! Get help! Please! My leg's pinned! The car's slipping!"

Bleeder said nothing.

The car shifted and slipped deeper under the water. Kyle's voice broke sounding almost like a child pleading.

"Jesus Christ, Bleeder. Help me!"

Bleeder glanced around, cocked an ear for any oncoming traffic.

The Camaro shifted again and dropped another few feet underwater.

"God! Bleeder, it's up to my chin. Please!"

At this point Kyle's pleas gurgled until they ceased.

Bleeder shoved his hands in his pockets and watched the water swallow the Camaro, watched Kyle's farm-boy hand shoot up, breaking the surface, his ring catching the moonlight as it thrashed for about thirty seconds until it vanished too.

Bleeder climbed the slope to the road. Got in his father's car and drove down Hangman's Lane back to town.

47

After conducting a threat assessment, the San Francisco police determined that enough time had passed and it was safe enough to move Molly Wilson from the house in Union City in the East Bay.

"But you can't go back to your apartment yet," Sydowski said, agreeing to let Molly move in with a friend.

Della Thompson.

She had a small, gorgeous cottage of a home way down south in Glen Park. Thompson had scraped, saved, shopped, and networked some real estate sources to land a remarkable deal on the place at the edge of one of the city's more upscale neighborhoods.

It was her dream.

Almost hidden from the street, her house was sheltered by huge eucalyptus groves, thick shrubs, and a wrought-iron gate.

It was a Mission-style home, made of white stucco with a red clay tile roof. It had a garage, living room, kitchen, bathroom, and two bedrooms. The house was like balm for Molly. She'd felt the first stirrings of normalcy when she moved in. At least she had a piece of her life back.

Violet Stewart, the *Star*'s managing editor, had insisted Thompson take a few days off to stay home with Molly.

"You think you're capable of handling my idiosyncrasies, girlfriend?" Thompson joked as she helped Molly settle in.

"I've just spent the last few days cohabiting with strange, disgusting male members of the species. I think I can handle you."

After unpacking, Molly held Thompson's eyes in hers for a serious moment. "Thank you," she said. "This means so much."

Thompson gave her a reassuring hug.

Later on that first day, Sydowski dropped by. He told them that unmarked district cars would be rolling by on a regular basis twenty-four hours a day.

"We may be overdoing it, but we think that this is the best way to go for the time being," he said. "You've got all our numbers."

"I just hope you catch the creep soon, Inspector," Thompson said.

"Sounds like a plan," he said.

After Sydowski left, Thompson passed Molly an envelope thick with messages, cards, and letters for her, then promised to keep screening her calls. Many were requests for interviews. Some came from story scouts and agents wanting her rights, or pitching book deals. Molly's answer was no to anything for now.

The women made a salad and pasta dinner. It was ambrosia after the endless diet of pizzas, burgers, and Chinese takeout Molly'd had with her protectors in Alvarado. As night fell on Glen Park, they sat on the floor before a crackling fire and sipped white wine.

"Oh, Del," Molly said, "this one guy, Inspector Schwartz, you should've seen how he groomed himself with his car keys."

"Gawd!" Thompson watched Molly demonstrate.

"I'm not kidding, every orifice."

The two woman laughed, cathartic, knee-slapping laughter, until tears came. They sighed and sipped more wine while watching the flames. A long moment passed in silence before Thompson turned to her friend.

"So how was it, really?"

Molly's face grew serious and her eyes never left the fire.

"More horrible than you could imagine," she said. "I see them in my dreams. They come to me bleeding, begging me to find the killer. But I don't know who, or why? Why? Then I feel I should be working with you guys, helping everyone hunt down the bastard. But there are times when I just can't move. I mean I just can't —" Molly covered her face with her hands and Thompson rubbed her shoulder.

"You've got to be strong, now," she said. "Sydowski's going to nail the sicko and you're going to heal. I promise you. You got that?"

Molly nodded, touching the corners of her eyes. She attempted to smile.

"And no one's going to bother you here. That is my pledge to you. They'd have to go through me first. And that would be a fatal error," Thompson said, downing the last of their wine before hitting on an idea.

"I think we should invite some of our friends over. Maybe tomorrow. Just a few. Have some laughs. Heal your soul. How's that sound?"

"As Sydowski said, sounds like a plan."

48

Tom was at his desk in the *Star* newsroom staring with mounting frustration at his cell phone. One of his street sources had called but the call had been cut off. He took a chance and dialed a number he was cautioned to use sparingly.

"Yes."

"This is Tom. Lois just called me but we got cut off."

"Please wait."

A full minute passed.

"Hello, Tom. Yes, she's still around."

"Would you please tell her to meet me in one hour at the usual place?"

"The usual place."

Again, Tom made a point not to use a staff billboard pool car with the *Star*'s logo painted all over it. He took his own Taurus and headed to the Mission District, to Hector's Cantina, a little restaurant he knew near the BART Station. He took a table, ordered coffee, and waited. About ten minutes later Lois Hirt entered alone.

She had short brown hair and walnut-shaped eyes. Her ears, eyebrows, and lip were pierced. Her skin was blotched. She weighed about ninety pounds. Her thin, feeble arms had bracelets of needle tracks. She was twenty-five.

Tom was relieved to see her.

"Would you like something to eat?"

She asked for a danish and tea.

Lois didn't speak. She gazed out the window, or maybe it was her reflection. Staring at nothing as if she were haunting her own life. Before she became a heroin addict Lois was studying dentistry at the University of the Pacific. Her fiancé was studying criminal law at Berkeley when he was killed in a car crash several years ago. Lois had lost her will to live and descended to the street.

Tom met her when he was doing a series on drug murders. Unlike many addicts, she circulated throughout the Bay Area. She had a network of drug addict friends and remembered what they told her. Through them she heard who was plotting, stealing, dealing, who got killed, who got robbed, who was hiding, lying, or dying. Because in the end most crimes were tied to drugs. Tom realized that Lois was a powerful receiver of invaluable street data. Trouble was she was difficult to track down. At times it took weeks.

"Paco said you needed to see me."

"I need your help. Two police officers were murdered in their homes. Detectives."

"Yes, it's big news."

"I need to know if anyone has heard anything about it. Someone who may know something. If their deaths are connected to anything from the street."

Lois dripped cream into her tea, then pondered the clouds it made.

"I remember reading about the first one in the papers. And I remember I was with Paco at some place, a party, and this girl was talking about it."

"In what way?"

"She said that maybe she knew something about it."

"Knew what?"

"She said some guy came up to her on the street and started talking to her about it right around the time it happened."

"Talked to her about what? The murdered officer? His killer? Can you recall?"

"Well, we were all getting pretty blasted."

"Think, Lois, please."

"Something like how this guy needed her to help him, to pass on some information about the murder."

Tom's pulse skipped ahead. He glanced around to ensure that no one was eavesdropping.

"What sort of information? Pass it to who?"

"I don't know. Just to make some calls."

Lois cupped her hands around her tea and stared into it. Discomfort passed over her

face. Tom knew she was going to need something soon.

"Did she make the calls?"

Lois shrugged. "I think so. Maybe. I'm not
sure."

Tom studied her.

"Do you know who she called?"

Lois shook her head.

"Did this girl know who this person was
that she was helping?"

Lois shrugged.

"Paco said she was full of crap but we
were all wasted."

"Do you know this girl from the party?"

She began rubbing her upper arms and
shoulders as if she was cold. She stared out
the window.

"I know she's got a rough life but I've seen
her."

"Do you think you could find her again,
like if you very quietly asked around, could
you maybe help me get in touch with her?"

Lois's head started moving up and down.

"I can try."

"Real soon?"

"Yes."

49

"Where was I the nights they were murdered?"

Any hint of warmth on FBI Special Agent Park Williams's face evaporated after Sydowski had clarified his request for help. Williams rubbed his chin, then asked: "Can we take a walk around the building?"

He had an athletic build, chiseled features, deep-set eyes, and a smoldering intensity that most women found attractive, including Molly Wilson. They'd dated for about four months nearly two years ago.

Once they were outside the Phillip Burton Federal Building, which houses the FBI's San Francisco Division, Sydowski again asked Williams to account for his whereabouts on the nights Hooper and Beamon were murdered.

"We just want to cross you off," Sydowski said.

Williams put his hands on his hips, spreading his jacket.

"We went through this with Hooper. I was in Los Angeles when Hooper was killed, and when Beamon was killed I was in Portland."

"Can you prove it?"

"There were meetings. Hotel receipts. Plane tickets. People I talked to."

"Fine, we'll need details and records if you'd care to volunteer them."

Williams eyed Sydowski and Turgeon, then glanced up toward the thirteenth floor.

"You speak to my supervisor about this?"

"No."

"Then I will." He shook his head. "I don't hold it against you. I mean, two of your own." Williams bit his bottom lip. "How's Molly doing?"

"This isn't a social call," Sydowski said, passing Williams his card. "Fax over the information as soon as possible. Until then, your name stays on the list." Williams looked at the card as Sydowski added, "I understand the press is sniffing around Molly's old boyfriends."

That should speed things up, Sydowski figured on their way back to the Hall of Justice. During the drive Turgeon reviewed their progress on the list. Glazer was on location with a film in Toronto where he'd been for the last four weeks. Toronto police confirmed it. Cecil Lowe and Pete Marlin were on assignments and wouldn't be available for at least a day. It was going to take longer for Steve Murdoch. He was in town during the murders. But he was now flying over Europe. Duane Ford and Manny Lewis had been cleared. Yarrow was out of town and, so far, unreachable.

When Sydowski and Turgeon returned to the detail, a padded sky-blue envelope from *Breaking News of the World Inc.* was waiting on his desk.

"Vincent's producer from *Crime Scene* sent it over," Gonzales said. "She said it's a cassette tape, volume one, of nut-bar voice mails left for Wilson on the show. She's got more material coming for us later."

Impressed, Sydowski raised his eyebrows. The producer sent a data sheet with dates, numbers, times, call durations. He collected his tape player and the information and went to the interview room.

"Coming?" he asked Turgeon. "There's only a few."

"Let me get my muffin."

The tape hissed, then began with call number one, which started with a long silence before a male voice said:

"Yes, this is for Molly. I watched you the other night and I just want to say that you're a coldhearted bitch. You're such a bitch. The way you just sit there so smug. If you were my girlfriend, I'd slap you, you bitch!"

Turgeon glanced at Sydowski, shaking her head. The next message echoed as if the man were calling from a cave. "Ms. Wilson, uh, yes. Enjoy the show . . . but one thing, uh, yes, you ever wonder, I mean really think about what it's like to *off* someone? I mean, uh, yes, *kill* them? You and Vinnie talk about crime so much, but do you have any concept of what it feels like to kill, *to end a life?* Yes, uh, just wondering . . . maybe you should address this on the next program."

Sydowski's face revealed nothing as the third one began.

"This is for Molly. Why haven't you called me!" the caller was screaming in a voice that was hard to identify as male or female. "You're such a lying whore! You sit there and I watch you and I beg you to call because we belong together. And don't you lie to me, you know it too! But you don't call! You're such a lying little whore who should be taught a lesson. Maybe I should come down there and instill in you some respect! An appreciation for decorum! For human dignity! You lying, cheating —"

The tape ended.

Sydowski was motionless, thinking.

"We'll get General Works to run the numbers down, get names and addresses. Background. Meanwhile, we'll get Molly to listen in case she recognizes any of these heroes. Frankly, I don't think our guy is among this selection."

Sydowski's stomach rumbled. He hadn't eaten all day.

After finishing with the tape he went downstairs to the cafeteria and grabbed an orange, sat down, and began peeling it while reading over his notes. Peeling helped him think. He wanted to go back on his driving records check for Frank Yarrow in Kansas and Missouri. Molly thought he was from Kansas City, possibly even Denver. Better query Colorado too. And call Yarrow again, he decided, tossing his peelings into the trash.

Sydowski's check for driving records had produced three hits for Frank Yarrow.

One Frank A. Yarrow in Joplin, Missouri, aged eighty-two.

One Frank Traynor Yarrow in Golden, Colorado, aged twenty.

One Frank F. Yarrow in Lawrence, Kansas, aged seventy-four.

Sydowski looked at the ages, sucking air through his teeth. *No way is my Frank Yarrow among this trio.* He went back to his notes. Molly had passed him a cell phone number for Yarrow. When he had tried it before, it rang about eleven times, unanswered. Might as well try again.

Illinois area code. Sydowski noted that, dialed, and waited. It rang once. Twice. Three times, then —

"Hello?"

"Mr. Yarrow? Frank Yarrow?"

"Sorry, he's out at the moment, can I take a message?"

"Oh, any idea when he'll be back? I need to reach him."

"I think he's in Costa Rica on business. Been there for a few weeks. I expect he'll be back in another week or so. Who's calling?"

"It's an old friend. I've been trying to reach him. Who've I got?"

"Len. Frank's partner. Can I help you or take a message?"

"No. I'll call again." Sydowski circled the area code. "Are you working out of Chicago?"

"No, I'm on the road right now. Somewhere in Texas or Oklahoma."

"I see, and how's business going for you guys?"

"Oh, not too bad. Could always use more, you know how it is."

"Sure do. Look, I'll call again real soon."

That was an odd conversation, Sydowski thought, after hanging up. He made several notes. For starters he wanted a trace on that cell phone number.

50

Across San Francisco, Frank Yarrow studied his cell phone after talking with the stranger who was looking for him.

Who was that guy?

The caller's number had been blocked. Yarrow had been caught off guard. Hoping the call was from Molly, he'd answered without thinking.

Saying that he was "Len," and that Frank was in Costa Rica, was quick. But he'd likely blown it. The stranger sounded smart. Said he was an "old friend." Yarrow didn't recognize the voice and the guy didn't give a name. He was smooth. Too smooth. And now he knew about Chicago.

Assume the worst, Yarrow told himself in the shower.

He didn't know who'd called or how the guy had gotten his number, but he had his suspicions. His ex must've somehow put them on to him and they were getting close. He'd likely been sloppy along the way, probably with bank or credit cards. Sometimes he just didn't think clearly. Old habits die hard.

His mouth went dry.

He forced himself to be calm. *Relax.* He needed to think now and it was difficult to think. He'd always known that sooner or later they'd pick up on something from Chicago.

And then they'd get the whole story about him.

Things had gone so bad back there. It was just a question of time that they'd lock on to him. But he couldn't let it happen before he accomplished what he'd set out to do.

Yarrow needed to get through to Molly. Needed to convince her of the deeper significance of their current circumstances. For chrissake, she had to have given some thought to what he'd told her. About what she meant to him. She had to realize, especially now after everything that'd happened, that she needed him as much as he needed her.

He got dressed.

She had to look into her heart the way he did and accept the truth. That they had something once. It wasn't perfect but it was good and they could get it back and make it stronger than ever before.

It was meant to be.

Why couldn't she see that?

Why, Molly?

How many ways and how many times did he have to communicate to her that she was not merely the right answer for his crisis?

She was the *only* answer.

If she would only understand that this was how it was supposed to work for them, then he could fix everything in the past. He could repair all the damage because he'd have her. And once he was secure in her love, there was nothing he couldn't do.

If she rejected him, then there was only one thing he would do. It was his final option. Yarrow gazed into the small framed photograph. A nice shot of him with Molly, both smiling. Happier times. He could make her happy again. If she would only realize it.

Without her he was no one. Nothing.

A zero.

He knew about all the high-powered guys she'd known.

The lawyers, the movie people, the pilots, the federal agents and detectives. How she'd met all kinds because of her profession and her work on the TV crime show. Exciting glamorous stuff. But he also knew her upbringing. Knew she was intelligent enough to accept that it was not the job, but the man, that counted.

A corporate security consultant. That's what he was doing now. It wasn't a lie. Not really. He looked across the room at his uniform hanging in the closet. He was an eleven-dollar-an-hour security guard.

Hold on. This was just temporary. He'd done better. And he'd do better again. The important thing was that he was here, close to her. Using all he knew to watch over her, to ensure that she was safe while she considered his proposal and their future together.

He was so vigilant.

At times when he watched her from a distance, it hurt. He wanted to get closer. Molly had to realize that no one needed her more right now than he did.

She was his only hope.

Molly had to admit that she needed him as much as he needed her. She had to understand that together they could get through this.

Yarrow closed his eyes and dreamed of the days when it was good for them. Days when he would take her hand and pull her close. It was a time when he believed he would always be with her and they would live forever. Then his life took a few wrong turns, forcing him on a long, hurt-filled road that led him back to Molly.

It was crystalline to him.

Molly had to see that he would help her through her pain as she would help him overcome his.

She was his answer.

Now more than ever.

Yes, the call just now was upsetting. It had unnerved him. They were looking for him because of Chicago. It was such a mess back there. They were closing in and time was running out.

He met Molly's eyes in the picture.

If time was running out on him, then it was running out on her too.

51

After considering the situation all day long, Tom Reed finally decided it was time to offer up a story about the San Francisco Police Department's suspect list.

He would not publish the names on it.

That's where he'd draw the line if Irene Pepper pushed him.

On one level it was straight-up reporting of basic homicide procedure. Detectives were going to Molly's ex-boyfriends and eliminating them as suspects. That was homicide investigation 101.

Most people in the city's police and press networks knew whom Molly had dated over the years. And if he crafted it carefully, the story would be fine. Solid. The angle would deepen the intrigue once *Star* newsprint was stained with something like this. He began to write:

The hunt for a suspect in the murders of two homicide detectives is reaching into the ranks of the SFPD, the U.S. Marshal's Service, the ATF, the FBI and the district attorney's office, sources have told the *Star*.

Tom pondered the first draft of his lead. He liked it. After further consideration he recognized how Sydowski had skillfully played him. This story would tick off the agencies named to move fast to get their people cleared, if they hadn't already. It was an effective way to tighten a key aspect of the investigation while letting the bureaucracy know the homicide detail was pursuing the case with righteous vengeance.

It was also a hell of an exclusive.

Della Thompson read over his shoulder when he finished. "It's wild."

"Think so?" Tom made a few adjustments before sending his lead to Acker, who would add it to the afternoon's story sked.

"Oh yeah. They ought to line that baby on front. You got a nice touch, maestro."

"Thanks. So how's Molly?" He reached for his coffee.

"You can find out for yourself tonight." Thompson bent down and quietly invited him to join others to visit with Molly at her house in Glen Park. "You're sworn to secrecy."

"What about Irene Pepper?"

"She knows, but apparently can't make it. Violet Stewart and Acker will drop by. Simon, Mandy Carmel, Henry Cain, you. That's it."

"I'll be there. I'd like to talk to her."

After he finished writing his story, Tom

called Ann and told her he was going to join some newsroom friends after work.

"That's fine," she said. "I'm taking Zach with me to the Berkeley store. We'll get a pizza and he's going to help with some inventory."

"He loves doing that."

"Did you find out what you wanted to know about roses?"

"*The roses*. Right. Not yet. Thanks, you just reminded me. I have to make a call. I'll let you know. Take care."

He began searching through stacks of newspapers, notebooks, press releases, and outdated police district reports for his map and notes on the flower shops. He was supposed to call back. He found the map. Which one was it? Here it was. He'd drawn a large asterisk beside *The Pacific Dreams Flower Shop*. Call and ask for Alice. Leeshann was very helpful, his notes said.

He reached for the phone.

"Pacific Dreams."

"Hi is Alice there?"

"No, she's not. This is Leeshann. May I help you?"

He explained how he was the guy who'd dropped in a little while back playing that office detective game.

"I remember. Office game boy. You gave us the list, the 'suspect' list."

"That's me. Did Alice ever get the chance to check it out?"

"I think so. Just a sec. She told me which guy it was. She marked it. Now, where did I put it?"

His fingers squeezed a little harder around the phone.

"Here we go. Now wait a sec, what do I get for helping you beat the other team?"

"Depends on if you can help me take it to the next level. We get extra points. But I doubt that you can." He smiled.

"Try me."

"What's the name?"

"Yarrow."

He circled the name on his suspect list.

"Frank. Frank. We should've known it was Frank."

"So what's the next level?"

"Well, did Frank walk in or phone in an order? And did he pay with cash or plastic?"

Silence. Tom held his breath thinking he'd lost Leeshann. Then he heard the clicking of a keyboard.

"He phoned it in, but look, I'd be fired if I gave you his card number."

"I know. Don't worry. I don't need his card number. Actually, what I'm looking for is his middle initial."

"That's it?"

"That's it."

"Are you absolutely sure no one's going to know?"

"Going to know what?"

Leeshann let a long moment pass.

"So is it there?"

"G."

"Excuse me?"

"It's G," she whispered.

Tom wrote it down after thanking Leeshann and assuring her that no one would know how she'd helped him.

Frank G. Yarrow. *Gotcha, flower boy.*

He wanted to learn everything he could about Yarrow and he was reaching for his phone just as Irene Pepper landed at his desk.

"I read your suspect story. Page one wants it."

Tom waited for the problem.

"It's not bad. Do you have names of the suspects?" she asked.

"Some but not all. We'd be irresponsible to run a partial list."

"But we're casting suspicions on entire agencies."

"No. The story says Molly dated individuals from those agencies and police are going to talk to them. You're asking for trouble if you publish names."

"Can't you go to them and see if they'll confirm that they've been questioned by homicide detectives?"

"Tried that already. No one's talking. Understandable when you consider the stakes. It's serious stuff. Look, if you want to hold the story and read about it in another paper, that's fine with me."

Pepper bit her lip and thought. Then she reached for Tom's phone and punched an extension. "Hi, it's Irene. Let Reed's story go as is. Right."

Pepper hung up, then crossed her arms, leaned against his desk, and lowered her voice.

"I understand you might be seeing Molly tonight?"

He nodded.

"I think it would be a good opportunity to nudge her on doing a first-person account for me, now that some time has passed."

"She knows about your request. I think she'd come to you when, or if, she agrees to do something."

"Consider it an assignment from me to persuade her to do this."

Another shot for challenging her, Tom thought after Pepper disappeared. He shook his head and took a deep breath. Then he headed to the counter of the *Star*'s news library, buoyed to see that Lillian was pulling the late shift. She was twenty-eight with a PhD in library science. The paper's best librarian for what he wanted.

"Lil, I need you."

"What do you need, Mr. Reed?"

She smiled, then poised her pencil over her notepad as Tom looked to the left, then right to ensure that no one else would hear.

"I was going to do this myself at my terminal but you've got access to more data banks. And you're better than me."

"Quit sucking up, buddy."

"The guy I'm interested in is Frank G. Yarrow." He spelled the name. "I want to know everything about him."

"What do you need?"

"Run a shotgun search of all news sources, big and small. All archives. I want any hits fitting him. Anything and everything, like Little League, school science fairs, arrests, car wrecks, cutlines, obits, family tree, military duty. Online newsletters, community papers. Nothing's too small. The guy should be in the mid-thirties range and might be involved in security of some sort. But don't limit the search to that."

"How far back?"

"As far as you can go."

"When do you need it?"

"I'm going out shortly. So how about for tomorrow morning?"

"Okay. I've got to do some filing in the back. It'll get real quiet later, so I'll likely finish it tonight."

"Sounds good. And, Lil, let's keep this search between us."

Heading back into the newsroom, Tom chided himself for not jumping on Yarrow's name sooner. Well, he sure as hell wasn't going to sit on his hands waiting for anyone to feed him stuff on Yarrow.

He'd launch his own full-court press now.

52

Since he'd arrived at Della Thompson's house in Glen Park, Tom was anxious to talk to Molly alone about Frank Yarrow.

He'd considered pulling her aside but rejected the idea, deciding it would be better to wait until the others left. She might be inclined to open up to him a little without a small audience.

The evening wasn't what you'd call a party but rather a gathering of trusted colleagues and friends, who'd come to support Molly in the wake of the tragic events. The wine, finger food, and inside jokes seemed to help. It was good to see her smile and hear her laugh, Tom thought.

Violet Stewart and Acker left early. As well-respected managers, they kept a professional distance, never discussing rumors about pending corporate strategy, leaving the hard-core gossip for the staffers.

"What I hear is that the corporation's debt has ballooned and there may be cuts," Mandy Carmel said.

"That would explain why they'd put Irene Pepper in charge of Metro, the largest news department with the most fat," Simon Lepp said.

"She's lethal with the cost-cutting knives," Tom said.

"Well, when all is said and done, my girl Molly's going to be just fine." Thompson patted her knee. "I've been screening her messages. Agents have been calling about a book deal when this is over."

Tom mentioned that Pepper was pushing for Molly to write a first-person story for the *Star*.

"No way! Save it for the book, girl." Thompson poured more wine for herself and Molly. "Listen to me. Don't give it away to Pepper. Take a leave."

Lepp was taken by Thompson's home and how she'd gotten it for a steal.

"Your place is a gem. Mind if I take a tour?"

"Be my guest," Thompson said.

Not long afterward, Henry Cain, a *Star* photographer, and Mandy Carmel left. As Tom helped himself to another ginger ale, he noticed white roses in a vase near a corner window. Had to be the most recent ones from Yarrow. He was inspecting them when Lepp decided to go, leaving him alone with Molly and Thompson.

Tom wasted no time.

"I've got a story on Sydowski's suspect list coming out tomorrow. I'm not naming people. But mostly all your old boyfriends, the ones you dated for more than a month, are on it."

Molly said nothing as Tom assured her he was not publishing the names but wanted to review them with her. They discussed the likelihood that Duane Ford, Rob Glazer, Cecil Lowe, Manny Lewis, Steve Murdoch, Pete Marlin, or Park Williams could've killed Hooper and Beamon. On the face of it, none seemed a plausible candidate, Tom agreed.

"It could be some head case who's seen me on the show," Molly said.

"Do you know who's been sending you the white roses with these cryptic notes?" he asked, showing her copies he'd made.

Molly poured more wine, looked at them, and shook her head.

"I got so many flowers, and I get strange stuff through the paper and Vincent's show. So no, not really."

"I did some checking and I found out. It's Frank Yarrow. I didn't recognize his name, but he's on Sydowski's list. You know him?"

Molly nodded, then set down her glass and said nothing.

"Aren't you concerned he could've had something to do with the murders? Look at his strange notes and the timing of the flowers," Tom said.

"I told Sydowski all I know about Frank a long time ago, right after Cliff's funeral. I told him that he'd come to talk to me."

"He came to see you after Hoop's funeral! Jesus! That's chilling timing. What did he talk about? Did he threaten you?"

"No. Nothing like that. Frank doesn't even live in California. It was coincidental that he was in town on business. It's a little complicated with Frank and me."

"Uncomplicate it for us. Tell us about him."

Molly cupped her face with her hands and gazed at the small flames dying in the fireplace.

"We were teens in Texas when I got pregnant. It all ended badly."

This part of Molly's life was a revelation. Thompson exchanged glances with Tom. After hesitating, Thompson said softly, "You were pregnant?"

Staring at her glass, Molly journeyed back through the years of her life.

"I was seventeen," she began. "Frank was the father. He wanted me to keep it. I didn't know what to do. I was torn. Frank and I argued during this whole time. God, he wanted to talk about wedding plans. I was *seventeen*. He came by my parents' home one night and picked me up in his truck. Said he wanted to drive to the river to talk but we argued. I started running from him and I fell and I lost the baby." Molly drank more wine.

"We broke up and moved on with our lives. I went off to college. I think he, or his family, moved around Texas, then around the country. Sometimes he would write and call me. I always put him off. Anything I ever shared with him died years ago on that riverbank. I left it all behind and moved on. We were kids. It was sad. It's over."

"So after all these years he comes looking for you in San Francisco at your boyfriend's funeral?" Tom asked.

"He was in town on business when he'd learned of Hooper's murder," Molly said. "Wants to take up with me again. He got divorced recently. He wanted me to consider starting over with him. I told him no, get on with your life. He was just reacting to his divorce. He's kind of shy and withdrawn. It makes sense that he would send me the flowers with these odd little notes."

"What does he do?"

"Corporate security consultant or something like that."

"You're not concerned that he could be linked to the murders?"

"I really think his problems coincided with mine," she said. "Frank's not violent. How would he even know about Cliff and Ray after all these years? He doesn't even live in California. I told Sydowski all about him. I doubt he's a serious suspect. It makes no sense."

Tom looked at her for a long moment as he considered her history with Frank Yarrow.

"Nothing in this case makes sense," he said.

53

Ida Lyndstrum was awakened at her large home in the Western Addition. The green digits on her bedside clock glowed 2:45 a.m.

"Oh, for goodness' sake."

It had to have been her upstairs tenant with his comings and goings at all hours. She was becoming disappointed with him. He had been so well mannered and quiet. A non-smoker who kept to himself. A gentleman, really. But he was always trudging up and down the outside stairs to the apartment at such ungodly times.

Don't you ever sleep, Mr. Night Owl?

Ida had a vague memory of a car door thudding.

She drew back her curtain on the window facing her driveway. His car was gone. It must've been him. Where was he going at this hour? *My word.* Oh, what did it matter? Ida sat up. He had every right to come and go as he pleased, but he might try to be considerate some of the time. If he kept this up she was going to have to speak to him about it.

Ida slid her wrinkled fingers along her

quilted bedspread for Clementine's soft fawn and white coat. But her fat tabby cat wasn't there. She was likely off prowling, or sulking.

"Where are you, Clemmie? Did Mr. Noisy wake you too?"

In the silence, Ida heard a distinct but distant meowing and immediately knew she was in trouble. Her old house had a sealed-off interior stairway and air duct system. Clementine could slip into the passageway where she occasionally prowled for mice. It led to the upstairs apartment. And judging from the meowing, Clementine had used it tonight. It sounded as if she'd intruded into the apartment and was crying to be rescued.

Ida knew Clemmie would not come back out on her own. She also knew she was a big baby who'd be frightened in the apartment. Her fear would lead to damage, which was the case three years ago.

That had cost her six hundred dollars to repair a tenant's sofa.

"Oh! Clemmie!"

Ida was forced to break a rule, and likely some sort of law. She grumbled as her feet found her slippers and she pulled on her sweater. She snatched her keys from the kitchen peg, trudged outside and around her house to the backstairs. Her intention was to enter the apartment, scoop up Clementine, and leave.

No one would be the wiser, Ida reasoned,

hoping her naughty cat had not wreaked havoc in the premises. After knocking and ensuring that no one was home, Ida entered.

"Clementine," she whispered. "Come here this instant."

There was no sign of her. Ida heard a meow from the bedroom and switched on some lights. The one-bedroom apartment was very tidy and clean. Ida approved. The walls were bare, save for a nice landscape painting of the coast. A laptop computer on a desk. Some orderly files. A few newspapers set neatly to the side.

Oh, that's nice, Ida cooed like the grand-mother she was, as she bent down to examine a framed photograph of a man and a pretty woman. It was taken some time ago. It looked like her tenant. And the girl looked familiar. Ida squinted, didn't have her proper glasses.

She straightened and tapped her finger to her lips. Now, why did that woman look so familiar? She was pondering that question when something nudged her from behind. Her breath caught in her throat.

She turned to find her cat.

"My Lord! You bad, bad cat!"

Ida collected Clementine into her arms, locked the apartment, and hurried downstairs back into her house. She continued wondering about the woman in the picture for nearly an hour before she fell asleep.

54

Driving home from Della Thompson's house, Tom was still troubled by Molly's history with Frank Yarrow. Showing up the way he did at Hooper's funeral was disturbing. Even if a man were traumatized by a divorce, he'd have better sense than to hit on his old high school girlfriend at a time like that. And the flowers with those cryptic sophomoric notes.

Yarrow was a whack job.

Tom stopped at a red light. The more he considered Yarrow the more it concerned him. He checked the time. It was late but he was too jacked up to sleep. He'd swing by the paper and see if Lil got any hits from her search.

He signed in at security.

"You're working late, buddy boy," Lester the guard said.

"Always working, pal. Whether I'm here or there, I'm always working."

The night desk staff was gone.

The building trembled ever so slightly with the hum of the *Star*'s big German presses several floors below. The newsroom was deserted except for Josh, the twenty-two-year-old news assistant-slash-intern. He was listening to a portable police scanner and watching *From Here to Eternity*.

Tom waved as he strode by to his desk, taking in San Francisco's skyline from the windows at the far end of the floor. At his desk, Lillian had placed a blue library folder on the seat of his chair, with a note that said *This is all I could find so far, Lil.*

It contained two pages. A printout of a color photo. About a dozen smiling men and women wearing ball caps, jeans, and T-shirts. The credit was the *Bryan-College Station Star-Journal*. Texas, Tom thought. The undated cutline identified the players as members of the Barner County Sheriff's Department. Lillian highlighted a name, Deputy Frank G. Yarrow.

Yarrow's a cop?

Tom studied the team shot and Yarrow standing among the men and women grinning from the back row. Good looking. Tall. Well built. Then he went to the next page, a printout of a short news hit well over ten years old, from the *Star-Journal*.

BEAUTY FINALIST ALLEGES
BARNER COUNTY DEPUTY STALKED HER
STAR-JOURNAL STAFF REPORT

A 26-year-old former Miss Texas finalist has lodged a formal complaint alleging a Barner County deputy sheriff followed her home, then made calls to her after a routine traffic stop.

Stacie Dawnne Lehe, of College Station, was returning from a church meeting Friday, traveling westbound in her 2002 Chevy Blazer on U.S. Highway 190, she said in her statement filed Monday.

Lehe was about 15 miles from Bryan when she was pulled over by Barner County deputy sheriff Frank G. Yarrow. Lehe alleges that after Yarrow issued her a traffic ticket for speeding, he followed her to a mall, then later followed to her home.

Yarrow then telephoned Lehe at her home in College Station the next day, Saturday. He was also witnessed parked near her residence Sunday, Lehe said in her statement.

Lehe was not available for comment. Nor was Yarrow.

It is believed that Lehe's vehicle had faulty equipment and Yarrow was ensuring her safety, a spokesman for the Barner County Sheriff's Department said, adding that Lehe's complaint was being investigated.

Man, oh man, that's a heck of a thing, Tom thought. Stalking a Texas beauty contestant. Molly never said a word about her old boy-friend being a cop who stalked pretty women. Tom didn't care about the time. He had to tell her.

Now.

Tom punched Della Thompson's number.

55

In the darkness Bleeder slowed his breathing.

His heart was beating so fast, slamming against his rib cage. His ears roared with pulsations so deafening he feared his enemies would overwhelm him.

But nothing happened.

Not a single thing.

Because right now, at this moment, Bleeder owned this part of the world and everything in it. Standing as still as a corpse in a darkened corner, he waited a full twenty minutes for his breathing to relax. For his eyes to adjust. For his ears to become attuned to every tick and creak of Della Thompson's home at a secluded edge of Glen Park.

Molly's time had come.

Never in his wildest fantasies had he believed it would be like this. This was not what he'd envisioned. But his project had endured so many obstacles he could not risk another. The line of empty wine bottles and glasses on the coffee table assured him that the women would be sleeping the deep sleep of the inebriated.

Bleeder's senses were tingling beyond his

311

expectations. Excitement shot through him like an electrical current. Look at what he'd accomplished for Molly. He'd eliminated two homicide detectives and left their grieving compadres bewildered. What was their little Boy Scout slogan, "Gold in Peace, Iron in War"? Well, this was war. And check out the graves.

You're losing.

Big time.

No longer was Bleeder the watcher from the shadows. The timid voyeur in the distance. He was the power and the glory. The undefeated champion who'd come to claim his prize.

Get ready, Molly.

Bleeder adjusted his latex gloves and moved down the hall to the bedrooms. Even before he got to Thompson's door he heard her snoring. He entered her room and stood over her. She was a veritable sawmill. He could've dropped a pyramid of wineglasses on the floor next to her bed without waking her.

Carefully, he pulled Thompson's bedroom door closed after he left.

He glided into the room where Molly slept and crouched beside her. He drew his face next to hers until he felt her soft breathing against his skin. He was ecstatic. His heart swelled as he slowly moved his hand near her brow, aching to touch her, to celebrate this moment with her. He closed his eyes and drank in her aura. His skin and scalp prickled. God, he was enthralled.

Not a moment to waste.

Be right back.

In the kitchen, Bleeder examined the knives in the butcher's block. He selected a ten-inch chef's knife. Looked like it had a strong, thick forged blade. The wooden handle was secured with brass rivets and felt good in his hand. This would do nicely.

Bleeder returned down the hall to the bedrooms.

Gently he swung Molly's door shut, then inched toward Thompson's closed door. He stood motionless, slipping into a trance of preparation. Holding the knife with both hands, he bowed his head.

Swift and sudden fury.

He repeated it like a prayer.

Swift and sudden fury.

He'd use his left hand to seal Thompson's mouth. Swift and sudden fury. His right hand would drive the blade into her heart with every ounce of his strength. Swift and sudden fury. To the hilt. Swift and sudden fury.

She'd be dead before she awoke.

With the last obstacle cleared, Molly would be his.

Bleeder spread his fingers against Thompson's door. The instant he touched it the phone beside her bed rang.

Bleeder froze.

Nothing happened.

It rang again. He heard stirring from Thompson's bed. It rang a third time and he heard her mumble. Then the rattle of plastic as she groped for the phone.

"What is it?" she said. "Damn it, Tom, do you know what time it is?"

Bleeder stepped back into the darkness and disappeared into the night.

56

Short spikes of orange hair shot in every direction like pyrotechnics, embodying the explosion of pain in her head, her bones, her soul.

It hurts. It hurts. It hurts. It hurts so bad.

Her knees buckled and she caught herself on a Market Street trash can.

The clonazepam had taken the edge off but its effects had faded long ago. She didn't have the strength or the will to go back to the clinic for more this afternoon. She craved her stuff. God, she needed it. Snot flowed from her nose, mixing with her tears. Droopy-eyed, she stumbled toward the corner hoping Gator would be there. She barely sidestepped a used condom in a pool of urine. It forced a reflex gag and she fell against somebody in an alley.

"Hey, bitch, watch your ass!" said a man, his face hidden by long matted hair and a beard flecked with cracker crumbs. His filthy fingers gripped a bottle wrapped in a paper bag.

Her palms slapped against brick as she kept moving toward the corner. *Please be there. Baby be there. Is that him? That's him! Thank you, Lord!*

Behind his dark glasses, Gator had been eyeballing her progress since he'd stepped off the BART from Oakland and got busy. He was gaunt with a face pocked and scarred by the ravages of acne and the life of a dealer. Annoyed at the sight of her, he sneered.

"Yo, Skin Popper, come take care of your bill."

"Gator, baby, you got to fix me up. Please. I'm sick."

"You see your doctor for that. With me, it's business." He looked away.

"You got to."

"I *got* to?" Gator's head snapped round. He inventoried her black spandex dress and ruby pumps. Arms striped with needle tracks, and sores that looked like lesions.

"How *do* you keep yourself looking so fine?"

She held out an open hand. "Gator, please."

"You got what you owe?"

"I'm short, but I'll pick up some work. Promise."

"Ah. That's sweet. See me when you got some dead presidents for me."

"Give me something to get me through."

She opened her purse, grabbed her leather wallet. It was personalized. Her name, Gloria, was written in a small elegant script in one corner. A handmade gift from her ex. He was in Folsom for a murder he didn't commit. She had to believe that for the sake of their two-year-old daughter, Sunny. Social services was taking care of her. *Just until Mommy gets all better.* Sunny smiled from her color photo, the one next to the worn tens and twenties. It was money earned an hour ago after letting a tourist do depraved things to her for ten minutes in the back of his family's rented van. And the few bucks she had left from that strange phone call she'd made for the weirdo.

She held out the cash.

"That should cover half a gram and some of what I owe, please."

He stared at her palm as if it held an insult.

"Girl, you're not doing the math."

She thrust the money under his nose. "I'm dying."

He swatted her hand away. His voice was stone cold.

"You owe me five hundred."

"But I'm dying. I'm sick. Take this. I'll get more."

"Either way you slice it you're diggin your grave, Skin Popper."

He snatched her money, shoved it in his pants, and stared at the Market Street traffic. Chewing and grinning at the undercovers with their gold chains and Vandykes, rolling by in their customized Honda. He knew they weren't interested in a bottom-feeding minnow like him.

"I need something. I'll take anything."

Eyebrows appeared above the dark glasses.

"Anything, baby?"

"God, yes."

He debated with himself, then worked his tongue until it found a small saliva-slick ball that looked like white candy. Extracting it, he placed it in her palm. "I'm testing a new product line. You're my first customer. It's fresh. Very potent. Very pure. Cook yourself up a dream." Her fingers closed on the balloon ball of heroin, then Gator crushed her wrist until it hurt. "Next time I see you, you better have my money."

Sobbing with pain tempered by the knowledge that relief was on its way, she vanished into a dark alley and crouched behind a Dumpster near a doorway that had coils of week-old excrement. She emptied the contents of her purse on the ground. She poked through tampons, condoms, spermicide, chocolate bars, and the folded note from the weirdo until she found her needle kit. Fingers shaking, she set to work quickly. She boiled the impurities from the heroin on a spoon, then injected herself under the skin between her thumb and forefinger. As relief flowed through her veins, she dropped her head against an obscenity scrawled on the wall and met her daughter's eyes staring up at her from the pavement.

She stayed that way for a while, letting the drug fill her with a warm sensation of well-being. Then she strolled off toward a corner coffee shop promising herself for the millionth time that she would get clean.

For Sunny.

As she walked, a sharp ache rocketed through her brain. Something was not right. Something was wrong. Then she heard a voice.

"Gloria?"

She turned to see a friend. The one she'd met at a party not long ago. The smart one who'd gone to college. Lois Hirt.

"College Girl Lois, hey, hon."

"I've been looking all over for you, Gloria, asking everybody where you went." Lois was nearly out of breath. "I think I can get you into detox, get you some money. Maybe a job."

Gloria's face brightened. "No shit?" Then her brain spasmed again. She rubbed her temples.

"Remember at the party, you told me some guy gave you money to read some joke into a phone?"

Gloria remembered. It happened down near Garfield Square. She shuddered with another jolt of pain. Something was happening to her.

319

"I got a friend who needs to track this guy down. He needs a little information. He's got connections who can help you get better."

Gloria had heard talk about Lois Hirt's friends. She licked her lips. Her stomach was quaking.

"Is this friend of yours a cop, Lois?"

"No. Hey, are you okay?"

"I don't know."

They found a bench.

"My friend's a good guy. He'll protect you."

Defeat washed over Gloria. She shook her head. Then felt cold.

"What does he want?"

"He needs you to help him find your telephone guy."

Gloria pressed her temples. It was as if corn were popping in her brain and her skull were about to split open. She gasped.

"But I don't know where to find him, I think he was wearing —"

The sidewalk rushed up to hit Gloria. Her last conscious thoughts were blurry images of the strange phone man and Lois Hirt's screaming.

57

Tom Reed had overslept and was running late. The shower's hot water soothed his sore muscles. He'd gone to bed coiled with tension after discovering Yarrow's incident with the Miss Texas finalist. Now he was uncertain it mattered.

It had happened over a decade ago. Sydowski supposedly knew all about him and was checking him out. Yarrow was recently divorced and not in the city when the murders took place. Showing up at Hooper's funeral was a strange coincidence; all valid points Molly had raised sharply during his call last night.

All right, maybe he'd overreacted. But Yarrow's case simply did not look good, Tom reasoned after dressing and driving to the paper. Yarrow's behavior gnawed at him. It didn't sit right. No, he wasn't ready to cross him off without digging a little more. And he'd chase his other leads. He was stopped at a red light when his cell phone rang.

"Reed."

"Yeah, this is a friend of Lois's."

"Hi. I was trying to reach her today."

"Something bad has just happened, like, a little while ago."

"Bad? Like what? Is she hurt?"

"No. She just called me crying, saying to tell you something went wrong on that thing she was checking for you. She's going to tell you more later."

"What? Jesus. Where is she? Do you know? Hello?"

The line went dead.

Tom immediately detoured from the *Star* for the Sixteenth-Street BART Station in the Mission District. He spent an hour searching the streets in vain for Lois Hirt before giving up and going to the paper.

The call about Lois worried him. What could it be? Any one of a million scenarios, that's what. And there wasn't a damn thing he could do but wait. At least Lois had got word to him. He had to trust her. She'd never let him down before, he assured himself as he settled in at his desk.

Get busy.

He reached into a file and reread the short article from the *Star-Journal* about Yarrow, then shook his head. There was no follow-up. Nothing. Yarrow's name hadn't made the paper again, or Lil would've found it.

Tom got on the Internet for contact information, then called the Barner County Sheriff's Department in Texas.

"Sheriff," a woman's voice said.

"Tom Reed from the *San Francisco Star.* Do you have a press person?"

"You're calling from San Francisco?"

"Yes. Do you have a person who handles press calls?"

"What's your question?"

"I'm trying to locate a deputy. He was with the department a few years back."

"Name?"

"Yarrow. Frank G. Yarrow?"

"Doesn't ring a bell with me. Hold on a second."

The line clicked and he heard a Dixie Chicks song. Tom loved their stuff. Then the woman came back.

"The man you want is Will Zotta. He's stepped away for a bit. I'll have him call you."

Tom went downstairs to the cafeteria. He was at the register paying for his bagel and tomato juice when old Hank Kruner grunted in his ear.

"Hear the latest?"

"About what?"

"The profits are down and the board's rigged some secret deal with managers," Kruner said. "Cash bonuses for every salary cut from their departmental payroll. Watch out, Ace."

At his desk, Tom finished his bagel and juice then looked around for Simon Lepp. He'd wondered if Lepp had made any headway on the foggy thing about old drug accusations against Hooper. Maybe *that* was a connection to Lois and the street? He couldn't recall if Lepp had said he was off today.

Tom was stretching when his line rang and Irene Pepper summoned him to her office. He sat while she remained standing, leaning against her desk with her arms folded.

"Did you ask Molly about doing a first-person account on the murders like I asked you?"

"She knows about your request."

"And?"

"Irene, I'm uncomfortable with the way you keep pushing me for this."

The polished nails of her fingers began drumming. The corners of her mouth courted a grin.

"Refusing an assignment is tantamount to insubordination, solid grounds for termination. To be blunt, I can fire you. End your career with this paper here and now."

Tom's jaw muscles tightened. He stared at her wondering, *How did it come to this?*

All the late nights pumping cops, hanging out at bars, riding along, working street sources, knocking on doors, and stepping into the lives of heartbroken people in pursuit of stories no one else dared chase, stories that pierced the city's soul. Stories that swallowed him whole, before chewing him up and spitting him out.

For that, he'd earned a Pulitzer nomination. He'd also earned a drinking problem and a marriage that had been patched over more times than he could remember. So how did it come down to someone like Pepper, standing over his career like a gravedigger waiting to throw the first spadeful of earth on it?

It doesn't.

No way in hell will that happen.

"Tom, if you've got something to say, something to get off your chest to clear the air in my newsroom, then take your shot. Tell me. Journalist to journalist."

Journalist to journalist.

"That's the problem, Irene, you're not a journalist."

"I've been an editor here for nine years."

"You've been on the desk here for nine years."

"Do you know how many times I've saved you at the *Star*? How many times I've put *your* name on *your* page-one stories, after *I* routinely rewrote the entire things on the desk?"

"That's not true. You tell yourself these lies to justify your existence here," he said. "You have nothing but disdain for reporters because you've never covered a single hard news story on the streets of this city. And you can't stand the fact that I, and most of the others at the *Star*, do it, day after day after day. It magnifies your incompetence. And now, here you are, by some horrible twist of fate, overlord of those you despise."

She glared at him for a long silent moment.

"You're on thin ice," she said. "I've assigned you to convince Molly to do a first-person account for me. Do it!"

"Or else?"

"Or else you're gone."

Anger bubbled in Tom's gut when he left Pepper's office, but it stopped when Acker yelled to him.

"Reed! Call for you! Some guy in Texas!"

"I'll take it at my desk."

He jogged to his phone and seized the line.

"Will Zotta with the Barner County Sheriff's Department in Texas returning your call."

"Mr. Zotta, thanks."

"What can I do for you?"

"I'm trying to locate Frank G. Yarrow, a deputy."

"And what is this in regards to?"

"I'm doing a story on police officers. A little biography work and Yarrow's name came up here and I'd heard he'd been with Barner County. Has anyone else called you on this?"

"No. But you're right. He was with us. He left the department years ago."

"Oh, I thought he was still with you. Any idea where he went?"

"Why are you interested in Yarrow?"

"It's kinda complicated. All part of a San Francisco story."

Silence filled the time that passed. Zotta was not stupid. He sighed. "Last we heard, Yarrow went to Chicago. Got into some trouble there."

"What kind of trouble?"

"You'd have to ask the Chicago PD."

Chicago Police Department?

"That's all I can say." Zotta was ending the call.

"Wait. There's something else. Can you tell me how, or why, Yarrow left your department?"

Another long tense moment passed. Tom fought the urge to push Zotta, who seemed a little uneasy that someone would call about Yarrow.

"He resigned."

"Resigned? Why?"

"Like you said, it's kind of complicated."

Okay, time to show his cards. "Can you tell me if there were ever any charges out of that old stalking complaint against him by that Miss Texas finalist?"

Zotta paused, realizing Tom had done his homework.

"No charges. It never got that far."

"You sound like you're familiar with the case."

"Yarrow was under my command."

"So he was never charged?"

"No. He volunteered to resign, and frankly, we weren't too choked up to see him go. Now, son, that's all I have to say."

Tom hung up.

He looked at Yarrow's ball team photo, then the story about stalking. He looked at Molly's empty desk and thought of the flowers and notes Yarrow'd sent her.

White roses.

They meant silence, secrecy.

Something was not right here. He was going to need more help fast and he knew just where he could get it.

Tom flipped through his Rolodex and reached for his phone.

58

Lois Hirt pleaded in vain to the hookers, addicts, and Tenderloin zombies who stepped around Gloria as her body convulsed on a Market Street sidewalk.

"Please, somebody call 911!" Lois knelt over Gloria, supporting her head, cursing when she spotted a tourist in plaid shorts, his eye clenched behind his camcorder. "Can't you see, she's dying! Call an ambulance!"

Fear slithered up Lois's spine as Gloria's body went cold and her lips turned blue. Her shoes clicked together until they slipped from her feet, exposing her cracked, painted toenails. Lois tightened her arms around her and their bodies shook in unison. She refused to let her friend die alone on a San Francisco street.

"Hang on, honey. Please hang on."

"Yo, that ho got some bad shit happening," a passing voice said just as a stream of vomit erupted from Gloria's gloss-lipped mouth.

"Somebody, please! Help us. Please!"

Lois stretched her own blouse, using it to wipe Gloria's face just as her eyes fluttered open and she moaned, attempting to speak.

"He-he-he-he wanted me to talk on the phone —"

"Shh. Don't talk."

Amid the street and traffic noise a scream surfaced from someplace distant. Gloria's eyes widened at something far above her in the blue sky.

"The phone man had nice clothes —"

The scream grew louder.

"Honey, please don't talk. I'm going to get you to the hospital."

Horns honked.

"Gloria?"

Her eyes rolled back into her head exposing the whites.

"Gloria!"

Sirens wailed. An engine growled. Brakes squeaked. Ambulance doors opened. The rattling aluminum sounds of a stretcher unfolding, wheels dollying on pavement.

"Miss, excuse us, please."

The paramedics were battle-weary street veterans. Not cold. Just efficient as they worked on Gloria. They refused to let Lois ride with her to San Francisco General. They loaded her. Doors slammed and they drove off, leaving Lois standing alone on the street hugging Gloria's purse and shoes to her stained shirt.

At the hospital, Lois showed Gloria's California driver's license picture to an emergency nurse, then detailed what happened.

"You're a family member?"

"Her sister," Lois lied.

"She was the overdose on Market they brought in a while ago." The nurse consulted admissions information on her computer screen.

"Yes."

"You know who her provider is?"

"No. We were estranged. Lost her to the street."

"Have a seat and we'll let you know when you can see her."

Lois spent nearly two hours in the crowded, depressing waiting room, fingering Tom Reed's card. She wondered if he could help her and Gloria. Or maybe Lois should call Gloria's case worker. Did she still use her case worker? Lois snapped through the pages of year-old copies of *People* and *Newsweek* before a nurse wearing green scrubs led her to Gloria's room.

"She's groggy so keep it short. Doctor says it's still touch-and-go."

"What was it?"

"Either an overdose or a bad batch. How long has she been addicted?"

Lois shook her head.

Two other patients shared the room. A withered bearded old man, asleep with his mouth agape. A large woman sitting on the edge of her bed, staring forlornly at the floor.

Gloria was near the window. A tube under her nose. IV running into her arms. Her orange hair against the white pillow livened up the room. Lois smiled as she sat next to her.

"Hi."

Gloria raised her hand. Her head lolled. She was far away.

"Thank you for saving my life."

"You'd do the same for me, honey." Lois put Gloria's bag on her table, then fished something from it. "It's time to get into detox and get clean." She passed Gloria the little snapshot of her daughter, Sunny.

Gloria stared at it. An agonizing cry, originating in her aching gut, escaped before she could mute it with her IV hand. Tears spilled from her eyes.

"Listen to me." Lois dropped her voice. "My friend might be able to help you get a job. Then you can get well. Pull it together. Get Sunny back. We'll do it together, okay?"

Gloria nodded, then began coughing.

"I need help."

"Good. We just got to tell him what he needs to know about that phone guy. The one who paid you to read something — want some water?"

Gloria fell into a violent fit of coughing. Water spilled, dampening her sheets as she sipped. She wiped her chin and sighed.

"I remember. It was around Garfield Square. I never saw him before. He sort of picked me out. I thought he wanted to date me." She swallowed more water. "But he gives me a slip of paper with a number and a short message. Tells me to call, wait for an answer, read the message, then hang up. He gave me a hundred. Weird. So I did it. That was it. He said it was a practical joke on a friend. We had a laugh, then —"

The bed clanged as Gloria's body spasmed. Her eyes rolled back and she puked, triggering a convulsion. Then silence as she passed out.

"Nurse! Somebody! Oh no! Gloria!"

Lois reached for the buttons above the bed and began pressing the pager. Then she headed for the door as two nurses rushed in, one uncollaring her stethoscope.

"Please leave!" she said to Lois.

The curtain whipped as the second nurse pulled it around Gloria's bed. Lois heard a commotion, something about CPR, then a switch clicked.

"We need a crash cart in 415!"

Lois covered her face with her hands, stepped back into a far corner out of the way, and watched as a woman in a white smock rushed a wheeled cabinet into the room with a defibrillator.

Lois didn't know how long they worked trying to save Gloria's life. It could have been five minutes. It could have been an hour. She remembered hearing someone screaming, remembered the nurses attempting to console her, remembered her back slamming against the wall, her stained shirt bunching up behind her as she slid to the floor, remembered seeing Gloria's arm drop over the side of her bed and her hand drop her snapshot of her daughter.

59

Sydowski enjoyed a tiny triumph as he crunched on a shortbread cookie and glanced at the *Star*'s front-page story about the unofficial suspect list.

Seemed that Cecil Lowe, an ATF agent, had been cleared of all duty *that very morning* and was waiting for Sydowski at the homicide detail. He had photocopies of a duty roster in a valise tucked under his arm.

"Here's a list of names and numbers to verify the dates." Lowe kept rubbing the back of his neck and apologizing for dragging his feet getting back to Sydowski.

On his way out, Lowe nearly bumped into Pete Marlin, a U.S. Marshal, who, it turned out, was not on any assignment when Sydowski had first requested to see him.

"I was booked off. Don't know how the wires got crossed." Marlin was in jeans and a T-shirt and had rushed down to the Hall after Tom Reed's story hit his doorstep in San Bruno. "Whatever you need." Marlin had been on a course in D.C. during the times of the murders. He had paper to prove it.

It didn't take long to clear Marlin and Lowe.

That left Steve Murdoch, the pilot. He'd called from Berlin promising to verify his whereabouts. Sydowski grunted after listening to his message, then put in a formal request through Interpol for Scotland Yard to meet Murdoch when he landed at Heathrow, to remind him to keep his promise.

That left Frank Yarrow. While Murdoch would likely be tied up soon, Yarrow's file would take time. Sydowski glanced at the phone and started into another cookie while waiting for callbacks.

The trace on Yarrow's cell phone number came up to a phone rental company from Chicago. Yarrow had paid cash. The contact information he'd left was outdated.

Tom Reed had suggested that Yarrow bought flowers in San Francsico for Molly. A run of his credit card showed a few purchases over the phone, but did not confirm his location, or a current number.

Sydowski's check with Illinois DMV gave him Yarrow's address and he got a number. Again, it was outdated. Sydowski had rounded a corner a short time ago. After some further checking he'd learned that Yarrow was an officer with the Chicago Police Department.

How that fit with being a corporate security consultant, as he'd told Molly, was curious. Bearing in mind that Yarrow had been recently divorced, he may have been trying to impress her. Finishing off another cookie, Sydowski was hopeful he'd get some blanks filled in from Captain Tiggle of the Chicago PD, the guy tasked with handling Sydowski's query.

On the phone, Tiggle sounded as though he was more of an officious prick than a cop. It left Sydowski with an ugly feeling about getting any effective help. He downed a glass of cold water when the homicide receptionist alerted him.

"Walt, Captain Tiggle in Chicago's calling back. I'll put him through."

Before picking up, Sydowski started grinding on a Tums for good measure.

"Sydowski."

"Tiggle here. Inspector, with regards to your query, I can confirm that Frank G. Yarrow was an officer with the department."

"Was?"

"A few months ago, he lost his appeal of the superintendent's decision to dismiss him from duty."

"Yarrow was fired. Is that what you're trying to say?"

"Correct."

"Why?"

"The Chicago Police Board reviewed the appeal by Chicago Police Officer Yarrow and upheld the superintendent's decision."

What the hell was this? Tiggle sounded like he was reading from a prepared statement.

"What was his offense, Tiggle? What did he do to get fired?"

"I can't reveal that."

"What? You're joking."

"Inspector, Chicago police policy and Illinois state law keep such records sealed."

"Tiggle, I've got two dead detectives. I've got your boy on a suspect list and I've got you jerking my chain."

"You could seek a warrant, Inspector."

"A warrant?"

Sydowski swallowed the remains of his Tums.

"Tiggle, I think you'd be wise to help me now. Because when the dust settles, I swear to God Almighty, you're going to be asked by people higher up the food chain to explain why you didn't."

Tiggle said nothing.

"I'll repeat: two dead homicide detectives. I helped carry their caskets. I'm staring at their empty desks now. I'm the primary. And unless you want me to write in my file 'Tiggle of the Chicago PD obstructed investigation,' I suggest you reconsider helping me."

Sydowski heard Tiggle's breathing quicken and thought the guy was likely a career desk jockey.

"Let me see what I can do, Inspector. And I'll get back to you."

Sydowski couldn't believe this. He loosened his tie. Christ, he wasn't going to wait for

Tiggle. He was going above him. And while he was at it, Sydowski would see to it that Tiggle got pissed on, too.

The officious prick.

60

Bleeder had been following Della Thompson's blue Toyota Corolla ever since she and Molly left Glen Park earlier that day.

He needed to get Molly alone. Just one golden moment, but Thompson was in the way. *Be patient,* he told himself.

He followed them over the Bay Bridge east from San Francisco. The afternoon traffic on the Bay Area expressways was heavy, making it easy for him to keep up with them with little chance of being seen.

The risk of losing them kept him alert. Maintaining a distance of three or four vehicles, he analyzed the situation. Molly was with Thompson. They hadn't made any stops. And from what he could determine they hadn't made any cell phone calls along the way.

Why this sudden departure from the city?

Bleeder checked his mirrors, adjusted his grip on the wheel, and forced himself to relax.

Thompson stayed on 580 beyond Hayward, then exited later and went north into the San Joaquin Valley. Bleeder enjoyed the pleasant breezes, which grew fragrant as they rolled by the expanses of vineyards, the miles of walnut, almond, and cherry orchards. They were nearing Lodi.

Lodi.

Bleeder smashed his steering wheel with both hands.

Entering the city, Thompson stopped at a strip mall. Bleeder drove to a point out of sight from where he watched their car while weighing the wisdom of entering the mall to see what Thompson and Molly were up to. Too risky. They could spot him. In less than ten minutes, they'd emerged.

Molly was carrying flowers.

Thompson drove to Lodi's outskirts to the country cemetery where Hooper was buried. Bleeder's neck muscles tensed and he cursed under his breath. He remained out of sight, taking a dirt lane, bordered by tall grass. It threaded the perimeter of the burial ground, disappearing into the fringes of a vast cherry orchard where living trees stood among the dead and twisted ones.

The Toyota's doors thudded. Thompson leaned against the car. Molly went to Hooper's grave and lowered herself to her knees. She placed flowers upon the still fresh mound.

No, Bleeder thought.

Alone among the headstones, Molly was a

portrait of sorrow. She dabbed her eyes with a tissue as birds sang.

No. No. No.

Bleeder looked off to the sun setting in the west, the Sierra Nevadas in the east. Anger broiled in his heart. This was wrong.

Dead wrong.

Bleeder could not allow her to *mourn* Hooper. She had to acknowledge what *he'd* done for her. This was wrong. Wrong. *Wrong!* He seethed, watching Molly out there, weeping. He wanted to take action now. Go to her, yank off his mask. Reveal everything. He was so close.

Why was she here?

She didn't appear to be getting any closer to understanding why he had to remove Hooper and Beamon. That what he did, he did for her. He restrained himself from going to her and remained in the shadows.

The time for telling would come soon enough.

Following them back toward San Francisco, he resolved to adhere to his plan. So much was at stake. He'd worked too hard to throw it all away. As the sun sank, Thompson drove them to Colma where Molly placed flowers on Beamon's grave.

Bleeder maintained control. He risked nothing, following them into San Francisco and Glen Park.

Time was running out.

Molly was slipping from him. Her visits to Hooper's and Beamon's graves were an affront to all he'd achieved for her. The pain bored deep. Yet he never stood down from his secret vigil. Never gave up hoping beyond hope that she would break through the lies, the deceptions, the unspoken truths, to see him as he was.

To see his heart behind his mask.

He ran his hands through his hair.

Molly had become distracted, like Amy. But she was smarter than Amy. And he was wiser now. Much wiser. Yes, he'd made errors with Amy and Kyle. But the lessons he'd learned so long ago would serve him now, he thought as his mind returned to the aftermath of Hangman's Lane.

You would have thought the world had ended by the way the local newspaper reported the "horrific tragedy." From the outset with the big photos of the sheriff's deputies watching the crane hoisting Kyle's Camaro from its watery tomb. The "massive investigation and search for answers" while the community pulled together to confront such an "unexpected, terrible blow."

Nearly everyone in town went to the memorial service at the high school, including Bleeder, who watched it all from his folding chair in the back of the gym, the very gym where Amy had kissed his cheek that first night. Because Kyle, the farm boy, could

343

throw a football, they shoveled their praise. As if he truly were a wholesome warrior hero, instead of an asshole.

Few paid much attention to the investigation. Kyle's father, and Kyle's farm-boy friends, admitted sadly, but with a hint of pride, how he loved to "test himself in his car," which meant he drove like a maniac with a beer between his legs. Amy's father regretted how he wished he'd been firmer in cautioning Kyle to "ease up on that valley turn by the bridge."

It seemed to Bleeder that no one suspected a damned thing.

No deputy or state investigator had asked him about his encounters with Kyle. No one asked him about his visits to the bridge at Hangman's Lane. Or inspected the scrapes on the large rocks in the ditch nearby.

Kyle's friends ignored him. During the weeks after the tragedy, no one at school talked much about it. Then finally, the paper published a story on the front page that said the tragedy had been classified as an accident attributed to excessive speed. Case closed.

Bleeder had committed the perfect murder.

Several weeks later as Bleeder began thinking hard about his mistakes with Amy, Bleeder's father announced that he was being transferred immediately. They moved across the country, settled for ten months, then moved three more times over the next few years.

Then one night while checking out-of-town newspapers in the library, Bleeder came upon an anniversary piece, a historical look back at the haunting case of Lud Striker, the insane hermit who murdered a farm family. Striker, the article said, was the last person executed on Hangman's Lane.

No, not the last, Bleeder thought.

Through it all, he never forgot Amy. She was the genesis of his terrifying power, a reminder of what he could do when circumstances compelled him to step forward and take charge.

Now, outside Della Thompson's house, he reached for his files on the passenger seat for a photograph of him with Molly Wilson. Look at her. Her smile, her eyes. So dangerously, wildly attractive. How he ached to have her skin next to his. His jaw and gut clenched, trapping his rage. He'd given her chance after chance to understand.

In his mind, she belonged to him. He would clear the final obstacles. Then he would remove his mask.

Time was up.

61

The day after Gloria Carter died, Lois Hirt vowed to get clean despite her painful craving for heroin.

Fight it, she told herself. *Let the clonazepam do its work. You can do this. You've got to do this. For Gloria. For Sunny. For yourself.*

Stunned by Gloria's death, Lois had gone to a clinic and taken steps toward getting healthy. It might have been the shock making her move so fast. People told her to slow down and grieve for her friend.

But Lois couldn't be still.

She made an appointment with Gloria's case worker. She wanted to adopt Sunny. She was convinced she could make it back to normal, while in her heart she feared she was destined to join Gloria in the ground.

Now, sitting alone in Hector's Restaurant, Lois searched for hope in the job section of the *San Francisco Star.* She saw a few glimmers and circled them.

Out of sympathy, Hector said he would allow her to work a four-hour shift as a waitress for a few bucks, tips, and a hot meal. It gave her the courage to call one of her old college professors, a kind woman who knew Lois's story. She'd promised to personally look into the possibility of Lois resuming her dentistry studies through night courses.

Lois intended to ask Hector to advance her enough money for her to move from her fleabag rooming house to a clean apartment nearby where there were no dealers or gangs. It had several shops and office buildings where she could try to land another job.

"Lois," Hector repeated louder until she lifted her head from her newspaper. "I said, there's a call for you."

She accepted the phone at the counter.

"Lois, it's Mavis, Gloria's case worker. You'd left me this number."

"Hi, Mavis."

"I've got some of Gloria's personal effects. Right now I have her purse. And I've got to change our appointment. Move it up. Can you come down to my office right away?"

Lois took the bus.

When she arrived, Mavis was on the phone. She waved Lois into her office. Mavis ended the call, slid a form across her desk for Lois to sign, tapping the X by the signature line, passing her a pen.

"It's for the purse," Mavis said as Lois signed. "I'll have more from her room later. Gloria didn't have much."

"I told you on the phone I want to adopt Sunny."

"Just finished talking to the social worker."

"Is there any chance for me?"

"It's complicated. Sunny's biological father is involved."

"He's involved in San Quentin. On death row."

"I hear you. I told them. I said that other than her dad, Sunny's got no one in this world now."

"That makes two of us."

"I'll make some more calls. See what your chances are. But I got to warn you, the odds are against you."

"They have been for a long time."

"Before you even go down that road, you've got to get cleaned up, get a good job. Demonstrate a stable life and home environment."

"I'm working on it."

Later that day when Lois was alone in her room, she tried ignoring the bass thudding of someone's music from the floor above as she stared at Gloria's purse. The remnants of a young woman's life sitting on her kitchen table. Lois covered her face with her hands, blinking over her fingertips. To go through it was such an invasion.

I'm so sorry, Gloria.

Lois emptied the purse on her table. It had gum, a knife, a personal key-ring alarm, pepper spray, a MUNI Fastpass, condoms, pens, tampons, minipad, her wallet. Her wallet had a few credit cards, her California driver's license, bank card, eleven dollars cash, slips of paper. One looked like a grocery list, one torn from the classifieds, about an escort service, another torn from the yellow pages. Dating service. She found a small black book with a list of cell phone and pager numbers. Right. Dealers. Then a folded slip of paper with a number on the top and a message printed in neat blue-inked block letters, alien from Gloria's handwriting style.

Lois stared at the message and thought for a long moment before she grabbed the coins, went to the public phone on the corner, and dialed the number.

"Office of Citizens' Complaints," the receptionist answered.

Lois hung up.

She stared at the words on the paper, reading them over and over.

This is it.

The message Tom Reed was looking for.

62

"Oh yeah, I remember this one." Della Thompson studied the printout of an old story Simon Lepp had dug out of the archives.

DRUG COPS POCKETED DEALER'S CASH, ATTORNEY ALLEGES

DELLA THOMPSON
SAN FRANCISCO STAR

Officers with the narcotics detail held guns to the head of a man convicted of trafficking cocaine, then stole "hundreds of thousands" in cash from his home, his lawyer alleged yesterday.

"This pulls back a curtain on police corruption. It will shake this city like it's never been shaken," Smith Holland Smith, a flamboyant outspoken lawyer for some of the Bay Area's most notorious citizens, charged in a hastily called news conference.

"Time to wake up, San Francisco. Something's rotten to the core in your city," said Smith, refusing to name officers or provide any evidence of wrongdoing on the part of the San Francisco police.

Lieutenant Paul Varner, a department spokesman, likened Smith's claim to a circus act. "His client is going away for a lot of years and Smith pops up with this knee-slapper," Varner said. "All he's missing is the big shoes and a honking red nose."

Asked why Smith never raised his allegations at the trial of his client, Flavelle "Big Daddy" White, Smith said: "Stay tuned. I'll be delivering it to you in an 18-wheeler."

Thompson shook her head at the memory of the story as Lepp waited for her assessment.

"What do you think?" Lepp asked, proud of himself for tracking it. The story had been missed by the computerized data bank. "I went through microfilm. This took place back when Cliff Hooper was in Narcotics. It's got to be tied to his murder. Has to be White's people coming after him."

After going through it, Thompson passed it back.

"Afraid not. Smith's claim was all bogus. We went nuts trying to confirm this. Smith never delivered a thing. Typical. It withered. Tom went to the street on it. He got through to White in prison. The guy admitted he'd

351

concocted the claim because he was so messed up on drugs."

But Lepp was not ready to toss it even though Tom had told him the same thing. Especially now. This story fit. It pointed to a killer with the strongest motivation. Revenge. OCC must be aware of this. And Hooper's partner, Ray Beamon, would have been the one man who would've known the truth. What was it Beamon called Hooper at the funeral, his "brother"?

Lepp was convinced this story fit. "Tom dismissed it too, but I'm going to chase this down. I think there's something to it," he said.

Across the newsroom, Tom Reed was working on Yarrow while worrying about Lois Hirt. He'd put out calls in a number of directions in the hope of locating her. On Yarrow, he expected a call back any moment from a reliable contact.

The big mystery swirling around the metro desk was centered on Irene Pepper. She was conspicuously absent. Acker was running Metro. "Don't ask me. I don't know what's going on," was all he told reporters.

Tom spotted Della Thompson headed his way, bursting to share something. "Hey, you won't believe this one." She dropped her voice. "I think Irene Pepper's been fired."

"What happened?"

"I got this from Yolanda in Human Resources. She does termination letters," Della

352

said. "Irene secretly approached a big New York publisher about coauthoring a book with Molly. Claimed she had exclusivity to Molly's cooperation."

"I never knew that."

"Neither did Molly. She had no idea what Irene did, let alone agreed to work with her."

"That kind of misrepresentation is nearly criminal, I'd say."

"You know it, baby. Also explains why she kept pushing for Molly's first-person."

"Well, well, well."

"Violet got wind of it and nailed Irene to the wall."

"And how did Violet learn about it?"

"Someone screening Molly's calls caught one from a very chatty New York editor, who explained Irene Pepper's proposal, actually faxed a copy bearing Pepper's signature for Molly to review."

"You've made my day."

"Ding-dong, the witch is dead."

"And how's Molly doing?"

"Better. She wants to move back to her place and get back to work soon."

"Yeah, well, she shouldn't let her guard down until they nail the guy."

After Thompson left, Tom got a fresh coffee and returned to his desk in time to grab his line on the third ring.

"Reed," he said.

"It's me."

Tom knew the distinct raw voice of a cement mixer churning gravel.

"Marv, how are you?"

"Yeah, I got your message and I'm taking care of that little thing like you wanted."

"Anything there?"

"Yes, but not over the phone."

"Where then?"

"Tomorrow morning. The marina. Near Avila."

"Cripes, Marv, it's impossible to park down there. Can't you just tell me?"

"I got paper coming for you. If you want it, you have to come and get it. And remember, our business goes two ways."

"What time?"

"Elevenish. This stuff from Chicago on your subject is something you need to see."

63

Tom caught the opening riffs of "Layla" coming from his radio and cranked the volume as he ripped through San Francisco's Marina District. He was on his way to meet the man who could lead him closer to the truth behind the murders of two San Francisco homicide cops.

The name of his source was Marv. He never used a last name. He was something of a retired investigator who in a former life had worked for the federal government. He'd done things no one could ever speak of and no one would ever acknowledge. He was good at obtaining solid up-to-date confidential information on anybody fast. They'd met years earlier. Marv had called him to clarify facts in one of his stories on intelligence agents. Since then, they'd formed a casual relationship, trading data when it was mutually beneficial.

Like today.

It took nearly half an hour to find a parking spot within walking distance to Marv's favorite bench, which faced the bay and the Golden Gate. As usual, Tom waited and watched sailboats bob in the hazy distance.

"Morning," a man in his late fifties said. White hair curled from a golf cap and he gazed at the water through dark aviator glasses. He was holding a folded newspaper.

"I ran that subject for you."

"What'd you find?"

"His last official address was Chicago."

Marv passed his newspaper to Tom, who opened it to a copy of an Illinois driver's license with a photo.

"That's it? This is all you've got for me? I could've gotten that."

"I've got more. A lot more. I pulled a lot of strings. Big ones that reach to the heavens. First, you're going to guarantee me help when I need it."

Tom momentarily considered the unknown risks before setting them aside.

"You've got my word," he said.

Marv looked at the Golden Gate in the distance.

"It'll have to do," he said. "Judging from what I've found out, Mr. Yarrow's got problems."

"What kind of problems?"

"Read for yourself. And this is all the help you're getting on this one." Marv walked off, leaving a white envelope on the bench.

Inside were three pages on Chicago Police Board letterhead, the result of a confidential board review of an appeal by Chicago Police Officer Frank G. Yarrow. He had unsuccessfully appealed the superintendent's decision to fire him, a step arising from a woman's allegations that Yarrow had assaulted her.

The pages were grainy photocopies of faxed photocopies. Summaries, stating that a woman, whose name had been blacked out, had filed three complaints over three years accusing Yarrow of physically abusing her. Twice when he was in uniform and on duty. What the hell happened? There were few details.

Tom read it over, going back on phrases like *reasons for dismissal . . . misconduct . . . assault . . . stalking.*

In addition to upholding the superintendent's decision to fire Yarrow, the board had ordered him to undergo counseling or face possible criminal charges. No other details.

Damn.

So as a young deputy, Yarrow stalked a woman in Texas, then left the department. He emerged as a cop with the Chicago PD, where he was fired for assaulting a woman and ordered to undergo counseling. Yarrow then surfaced and looked up Molly, his high school sweetheart, around the time her detective boyfriend was murdered.

Tom shuddered at the ramifications. He had to get to Sydowski. He had to get to Molly. Christ, they had to grab Yarrow.

Now.

64

The growing pile of messages from Captain Tiggle in Chicago remained unanswered on Sydowski's desk. They seemed to increase with desperation.

Urgent, please call. I have info as per request.

Sydowski peered sadly over his bifocals. Tiggle's career had suffered a self-inflicted injury. Sydowski no longer needed him, he'd gone directly to Captain Ronan in Chicago Homicide, who'd moved mountains for him.

Sydowski finished studying the Chicago Police Board's file on Yarrow, which Ronan had e-mailed earlier in the day. Photos, reports, everything. Ronan had grasped the significance of Sydowski's request. Not only did he furnish Sydowski with Yarrow's file but he'd arranged to go one better.

A few moments ago, Ronan had advised Sydowski to expect a critical call on Yarrow from Chicago at any moment.

Sydowski sipped his tepid coffee as he waited, moving on to reread the inventories of Hooper's and Beamon's crime scenes. He still had the feeling they'd missed something. No matter how many times they'd reviewed or gone back, he was convinced they'd over-looked one tiny thing. But he couldn't put his finger on it.

His phone rang.

"Sydowski."

"It's Ronan. Here's the number. She's waiting for you to call now."

"Thanks, I owe you."

Sydowski dialed the number, a 312 area code. It was answered on the third ring.

"Hello?" a woman said softly.

"Hello, Joy?"

"Yes."

"Hi. Walt Sydowski with the San Francisco Police Department. I'm told you might be expecting my call?"

"Yes." The woman cleared her throat.

"You also want anonymity?"

"Yes. Can you give me that assurance, In-spector Sydowski?"

"Yes."

"I'll only give you a few minutes."

"Why did you agree to talk to me?"

"Captain Ronan is someone I trust."

"How do you know Frank Yarrow?"

"I'm his ex-wife."

"Why did you file three complaints against him? What were the circumstances?"

"Frank became increasingly abusive to me when we learned, after two miscarriages, that I can't have children."

"How was he abusive? Can you elaborate?"

"We were thrilled when I first became pregnant. But I lost the baby after two months. About three days after I got home from the hospital, Frank began talking like it was somehow my fault. Said I didn't pray enough."

"Was that the extent of the abuse?"

"About a week later, he came home during a shift. He was upset and accused me of not reading enough Scripture. He said that was why I'd lost his child. We argued and he punched me" — in the head, the documents noted — "I let it go. Made excuses. We were both still grieving, hurting."

"Was he okay after that?"

"It seemed. Time went by. I got pregnant a second time. I lost the baby after eleven weeks." A long silence passed as the woman struggled with her emotions before resuming. "The doctors then told me that there was little chance I could ever carry a baby to term."

"How did Frank take that?"

"For weeks he wouldn't speak to me. Then he hurled a Bible at me. Then he began accusing me of ruining his life, not being able to give him a child. At his worst, he accused me of being in league with the devil. He got angry. One day he started choking me. I filed for separation."

"Where did you go?"

"I moved in with my sister but he kept

360

stalking me, demanding I come back, pleading that he was sorry, that he was hurting, that we should see about a medical miracle."

"What did you do?"

"I told him it was over. He didn't say anything. Actually, he was okay until our divorce came through."

"How did he handle that?"

"Horribly. One night I was in the supermarket and he just showed up, in uniform, stalking me. Followed my car home. Showed up in the driveway. He said he knew how to deal with sinners. It was a threat. He scared me to death."

"What happened?"

"Nothing. Then two weeks later he showed up one night at my house. Accused me of destroying him. He slapped me. A neighbor, a firefighter, witnessed it all, came over the fence and protected me. In the morning, I called my lawyer and got an emergency order of protection from a Cook County court. My lawyer helped me file complaints with Chicago PD against him. I'm glad Frank lost his job. He has no right being a police officer. The Chicago PD was very good. They took my case seriously."

"Why didn't you press charges?"

"I'd considered it but I didn't want to deal with him anymore. His history is on record. I was relieved he moved away."

"When's the last you heard from your ex-husband?"

"He called me about a month ago in the middle of the night."

"To threaten you?"

"No. It was strange. He said he'd forgiven me. He said it took a long time for him to realize that there was only one woman in the world for him."

"Who was that?"

"An old girlfriend he knew growing up in Texas. He said that they were once in love, that she would give him a child. That they were meant to be together and he was happy because he was going to make it happen. It was strange."

"Did he tell you who this woman was?"

"Molly somebody."

Sydowski cleared his throat.

"Molly Wilson?"

"I don't know."

"Ever hear of Molly Wilson?"

"No. Look, that's all I have to say," she said. "This is still very painful."

"I understand and thank you. Oh, just one last thing. Do you have any idea where he's living right now? Is it Kansas City?"

"San Francisco," she said.

"*San Francisco?* I thought he was just visiting here."

"No, he lives there. That's what my lawyer told me when he updated the protection order. Seems he moved there just a few months ago for some job with a security firm. I mean, he's got court violations. He owes me alimony, he's supposed to take counseling. I'm sure he's hiding from creditors. I thought that's why you were calling."

Sydowski hung up and called the SFPD dispatcher to request two units go Code 2 to Della Thompson's house in Glen Park and check on the welfare of Molly Wilson. Then he immediately tried calling Thompson's number. While it rang, he pulled out his cell phone and tried Molly's cell phone number.

He felt a trickle of sweat meander down his back.

Answer. For God's sake, somebody answer.

65

Della Thompson was waiting in line at the supermarket scanning the tabloid headlines and diet books when her cell phone rang.

"Hello."

"It's Tom. Is Molly with you?"

"No. I dropped her off at her apartment this morning. You sound panicked. What is it?"

"I've been calling there and her cell phone. I've got to reach her."

"Miss —" The woman behind Thompson had a wrinkled prune of a face as she indicated it was Thompson's turn to unload her items on the conveyor.

"She was going to go for a run," Thompson said, "then drive back to my place with her own car. Tonight was going to be her last night with me before she moved back. We were going to have a nice dinner —" Thompson heard a horn honk, screeching tires, and cursing. "Tom! What's going on!"

"I'm on my way to her place now. Tell her I think it's Yarrow. Keep calling. And call Sydowski."

"Miss — please, are you checking out now or not?"

Thompson hung up and quickly unloaded her cart. But her mind was on Molly's safety when her phone rang again. This time it was Sydowski asking about Molly.

"I just told Tom, she's at her place in North Beach, running through Telegraph Hill."

"I called there. Her answering machine is jammed. Can't take any messages. Did she take her cell phone with her?"

"Not when she jogs. She was going to jog. Is she in danger?"

"We just want to talk to her as soon as possible."

"Miss — would you please —"

Thompson whirled to face the old woman.

"Step back, Grandma! Just step the hell back!"

66

At home in her shower, Molly scrubbed herself raw while struggling to regain control of her world.

A dark, overwhelming fact crouched like a wild thing in the back of her mind. The person who'd killed Hooper and Beamon, the person who lived in some perverted fantasy that involved her, was still out there.

She refused to cower, curl up, and die for him.

Not for this bastard. She demanded her life back. Her jog through her neighborhood this morning was her first since Sydowski had moved her. It was therapeutic, recharging her will to fight this nightmare. Not one minute passed without her struggling to figure out who the creep was. Was it one of the guys she'd listed for Sydowski? Or some jerk she'd interviewed for the paper? Or maybe a psychopath who'd seen her on the show, or on the street?

Or anywhere.

God. She didn't know. How could she know? Sydowski didn't know. No one knew.

Molly toweled off with such ferocity she

burned her skin and she cried out. She realized her unease — admit it, her fear — at suddenly being alone in her apartment was manifesting itself as rage. She switched on her hair dryer, then gritted her teeth. *If it's me you want, then come on, asshole, but I'm not giving up without a fight,* she told her reflection as she dressed quickly.

Before heading back to Della Thompson's house, Molly closed her fingers into fists. Took several deep breaths and calmed herself.

Anger is good. You have every right. Don't let him win.

Molly steeled herself. She was a strong woman. A fighter. A survivor. She would get through this. One minute, one hour, one day at a time.

Hurrying, she grabbed her cell phone, purse, and keys and trotted down the stairs to her car in the street. She never heard her apartment phone ringing behind her. She turned the engine, engaged the transmission, and began to inch away when tires squealed, brakes thudded and a motor roared. Out of nowhere a strange car T-boned her path, blocking hers.

Molly's heart stopped.

A man emerged, approaching her car fast. Molly locked her door and scrambled for her cell phone. It had spilled to the passenger floor, along with the contents of her purse.

Pepper spray. She had pepper spray. She'd taken self-defense. Frantic, she probed the litter on her floor.

Phone. Spray. Phone. Dial 911. Find it. Find it.

Her pulse raced when there was a knock on her window. *Her name?* He was calling her name. Her fingers found the spray. Holding it up defensively, she turned to the glass and met his face.

"Frank!" Molly caught her breath.

"Molly, please."

She dropped the window.

"What the hell are you doing here? Are you out of your mind, stopping me like this? You scared me to death," she said.

"I need to talk to you, please."

"We've been over this. I told you to go home."

"I know but please."

She scanned the neighborhood, keeping her voice down.

"This is the worst time. I told you, nothing will change."

"I'm begging you, Molly."

He looked upset. His eyes seemed red as if he'd been crying. She didn't want to risk a scene in the street. She didn't smell any alcohol on him. Collecting herself, she said, "I'll give you two minutes. First, move your damn car."

Inside her apartment, she refused to let

368

Yarrow sit. She stood near the door.

"Did you just get back into town? Did you talk to Sydowski?"

Yarrow didn't answer. He was staring at her.

"You'd be smart to call Sydowski and talk to him so he can cross you off his list. Frank, did you hear me?"

"Listen," Yarrow said. "Please, you've got to say there's hope. I've made so many mistakes in my life. Finding you, seeing that you're hurting too means we can help each other. We can get through our rough times together."

"Stop this. How many times do I have to tell you that there is no future for us, only a past that I want to forget?"

"No, I think it was meant to work out like this. If you would only see things the way I do."

"I don't."

His face tightened.

"You've got to give us one more chance."

"I don't."

"I told you, I've got nothing. How can you stand there and be so cold to me when I'm begging you for understanding?"

"Stop it. I don't owe you anything."

Yarrow dropped to his knees.

"Oh, for God's sake."

"We conceived a child together."

"Stop it. Stop it. *Stop it!*"

369

He raised his head to hers. Then slowly stood. Veins in his temple and neck began throbbing. She noticed how the tight shirt he was wearing emphasized his powerful shoulders, upper arms, the scar on his chin.

"Everything behind me is in ruin," he said. "Without you offering me hope, I've got nothing. You've got to give me one last chance."

"Are you crazy?"

"Don't say that."

"You are crazy for acting this way. Let's see, how can I make this clear to you? *Stay the hell out of my life.*"

It was as if the wall jumped from behind and slammed against Molly's back and head before she realized Yarrow had shoved her. His power and swiftness were terrifying.

"Calling me crazy is a mistake."

The blow had winded her. Molly blinked at the stars swirling around her. She stood against the wall gasping for the longest time before her breath returned. Her fingers slid into her bag and probed for her pepper spray.

"You're going to regret this," he said, "because the second I walk out that door, everything will be set in motion. And once a thing is set in motion, there's nothing you can do to stop it. Nothing."

Gripping the spray, she stared at him until at last she found her voice.

"You'd better go now, asshole."

"Just remember." He held his finger a quarter inch from her face. "I begged you not to make me do this."

67

As he drove across the city to Molly's apartment building, Tom could barely contain his fear. Stopping at a traffic light, he punched Molly's home number again. It went unanswered. He tried her cell phone. Still no answer. The light turned green.

He didn't like this.

He put in calls to the newsroom in case she showed up there. Messages were sent to *Star* photographers working throughout the city to search for Molly. Pulling up to her building, Tom saw no sign of her car. He parked, went to the front, and buzzed her unit.

Nothing.

He walked around the back in case she'd parked there. No sign of her car. He returned to the front. At that moment, a man and woman who appeared to be in their seventies had returned from a walk and were entering the building. They looked familiar. Politely, he stepped aside.

"You're a reporter." The woman smiled at him. "One of Molly's friends. We've seen you here before. We chatted a few times."

"That's right. Tom Reed."

"See your stuff all the time in the *Star*, Tom." The man's keys jingled.

"If you're here to see Molly, I don't think she's here," the woman said.

"Oh no," the man said, "I saw her out jogging this morning."

"Well, you just go on up," the woman said after the man opened the door for Tom.

"Thanks."

Arriving at Molly's door, he knocked softly, cocking an ear for any movement inside.

Silence.

He knocked again, a little harder. Nothing. Turning to leave, he looked at the door frame and froze.

He saw a dime-sized reddish smear about waist-level on the pearl-white wood. He drew his face near. It looked like a finger had trailed something. It glistened in the soft light streaming into the hallway.

Wet blood.

68

Come on girl, be strong.

The tear tracks had stiffened on Molly's cheeks as she drove her car south to Della Thompson's house. Adjusting her grip, she noticed her hands were sticky on the wheel from touching the damp spot at the base of her skull.

Blood.

From Yarrow slamming her against the wall. Violent asshole. He was lucky he left before she sprayed him. She should have him charged. The idiot was stuck in a time warp. Blubbering to her that his life was nothing because he couldn't get over their high school years. What happened to Frank Yarrow? He was a sweet, sensitive boy. Considerate. Protective. That's why she'd fallen for him.

That was another time. Another life. And now. *Now this?*

She couldn't deal with Yarrow's stupidity.

Truth was, he'd terrified her. She would tell Sydowski everything and swear out a complaint. She tried calling him on her cell phone but the battery was dead. Her spare was in her bag at Glen Park.

Molly's heart was racing as she pulled onto Thompson's street. Nearing the house, she felt faint. Did she have a concussion? Blinking rapidly, she massaged the back of her head until the feeling passed. Couldn't be serious. She wasn't bleeding much. Had to be stress.

What's with the black-and-whites? she wondered as she stopped at the house and got out of her car. Keys jingled from the utility belt of a uniformed officer who rushed to her.

"Ma'am, you're bleeding from your head."

Paramedics were called.

They said Molly had suffered a mild concussion and a few tiny vessels were broken. When Sydowski arrived he called it an assault and initiated a Bay Area alert for Yarrow.

69

Less than three hours after Yarrow had confronted Molly, news crews crowded into the Police Commission Hearing Room at the Hall of Justice.

By now, everyone in San Francisco's press circles knew the events.

Frank G. Yarrow's Chicago Police Department ID photo had been enlarged and posted on a corkboard to the left of the podium. On a corkboard to the far right, emphasizing the distinction between the hunted and the heroes, were pictures of homicide inspectors Ray Beamon and Cliff Hooper.

Yarrow was the suspect who'd emerged in the ritualistic murders of the two homicide detectives. National news networks were going live. The story of a disgraced violent ex-cop turned multiple-murder suspect, with overtones of sex and betrayal involving two detectives and a San Francisco crime reporter, would play large across the country.

San Francisco's police chief, accompanied by sober-faced senior officers, took his place behind the mountain of microphones and cassette recorders.

"The San Francisco Police Department is seeking the public's assistance in locating Frank Gregory Yarrow, age thirty-five. He's wanted on a charge of assault involving an incident that took place a few hours ago. As well, Yarrow is regarded as a witness to the murders of Cliff Hooper and Ray Beamon, inspectors with the department's homicide detail. Both men were found in their respective residences.

"Anyone with any information as to the whereabouts of Frank Gregory Yarrow is cautioned not to approach him, but to immediately contact law enforcement authorities. That is all we can say at this time. For members of the press here today, we've provided some further information on fact sheets being distributed now. I will not speculate or discuss case details. I will take no questions at this time."

As the chief stood to leave he was deluged with a barrage of questions.

He didn't stop to answer any.

Across San Francisco, Ida Lyndstrum set a saucer of milk before Clementine, her cat, sulking on the sun-warmed windowsill of her apartment in the Western Addition.

"Who could sleep with Mr. Noisy coming and going last night? And then all the hullabaloo upstairs today. My word."

Ida slid her wrinkled fingers along

Clementine's soft coat, sighed, then settled into her winged-back chair with her tea and needlepoint. She found her remote and switched on her TV to her favorite morning talk show. The racket from her tenant had displeased her. And the man had seemed so considerate. Said he'd worked in security in the Midwest. Weren't people from that part of the country supposed to be quiet types? Just went to show you really couldn't know a person's true nature.

Ida's tenant was still settling in upstairs after moving from his first San Francisco address, a hotel by the airport. Hadn't even connected his telephone yet. Oh, how she hated to sour things, but she couldn't tolerate inconsiderate behavior. Not one bit.

Clementine purred.

"Yes, I know, dear. I'll discuss it the next time we see him."

Ida's attention went to her television. It had flashed a BREAKING NEWS BULLETIN, then broadcast a terse report on the murders of the homicide detectives.

"My word."

The station cut to San Francisco's police chief with newspeople, and Ida abruptly felt the earth shift. The face of her upstairs tenant stared at her from her TV. Alarm rang in her ears. *Good Lord.* She fumbled with her remote to increase the volume in time to hear:

". . . Police Department is asking the public's assistance in locating Frank Gregory Yarrow. He's regarded as a witness to the murders . . ."

Murders! Ida gasped.

Her first reaction was to go upstairs and inform Mr. Yarrow the police were looking for him when she heard:

". . . cautioned not to approach him, but to immediately contact law enforcement authorities . . ."

Her mouth went dry as she lifted her head to the ceiling.

"Dear Lord. Oh, dear Lord, Clemie."

Ida patted her thighs. Clementine, sensing her unease, padded from the window and leaped into Ida's lap. She slid her arms around her cat, hugging its warm body to battle her sudden chill.

"Dear Lord," Ida repeated, transfixed by the news conference. When it ended she collected herself, reached for her telephone, whispered a prayer, then pressed three digits.

70

In the *San Francisco Star* newsroom Tom and Acker hunched alongside the intern listening to the emergency scanners.

Acker's face was taut. Tom was jotting notes fast.

"That's a lock on Yarrow's address," Acker said. "It's a good one. They're calling for the tac unit."

"Alert photo! Get Della, Simon, everyone you can spare," Tom called, heading for the elevator. "Every shooter we've got before they seal the neighborhood. Call me with any updates."

Across town in the Western Addition, the tactical unit's equipment truck lumbered through the neighborhood as every available officer in the district and from across the city offered to help with the takedown.

Everyone moved quickly without lights or sirens. Marked units set up an outer perimeter around the hot zone, shutting off all traffic a few blocks away. Plainclothed female officers quietly escorted Ida and Clementine from her building. They walked several blocks to the far end of a cross street, where the equipment van had squeaked to a halt next to a clutch of police vehicles that stood as the command post.

The officer in charge, TAC Lieutenant George Horn, spoke with Ida. Between talking on his radio and his cell phone, he studied street maps, blueprints, and the detailed floor plan sketches he'd asked Ida to make of her Victorian home not far from Alamo Square.

"And Yarrow lives alone in your two-bedroom apartment, on the top floor?"

Looking at photos, Ida nodded and hugged Clementine.

"And he has no phone, correct?"

"He told me it hasn't been connected yet."

"What about a cell phone?"

"If he has one, I don't have the number. Please, Lieutenant. This is all so frightening."

"I know, I'm sorry, ma'am," Horn said as Sydowski and Turgeon arrived.

"How's it look, George?" Sydowski asked.

"Just setting up. His landlady, Mrs. Lyndstrum here, is certain he hasn't left his apartment. His car's still there and she heard him making noises last night, then only a few hours ago."

"What kind of noises?" Sydowski withdrew his notebook.

After evacuating every resident within the line of fire of Lyndstrum's building, Horn's tactical team set up an inner perimeter around the house. Armed with copies of Ida's sketch, scouts went in first, to determine safety points for other team members. They were followed by the utility man, the breacher, the gas team, and sharpshooters. Without making a sound, they used an aluminum extending pole to place a fully operational cell phone at the rear entrance to Yarrow's apartment.

The large rear window came into sharp focus, filling the rifle scope of the sniper on the roof of the house nearby. He'd taken cover behind a brick chimney, while in front another sharpshooter put Yarrow's front window in his crosshairs.

"No movement inside," the rear sniper said through his headset.

"Nothing in front," the second sharpshooter radioed.

The third sniper, who had his rifle trained on Yarrow's south-facing window, also picked up his car in the driveway. He recited the Illinois tag to Horn, who relayed it to dispatch, to run through NCIC. It came back registered to Frank G. Yarrow of Chicago.

"Okay, it's time to talk to him," Horn said over the radio to Sergeant Dave Davis, his team leader, who was near the house. He'd taken cover by a neighbor's garage.

Davis raised his bullhorn, which crackled at the Lyndstrum building.

"Frank Yarrow, this is Sergeant Davis of the San Francisco police. We want to talk to you about an important matter. For your own safety, would you exit from the rear with your hands raised, palms forward, please."

A long moment of silence passed.

Davis radioed a nearby unit to sound his siren loud by giving it three yelps.

"Mr. Yarrow, this is Sergeant Davis of the San Francisco police . . ." Davis began again. He repeated this request four times over the next ten minutes, informing Yarrow to use the phone that police had placed by his door if he wanted to communicate privately. Nothing happened.

Horn checked with his sharpshooters. None reported any movement, none had a clear shot.

After half an hour had passed, Horn made a decision.

"Throw in some chemicals, flash-bang, then assault and extraction. You time it, Dave."

Davis alerted his team, who took their positions. Sixty seconds later the *pop-pop* and shattering glass sounds of tear gas canisters echoed down Lyndstrum's street. White clouds billowed from the upper floor, followed by a deafening *crack-crack* and lightning flashes of stun grenades as the tactical team rushed the rear entrance and kicked in the door to Yarrow's apartment.

Flashlight beams and red-line laser sights pierced the acrid fog. Darth Vader breathing of the heavily armed and gas-masked squad filled the small apartment in its pursuit of an ex-cop turned cop killer. The living room: empty. Bedroom number one: empty. Kitchen: empty. Halls: empty. Closets: empty. The ceiling, floors, and walls were tapped for body mass. Empty. Bedroom number two: empty.

Bathroom. *Bingo.*

Islands of bloodied pulpy brain matter adhered to the walls, from which ribbons of blood cascaded down the tiles to the tub where the corpse of a man was crumpled inside. His face was a wide-eyed death mask. A .40-caliber Beretta was in the tub by his right leg. No visible entrance wound. The mother must've swallowed a round, because the back of his head was gone, the team figured, as Davis called it in to Horn.

After Tac secured the Lyndstrum building, garage, and yard, and after the air had cleared in Yarrow's apartment, Horn turned it over to Homicide. Several marked units cordoned off the property. Sydowski and Turgeon slipped on shoe covers, pulled on gloves, then stepped inside.

Sydowski went to the tub and began inspecting the brain matter up close for any traces of a spent bullet. It was too messy for him to determine if the round was in the wall, or in Yarrow. He saw a shell casing in the tub.

Turgeon was at Yarrow's computer where she found a half-composed letter to Molly Wilson.

Molly:
I have no right to ask your forgiveness for all the pain I've caused. But as I look back upon my life and all my failures, your forgiveness is the only thing in this world I have left before I

"Better have a look at this," Turgeon said from the computer.

Squinting at the screen, Sydowski slipped on his glasses.

"That's it?" he asked.

"Yes, it ends like that. Wonder why."

"Maybe he couldn't find the words." Sydowski indicated the bathroom. "Actions speak louder."

As a seasoned investigator, Turgeon knew that not every suicide note was completed, or coherent. "Yeah, maybe."

Sydowski took out his small camera and photographed the screen, as he'd done with Yarrow's corpse in the tub. "Linda, can you check the time this note was created?"

"I'll print it first."

After they'd secured a hard copy, Turgeon displayed the time the file was created. A few hours ago. "That would be after he assaulted Molly."

Sydowski moved from room to room, taking stock of Yarrow's apartment. Orderly and clean. Bare walls, except for one large landscape of the Pacific coast. On a bookshelf he saw a framed photograph. It was Yarrow and Molly Wilson, taken years ago. They looked like kids. Sydowski stared into it for a long, sad time. Nothing in their bright faces foretold the monumental tragedy that would eclipse them.

"Jesus," Turgeon said. "Jesus."

Sydowski popped a Tums into his mouth.

"What do you think, Walt?"

He removed his glasses, folded them, slipped them into his pocket.

"We'll get Crime Scene to scour the place, then wait for the medical examiner to pry out the round from Yarrow, so we can compare it to the rounds from Cliff and Ray. Then we'll clear this thing."

"Fingerprints and dental records confirm the victim's identity as Frank Gregory Yarrow," Julius Seaver, the medical examiner, said.

Sydowski and Turgeon were in Seaver's office where he was going over his preliminary findings of the autopsy he'd done earlier that morning.

Cause of death was from a single gunshot wound to the head. The round recovered was a .40 caliber. It looked like an SXT Talon. Ballistics would conduct further tests. No other apparent trauma or injuries.

Sydowski and Turgeon then delivered the recovered bullet to ballistics, which already had the Beretta and the spent casing. Then they waited at Nick's Diner where Sydowski stared at the television above the counter and picked at his BLT. Turgeon chewed on a carrot muffin and looked glumly into the street.

"You're thinking hard on something. What is it?" Turgeon asked.

"We've got a loose end somewhere, but I can't put my finger on it."

"Like what? The case is a slam dunk.

We're going through formalities."

"I don't know. Some little thing I missed."

Sydowski's cell phone rang.

"Walt, it's Chico in Ballistics."

Sydowski took out his notebook.

"The kill-shot round from Yarrow is a .40-cal SXT Talon."

"We figured."

"Just like the rounds from Hooper and Beamon, .40-cal SXT Talons. Comparing all of them, by the twists and lands, I'd swear in court that all were fired from the same weapon, the .40-cal Beretta recovered from Yarrow. All of the recovered bullets came from the same gun."

"Did you image the casing from Yarrow, run it through the data banks?"

"Yes. Nothing. Nothing lights up in any database."

"What about the gun, Chico?"

"Untraceable. ATF gave it a priority. You must've scared them. They moved like greased lightning. They were thorough. It's a .40-cal Beretta, exactly what we use, but widely available to the public. It doesn't light up anywhere. It coulda been a throw-down, Yarrow was an ex-cop."

"Don't call him any kind of a cop."

"You know what I mean."

"Yes, thanks, Chico."

Sydowski slipped on his glasses, then called his lieutenant and told him.

"According to Chico, it all fits for Yarrow."

"Ident called. Yarrow's prints alone on the Beretta," Gonzales said. "Any surprises from the autopsy?"

"Nope," he said. "I'll call Molly, let her know it's all over."

Back in the homicide detail, Sydowski stared at the empty desks that belonged to Hooper and Beamon and rocked pensively in Hooper's old chair, taking stock of himself.

Over twenty years with the squad. Maybe the time had come for him to punch out, spend more time with his old man. Was he really ready to hang it up? Being a homicide detective was who he was.

Sydowski smoothed his hand across the desktop. This case hurt. Had thrown him badly. He never really had a handle on it. Was he losing his edge? There was a loose end but he couldn't put his finger on it. He sighed, went to his desk, cleaned his bifocals, and examined the case files again.

Maybe the loose end that was gnawing at him would reveal itself, so he could put it to rest, he hoped, going to Seaver's autopsy report on Yarrow.

There was gunpowder residue on Yarrow's hand and shirt. Sydowski reached for the reports on the Beretta. He snapped pages. The reports confirmed that Yarrow's prints were on the gun. Blood and tissue from blow-back were on the muzzle. The reports also showed significant amounts of residue and soot inside Yarrow's mouth and on his tongue. Sydowski read the observation that Yarrow placed his gun in his mouth and closed his mouth around it.

But what if the Beretta was shoved into his mouth and he grabbed at it to resist when it was fired? Residue and prints would still be present.

Come on. Drop it, Sydowski rebuked himself, removed his glasses. It was a suicide. Yarrow had twisted the wreckage of his life with his fantasies about Molly. Stalked her, Hooper, Beamon. It was all there. The physical stuff, the bullets, his note, his history.

Something continued niggling at Sydowski and he'd be damned if he knew what it was. He leaned back in his chair and let his eyes travel around the room, trying hard not to let this thing distract him until he glimpsed the receptionist working at her desk. A shaft of sun lit on her and then it hit Sydowski.

His loose end.

He went back to the files on Hooper's homicide. *How could he have missed this?* He flipped through Hooper's credit card receipts. Then through the inventory of items found at his apartment, his desk, his locker, his car.

"It's not there," he said aloud.

He did the same for Beamon, then Yarrow.

"It's not anywhere."

He made a phone call.

"Molly? Sorry, it's Sydowski again. One quick question."

"What is it?"

"It seems Cliff's credit card records show that a few weeks ago he bought a ring."

"Ray had said Cliff had planned to propose to me."

"Yes." Sydowski listened for a reaction. Hearing none, he resumed. "By any chance have you seen the ring or heard anything about it?"

"No." She cleared her throat. "Why? I mean, you know as well as I do he never got the chance to propose. I never got the ring. I'd always assumed you had it for evidence, or something. Why are you asking me now?"

"Because the ring appears to be missing."

72

At her apartment Molly didn't have time to sort out her feelings. She was too busy clawing her way back to normal.

"Go with the flow," the shrink had advised after her little visit this morning.

Now Molly was scrubbing her bathtub just as she'd done after Hoop's death. A normal reaction, the shrink had said. "People try to wash the bad away." Exhausting herself physically had helped her cope. So did her closest friends who'd called or dropped by. She loved them for it but kept their visits short, as she'd likely do with this one.

Her apartment buzzer sounded twice more before she got to it.

"Who is it?" she said into her intercom.

"Simon."

Simon? Oh, shoot, she'd forgotten he'd called.

"I said I was coming over, remember?"

"Yes. Simon, I'm sorry but I've changed my mind. It's all so soon and I've got a lot to do."

"Are you sure?"

"I'm kind of busy with something. I'm really sorry."

"But on the phone you said you'd like to get out. I've got a surprise I know you'll love."

She reconsidered as he coaxed her. "Come on. It's a gorgeous day."

Smiling, she wavered. He'd been so good to her during this awful time. Sweet. Genuinely concerned. Considerate, actually.

"What did you have in mind?" she asked him.

"A drive along the coast and a few things I'd like to keep secret for just a bit longer."

Sydowski was supposed to call her back about the ring business, but she couldn't bear to dwell on that. Besides, it was a beautiful day and she hadn't been outside as much as she'd like. Why not go have some fun?

Go with the flow.

"All right. Wait there. I'll be down in five minutes."

Molly changed into a fresh top and jeans, grabbed her bag, then went down to the street where Lepp opened the passenger door to a new silver Mercedes 450 SL.

"Hi, Simon. I'm sorry for waffling. It's been hard."

"No apologies necessary. The worst is over now."

"Nice car."

"Got it just for us."

He shut her door and got behind the

393

wheel, fearful he was going to explode as he slipped on his dark glasses. He almost grinned. This was such a glorious day.

Every obstacle had been removed.

73

Tom's line rang at his desk in the newsroom.

"Reed."

"It's Tammy out front. You've got a visitor. Lois Hirt."

"Lois?" His street sources never came to the *Star*.

"Want me to send her to you?"

"No. I'll come out. Thanks."

Lois was wearing faded jeans, a peach top and jacket. She looked well. He led her to a meeting room where he offered her a cushioned chair.

"Would you like coffee, tea, soda?"

"I'm fine, Tom."

He shut the door.

"Lois, I tried calling you through Hector. I left messages. He told me about your friend, Gloria Carter. Her overdose. I'm so sorry."

Lois nodded.

"You look good, Lois."

"Thank you. I'm going to take things one day at a time. Working at getting healthy." She twisted the straps on her purse. "This is weird, but Gloria's death and my coming

395

here, it's sort of all related to you."

"How so?"

"The reason I never got back to you, when you asked me to help you find the person who called OCC, is that, well, it was Gloria."

"It was Gloria?"

"She was the one I told you about. The one who was approached to make the tip call about Hooper with OCC. I wasn't certain at first. She'd talked about it at a party, then disappeared. When I found her, she was sick." Lois pulled a sealed letter-sized envelope from her purse and passed it to Tom.

"What's this?"

"It's a note. It was in Gloria's wallet. I went through her things," Lois said, "I think it's the note the guy made her read into the phone. The guy you were looking for."

Tom stared at the envelope without opening it, then sighed, feeling a wave of exhaustion wash over him. The Yarrow story was done.

"Look, thanks." He tucked the envelope in his pocket. "The story's finished. It's over. Frank Yarrow was 'the guy.' He was an ex-cop. He's dead. He left a suicide note. Did you see our stories today?"

"Yes, but I'd promised to help. I wanted to keep my promise."

"I understand." He patted her hand, letting a moment pass.

"I feel I should have done more to save Gloria," she said.

"You had no control over that. You have to take care of yourself now."

Lois nodded, collected herself, then stood.

"If you're still looking for a job," Tom said, "there are some openings in our mailroom. It's physical shift work but it pays well. I can talk to Human Resources if you want?"

"I'd like that."

"Can I reach you through Hector?"

"Yes."

They hugged. Then Tom got a fresh coffee from the kitchen and returned to his desk feeling melancholy. Hardly anyone was around the metro section today. He was nearly done with his follow-up story on Yarrow's history. Nothing else happening in town. A small news hole. A real dead day.

He felt the envelope from Lois sticking him. What the hell? Maybe he could use it. He found his scissors and slit the top, which revealed a small sheet of paper folded into quarters. The page struck him as familiar. A telephone number was written on the top. It was OCC's number, followed by a short handwritten message, neatly printed in block letters.

HEY, OCC, YOU BETTER LISTEN TO THE WORD DOWN HERE ON THE STREET. HOOPER HAS BEEN

SHAKING PEOPLE DOWN, ROBBING
DEALERS, POCKETING THEIR CASH,
MAKING ENEMIES BIG TIME. WHAT
HE GOT WAS PAYBACK.

Something cold spasmed in the pit of
Tom's stomach.

He turned the sheet over. Nothing on the
reverse. This page was from a reporter's
notebook. Torn from the wire spirals. A four-
by-eight-inch sheet, blue-lined with Pitman-
style spacing. The exact kind used by *Star*
reporters. Bundles of them were in the
supply cupboard. But this page had a blue
tint, and only a couple of *Star* reporters preferred blue tint.

His pulse increased.

Every reporter had a unique note-taking
style, as distinct as a voice. He recognized
the neat block letters of this note. His
breathing quickened. He raised his head. The
newsroom was nearly empty. He swallowed
and walked to Simon Lepp's desk.

Used notebooks were stacked in neat towers
on the right of Lepp's terminal. Tom set the
OCC note down, then opened a notebook at
random. Blue tint pages. Neat block letters.
Identical to the OCC note. He opened another one. Blue pages. Block letters. Christ.
The last line of the note screamed at him.

WHAT HE GOT WAS PAYBACK.

Tom felt a hand on his shoulder.

"What do you think you're doing?"

It was Della Thompson.

"Del, where's Simon?"

"I told you, he's off today."

"Off?"

"Said he was going to drop by Molly's place. Tom! What is it? *Tom!*"

He hurried to his desk and began jabbing numbers on his phone.

74

Bothered by the missing ring, Sydowski contacted Turgeon on her cell phone as she was driving into work.

"Don't you remember me telling you?" she said. "I had called the jewelry store where Hooper bought it, to see if they were holding it."

"And?"

"Nothing came up. The manager was going to check in case it was a custom order and get back to me. But I never heard from him. Then Ray happened, then Yarrow happened, and —"

"Call him again right now. Push the store for an answer."

Sydowski popped a Tums into his mouth. Grinding on it, he hoped that the ring hadn't disappeared from the scene. He combed the files again in case a note was misplaced. Turgeon called back.

"It's not with the jeweler. The manager checked, then put me on the line with the clerk who sold Hooper the ring. She insists Hooper took it, even has a signed receipt."

"Christ."

"What do we do?"

"I don't know," he said. "My other phone's ringing. Just get in and we'll figure something out."

Sydowski hung up his office line and answered his cell phone.

"It's Reed. Where are you?"

"At the detail."

"Check your fax, I just sent you something."

"Tom, this is not a good time."

"You *have* to see it."

Sydowski went to the machine and studied the note.

"What is this?"

Tom explained as quickly as he could.

"Hold the line, Tom. *Leo!*" Sydowski waved the fax at Gonzales, then told him about the OCC tip, about Simon Lepp and Molly. Then got back on the line.

In the newsroom, Tom's finger traced down a coffee-stained staff list pinned on his half wall, stopping at the Ws. He first recited Molly's address.

"We already have hers. Give me Simon Lepp's."

Sydowski shouted the addresses to Gonazales, who got on the line to the emergency dispatcher to send cars to Molly's building. Sydowski called Turgeon as he hurried to the elevator.

Gonzales called the Northern and Central

District captains to send bodies into the area. And he alerted the Richmond District to send units to Lepp's address and called communications to put out a Bay Area lookout for his car. Then they alerted the California Highway Patrol's air unit.

Outside the Hall of Justice, Sydowski flagged Turgeon as she pulled up. They drove to North Beach, coming upon five SFPD units in front and two behind Molly's building. The flashing lights and excitement drew a crowd, which grew with the arrival of the TV news trucks.

Uniformed officer Luke Dinson was standing just inside the door taking notes from Molly's landlady. Sydowski and Turgeon arrived and saw the fear etched in her face as Dinson took them aside.

"Mrs. Collery got a glimpse of Wilson. She's positive it was her, getting into a light-colored sedan with a white male in his thirties," Dinson said.

"How long ago?"

"About an hour."

"Does Mrs. Collery know this guy? Get a look at him? Did Molly look cooperative or compelled to go with him?"

"It was casual, she said. No, she didn't get a good look at the guy or recognize the car."

Turgeon stepped aside to use her cell phone to update Gonzales. He said units in the Richmond District were setting up on

Lepp's house near Golden Gate Park and there was a lookout for Lepp's car. Out of the corner of his eye, Sydowski saw Tom Reed approaching. He turned and spread out his hands to calm him.

"Is she all right?"

"Hang on, Tom."

"I've been trying her cell phone. I can't reach her. Is she here?"

"No."

"Where is she?"

"She may have left with Lepp. We've got people looking and people at Lepp's home."

At the southeastern edge of where the Richmond borders the Haight, eight uniformed district officers toting shotguns took points on the house rented by Simon Lepp. The University of California, San Francisco, was not far and music strained from a student building. An old song by The Who.

No movement was seen around, or in, the small tidy bungalow. Lepp's car was not present. Letters and magazines peeked from the mailbox. A call placed to the phone inside went unanswered.

Officer Russ Rutledge, a fifteen-year veteran, took charge of the takedown. He spoke into his shoulder mike for the others to confirm their positions and scene status.

No movement was reported as the music echoed eerily.

Rutledge radioed his supervisor and apprised him of the situation, expecting to be ordered to hold their positions and await the tactical unit.

"Russ, this is a hot pursuit. Kick it. Go."

Rutledge swallowed, then alerted his team at the rear.

"On three. One . . . two . . . three . . ."

Rutledge and his partner kicked the front door open, while two other officers entered through the rear. Outside, four other officers held positions around the bungalow. Guns drawn, Rutledge and his crew completed a swift room-by-room search. The house was empty but for the menace that filled it.

"Hoe-lee shit."

All the blood drained from Rutledge's face as the officers stared wide-eyed at what greeted them.

One entire wall was papered floor to ceiling with pictures and news clippings of Molly Wilson. Closer examination showed photographs of Molly jogging, driving, shopping, entering the *Star*. Their grainy quality indicated they were taken using a long lens. The array of pictures also included several photographs from news stories about murders. Pictures of Cliff Hooper and Ray Beamon.

"I don't believe it," Rutledge said. "First it's Yarrow, freak number one, stalking her. Now this, freak number two. Jee-zus."

In every picture, Hooper's and Beamon's eyes had been blacked out.

The big-screen television dominating the living room was on. Molly's pretty face filled the screen, frozen from a videotape of an episode of Vince Vincent's show, *Crime Scene*.

Her head was circled with a thick line in red marker, which had bled onto the words scrawled below.

TIME'S UP, MOLLY

75

"This is a nice car, Simon," Molly said after they pulled away. "I thought you had a Ford. When did you get this? And how can you afford it?"

"It's a rental." He turned to her. "Part of my surprise."

"Any hints?"

He eased to a stop at a traffic light and thought for a moment.

"All right, what's the one thing you told me would save you, if your world was falling apart?"

"Gosh." She thought. "I can't remember."

"Ice cream," he said.

Molly blushed and a smile bloomed on her face.

Her beauty electrified Bleeder, turned the key in the vault of his unfulfilled desires. He ached to slide his arm around her at that very moment, pull her to him, and reveal who he really was.

Tell her. Remove your mask. Tell her now.

"Ice cream? Is that my surprise?"

"Part of it."

The light turned green.

"Ice cream." She giggled. "You're so sweet for remembering, considering we only went out two times."

"Three times."

"Three times." She nodded, then touched his shoulder. Her warmth was incredible, like that sweaty night in the gym and Amy's cherry-candy kisses. Molly kept smiling.

Good. Very good.

The ice cream shop was at the corner of Hyde and Union. After finishing their cones, they went to Golden Gate Park. Then they headed south along the coast driving for some time without speaking until Molly thanked him.

"I'm glad I came." She looked out at the shimmering waves of the Pacific. "This whole thing has been a living nightmare."

He said nothing.

"You know, I'm sorry that I ended things so abruptly when we went out. You know. You've been great."

She was beginning to understand. *Tell her. Tell her now.*

Molly searched the horizon, saying, "I don't know why these horrible things have happened. Cliff, Ray — what Frank did."

"What *he* did?"

"I mean he was — he was — *insane*."

"No, he wasn't."

"He had problems." She turned to him. "Not everything about him made it into the news stories."

407

"Like how he wanted you to keep the baby?"

Molly caught her breath.

"Did Della or Tom tell you that?"

"No."

"Then how did you — ?"

"Frank Yarrow told me."

"Frank told you?"

"Before I killed him."

Her heart slammed against her rib cage.

"Yarrow was an obstacle, like Hooper and Beamon. They were all obstacles between us. I removed them. *For you.*"

"This isn't funny."

"No. Not at all."

This can't be real. No. No. He's fantasizing. Delusional. Maybe off some type of medication. This can't be. She held her breath and struggled to be calm.

"Would you please pull over at the next gas station?"

"I'm afraid we're not stopping."

"I really would like you to stop. Please, Simon —"

"Stop calling me Simon. Simon's a pathetic loser. *Do you see any losers here?*"

"I'm sorry."

"I want you to listen and I want you to understand."

Her skin prickled at his calmness.

"Are you listening?"

"Yes."

"Day after day after day, I sat near you. Close enough to hear you flirting on the phone, close enough to know you wear Obsession. I love the chime of your bracelets whenever you slide your fingers through your hair. And in those rare times when you talked to me in the newsroom, sometimes you'd touch me. Sometimes you'd share the little dramas in your life. You never knew how much you meant to me. You were the sun in my life. I needed you but feared a woman like you would never actually go out with me. But you did. Being with you changed me. I realized we were meant for each other and prayed you'd realize it too."

"But we hardly went out at all."

"You're not listening!"

Molly's mind raced. *Think hard. Find a way out.*

"You never gave me a chance. You never got to know who I am. I handed you my heart and you threw it away. I waited, thinking you'd discover your mistake and come round. But you didn't. You dated others. Less worthy men. Do you think for one goddamned second that they would've done the things I did for you?"

"Please. I'm sorry." Surreptitiously she tried her door. He'd locked it from the driver's control panel.

"You left me no choice but to prove that I

am the only man for you. And I had to keep proving it."

"Please."

Her bag was on her right, resting against the door. She slid her hand into it, unseen. Oh God, she'd forgotten her spray. Wait. She had something else.

"I had to prove it with Hooper. With Beamon. With Yarrow. Over and over. I left you messages asking you why? *Why?* Why wasn't I getting through to you?"

"I'm sorry."

Frantically she probed her bag's contents. *Where is it? Where? Please be here.* Brush, compact, gum. There. There it was! The familiar shape. Present in her hand. Concentrating with every fiber, she delicately explored the surface with her fingers. This was her only hope. She began pressing the sequence.

"You wounded me deeply, treated me as if I were a bad movie you walked out on. It was as if you'd used me as a diversion between other men. Only one other person in my life did *that* to me. *Humiliated me.* She'd refused to rectify matters. So I worked on a special way of enlightening her. Unfortunately, things went awry."

Glancing off, his thoughts took him to another time until Molly found the words to ask, "What happened?"

"I killed her."

Oh Jesus. All the saliva dried in Molly's mouth. *This isn't happening.*

"It was a mistake. Her name was Amy. How was I to know that she was sitting in the car next to her 'boyfriend' when it went over the bridge on *that* night? Don't get me wrong, Kyle was an asshole. He had it coming to him. I enjoyed watching him die." He pounded the steering wheel. *"He had it coming!"* he screamed, then his voice softened. "But Amy was an accident."

Molly felt his hand patting her lap.

"I won't be making any mistakes with you."

He hadn't paid attention to how she'd shifted her open bag until it was resting on the console between them.

"I know what I'm doing. Older and wiser, as they say. I've worked so hard at this. After you ended it with me, I watched you. Praying you would see how wrong you were about me. I watched you with the others. It tore me up."

She had to think. Find a way out. She studied the rental company's tiny elegant seal near the console. Golden Pacific Luxury. *This has to work.*

"I watched every move you made. I watched you that night at Jake's where you waited for Hooper. I watched you weep over him. Then who did you turn to? Beamon. *You grieved for Hooper and turned to Beamon?*

411

Then Yarrow pops up. Pathetic Frank. He needed to be put out of his misery. You let these obstacles get in the way. It was all wrong."

He turned, saw her attention flicker to her bag, and followed it inside to her *cell phone!* And the goddammed thing was on!

"What the hell is this!" Rage twisted his face. "What the hell are you doing!"

"Let me out! God, please let me out!"

76

Tom was waiting on the other side of the police tape stretched around Simon Lepp's rented house in the Richmond District. TV news helicopters were approaching when his cell phone rang.

"Reed."

Loud highway noise spilled into his ear.

"Hello?"

Pushing the phone against his head, he heard the highway rush and the faint voices of people talking in a car.

"What happened?"

"Molly?" *Christ, it's Molly!* Reed could barely hear. He increased the volume, plugged his finger in one ear, then pressed the phone against the other.

"I killed her . . . it was a mistake —"

That's Lepp! Jesus! Molly's put out a call! Tom scanned all the uniforms and suits until he spotted Turgeon. He covered his cell phone's mouthpiece, then waved at her, holding up his phone, pointing at it. Turgeon trotted to him.

"What is it?"

Tom mouthed the word "Molly."

Moments later, Sydowski, Turgeon, several other detectives, and crime scene techs huddled around Tom over the hood of a police car. The whooping of the news choppers distracted them.

"This is no good! Move it into our truck! Quick! Let's go!" said one of the tac team's electronics experts.

The tac officer set a speaker amplifier next to the cell phone, boosting the sound after he'd taped over the mouthpiece. Tom switched on his microcassette tape recorder, placing it next to his phone.

"I've worked so hard at this —"

IT'S LEPP & MOLLY! Tom scrawled in big letters for the others.

"After you ended it with me, I watched you. Praying you would see how wrong you were about me. I watched you with the others. It tore me up —"

No one spoke. They held their breath. Sydowski called Gonzales at the homicide detail. Whispering, he got him to flip through Molly's file for her cell phone service carrier, knowing in his gut that it was unlikely they could pinpoint the location of the call.

"It's Ocean AirNet Systems," Gonzales said. "I've got Emergency Communications making the call now. Stand by."

Helpless to do anything, Tom and the others continued listening to Molly's call. How the hell did he miss that it was Lepp?

A nice guy who gave off a weird little vibe, which Tom had dismissed because Lepp probably possessed the highest IQ at the *Star*. That was the joke. Lepp should've been a rocket scientist, not a reporter. He blinked at Lepp's house.

Three homicides. Two detectives. An ex-cop. Now he had Molly. And there wasn't a damned thing anyone could do. Tom knew the odds were fifty-fifty the cell phone carrier could track Molly's exact location. Some systems had the capability, some didn't. *Come on, Molly, give us something. A landmark. An address. Anything.*

"I watched you that night at Jake's where you waited for Hooper. I watched you weep over him. Then who did you turn to? Beamon. You grieved for Hooper and turned to Beamon? Then Yarrow pops up. Pathetic Frank. He needed to be put out of his misery. You let these obstacles get in the way. It was all wrong."

Gonzales gave Sydowski the verdict. Ocean AirNet Systems had no way to locate Molly through her cell phone. Sydowski cursed. Turgeon stared off at nothing, just as Lepp discovered what Molly had done.

"What the hell is this! What the hell are you doing!"

"Let me out! God, please let me out!"

Static crackled through the line, causing the sound to break up.

415

"How long has this — give it —"

"No — we're in siller . . . ced . . . 50 S
. . . entel . . . den Pacific . . . stop please —"

"You stupid . . . ruin everything —"

Silence. The call went dead. The faces of
the investigators tensed with concentration.

"Replay your tape, Tom, the last bit,"
Sydowski said.

They heard the same garbled exchange as
they strained to listen.

"Again," Sydowski said. "Adjust the speed,
slow it down."

"We're in a silver . . . 450 SL rent . . .
golden —"

"Again."

"We're in a silver Mercedes 450 SL —"

"Again."

Tom replayed it several times at varying
speeds. Until they'd finally determined the
last thing Molly had screamed.

"We're in a silver Mercedes 450 SL rental
from Golden Pacific Luxury —"

One of the cops listening was Harry
Saguer, a bomb expert with OED working
with the tactical unit.

"A car like that should have Global Posi-
tioning Satellite or cellular tracking," Sauger
said. "We can get them to activate the system
as if the car were stolen, but don't shut it
down until we're on them."

Turgeon called emergency communications.
The 911 operator called Golden Pacific,

alerting the company to a life-threatening police emergency, then patched Turgeon through.

"Who've I got?" Turgeon said.

"Mark Jepson, district supervisor. How can we help?"

Turgeon passed the vehicle information to Jepson, hearing him typing on a computer keyboard before reading to her from his screen.

"We've got twenty 450 SLs, Inspector. Eight of them silver. All of them rented. Do you have a name?"

"Lepp. Simon Lepp."

The keys clicked. Then stopped.

"Sir, I'm not sure I can do this."

"Read off the rental agreements."

"We have privacy issues. Maybe a warrant would —"

"We'll get one. But if we're too late, you'll face a wrongful-death lawsuit. Your call, Jepson."

Turgeon heard Jepson gulp over the line before he nervously began reciting customer names. "Wong, Chambers, Klinner, Romaz, *Lepp*. Here we go."

"When was it rented?"

"This morning."

"Have you got location systems in that car?"

"Yes, GPS coordinated out of the central tracking station near Los Angeles."

"Can you get us a trace on that car immediately as if it were stolen."

"Well, don't you need a warrant for that?"

"This is a life-threatening emergency. We need to track that vehicle now! Just track it. Don't shut it down."

"I'll call them and get them to call you as soon as I —"

"Now! Get them now! Damn it!"

Helicopters thumped above them.

The *Star* had a cost-sharing deal with KKGW's news helicopter, which was hovering overhead with Henry Cain, a *Star* photographer, aboard. As Tom dialed the *Star*'s photo desk he got Sydowski and Turgeon to guarantee their help.

"Swear you'll give me Molly's location when you get it!"

"Tom, you can't —"

"Swear! I've been helping you and I'll stay out of the way."

Sydowski agreed just as Tom got through to the photo desk and quickly explained to the editor.

"Get them to pick me up," he said. "I think I can take them to Molly."

"Hang on, Tom, I'll get Henry on his radio." Less than thirty seconds later, the editor came back. "There's a vacant lot two blocks east of you. They'll pick you up there now. Run."

After Tom left, the California Highway Patrol requested Sydowski accompany their helicopter crew to assist with aerial observation of the vehicle suspected in three San Francisco homicides.

Turgeon stayed on the ground and on the line with Golden Pacific Luxury and the emergency dispatcher ready to relay the location and direction of travel.

77

Bleeder seized Molly's cell phone and studied the number on the call display. Recognizing it as Tom Reed's, he pressed it to his ear. He listened intensely for a long moment. Hearing nothing, he surmised that she'd probably got his message box.

He switched it off, smashed it against his door frame, then hurled it out his window along a windswept section of Highway 1, somewhere southbound between Swanton and Davenport.

Bleeder ran the back of his hand across his mouth as he glared at Molly. She could smell the strawberry farms, saw the hills rushing by as the Mercedes gathered speed along the twisting road near the sea.

"That was stupid, Molly."

"I was scared."

"I'm scaring you?"

"I think you want to hurt me, because I hurt you, the way Amy did."

He began shaking his head.

"I'm not going to hurt you."

"But I thought —"

"I told you, Amy was a mistake. You're

smarter than she was. I'd never hurt you, understand?"

"Yes," she lied.

She only understood that he was a deranged murderer and she would die if she didn't get away from him.

"I've got plans for us. Big plans. All part of my surprise."

"Are you going to let me go?"

"Don't ask me that. I've got something for you. A surprise. It's in the glove compartment."

She didn't move.

"Your surprise is in the glove compartment. Open it."

She hesitated, then touched the door but didn't open it.

"Go ahead, Molly."

She opened it and saw a small box.

"Open it."

Tears filled her eyes. It dawned on her. She knew exactly what was inside before opening it. She knew.

"Go ahead."

It was a small velvet-covered box with a gold hinge. She pressed her thumb on the lid, snapping it open to a diamond engagement ring.

"Oh God."

"It's for you."

She covered her mouth with her hand, swallowing the horror of knowing that this was Sydowski's missing ring. The one Cliff had bought to give her the night he'd planned to propose. The night he was murdered.

"See how things have worked out for us, Molly? We belong together."

She couldn't form words. Her heart raced.

"Give it to me. I'm going to put it on your finger."

No. God. No. She snapped it shut, replaced it, and closed the glove compartment. He reached into his jacket and in less than a second a .40-caliber Smith & Wesson semi-automatic pistol was pressed against her head. In feeble defense, Molly held up her hands and leaned away.

"Please don't."

"Get me the goddamned ring, Molly."

"All right. Please put the gun down."

The gun went back into his jacket, out of her reach. She passed him the ring box and he worked out the ring.

"Hold out your hand."

Molly's extended left hand trembled. She turned from him, unable to stop shaking. He snatched her hand and forced the ring on her finger. He slid it on roughly, then sighed as he pulled her hand close, examining his work.

"I'm so happy, Molly. I worked so hard. I didn't want to lose you."

Tears rolled down her face as she searched

the ocean, the smell of the berry farms fading with her hope.

It was a majestic place to die.

78

SpaceGuard Systems was headquartered at
Long Beach, California, in a ten-story
building, where its dark blue windows reflected a palm-framed sky over the ocean.
From that site, SpaceGuard monitored a network of satellites orbiting the earth, transmit-
ting data on the cars rented by Golden
Pacific Luxury, and forty other companies
from San Diego to Seattle.

Within seconds of the SFPD's request,
Rona Cortez, a dispatcher at SpaceGuard's
control center, entered the code for the
Mercedes 450 SL, rented on the credit card
of Simon Lepp.

A red blip began pulsating on Cortez's
computerized map. It displayed longitudinal
and latitudinal coordinates. She locked on
the California zone, south of San Francisco,
adjusted her headset, and sat up.

"Vehicle now on Highway 1, eleven miles
north of the Santa Cruz County line, traveling southbound at sixty-two miles per
hour," she said into her mouthpiece. She had
the ability to disable the vehicle from her
keyboard but she'd been advised to refrain.

Law enforcement agencies were scrambling to marshal resources for an arrest involving a hostage situation.

Cortez's line was patched to a San Francisco emergency communications operator. He immediately alerted dispatchers at the Santa Cruz County's Netcom Center at De Laveaga, and the California Highway Patrol's Golden Gate Communications Center, known as GGCC, which alerted the Monterey Comm Center. Monterey relayed data on the suspect vehicle to all units in the region. Down the coastline, the San Luis Obispo Comm Center made an immediate request for air support.

The helicopter assigned to the Highway Patrol's Coastal Division is based at the Paso Robles Municipal Airport, which is situated amid golf courses and sedate rolling farmland. Two flight officers hurried to the tarmac and clicked through their preflight inspection. Less than six minutes after the call, the new Eurocopter AS350 A-Star lifted off, its blue, gold, and white colors of the California Highway Patrol contrasting against the sky as it thundered north to Santa Cruz.

The alert also was received by the Highway Patrol's chopper out of San Francisco with Sydowski aboard. And as promised, the information went to Tom Reed, who was in the KKGW's news helicopter, which banked and pounded south.

★ ★ ★

On Highway 17, about twenty-five miles south of San Jose, Floyd Grimshaw, an independent hauler from Illinois, had a world of trouble on his mind. The woman at the other end of his hands-free speakerphone was crying.

"Tillie, Tillie, listen to me, darlin'." Grimshaw failed to get a word in edgewise to his wife back in Skokie. It was pissing him off to the point of distraction as he rolled southbound by the golf course.

"I don't believe it, Floyd. She knew too much about you."

"I'm telling you, Reb Denny put her up to it. You know Reb from Portland, he's the biggest damned joker. Probably had a big old bet going with Harley and those guys from Texas. He gave her our number, told her to call you and let on like she's my girlfriend and you're my ex. It's pretty funny really —"

"It's *not* funny, Floyd —"

"Tillie would you just listen —"

"No, *you* listen —"

The six-hundred-horsepower Detroit Diesel of Grimshaw's Freightliner growled as he shifted gears for his approach to the Fishhook interchange. He was pulling a tanker trailer fully loaded with nine thousand gallons of gasoline to deliver to gas stations in Aptos and Rio Del Mar. Taking the southbound off-ramp to begin the sweeping turn,

Grimshaw heard thumping in the sky.

"I'm serious, Floyd, I found a woman's T-shirt in your cab when you got back from Knoxville last week. You gonna blame that on Reb Denny?"

The pounding grew louder. Glancing up, Grimshaw saw the police chopper as he was merging onto Highway 1 southbound near Emeline. *What's going on?* At that moment on his blind side, he glimpsed a silver car streaking to beat the gap he was narrowing with his lane change.

"God Almighty!" Grimshaw jerked the wheel, yelling at the speeding car. "You ain't going to make it! You ain't —" The rig swerved, brakes screeched, he braced for the collision as metal sparked against the guard rail. "Son of a —" The truck jackknifed, Grimshaw's tractor was pinning the car against the guardrail, both of them sliding. The big tires began shredding, the tanker trailer vibrated, began bucking, until it broke free from the hitch, toppled onto the asphalt, and started to roll.

A short drive south, near Soquel, Santa Cruz County Sheriff's Deputy Mike Fuller, with the patrol division's B-Team on second watch, was at the top of his shift when his radio crackled with a Code 3.

A bad wreck at the Fishhook.

He hit his lights and siren and came upon

the scene in minutes. A tanker rollover across Highway 1's southbound lanes. Arriving at the same time as the first responders, a fire engine and a California Highway Patrol cruiser, Fuller saw the tanker truck's driver rushing between his overturned trailer and his tractor. It had vise-gripped a silver sedan's doors between its grill and the guardrail, blocking the passengers' escape through the car's doors.

The highway patrol unit closed the oncoming northbound lanes while Fuller used an emergency turnaround to come up behind the scene and block southbound traffic. He got out and jogged toward the site. The shaken driver hurried from the crash to Fuller and firefighters. His T-shirt was stained with blood webbing from his head, but he appeared to be all right.

"They just came up on me! I had to swerve! I'm fully loaded with gasoline and I'm leaking, get everyone back!"

"Wait by my car, sir. We'll have the paramedics look at you," Fuller said, glancing at the scene in the distance.

He could tell from the tail configuration the car was a new Mercedes. The airbags had deployed. Two people were inside. Fuller could see their heads moving. They were trying to free themselves. They had no way out. The woman in the passenger seat was screaming, her cries drowned by more sirens

428

wailing and whooping from every direction. An ambulance and more fire and police vehicles were arriving.

A couple of helicopters were already putting down now about seventy yards off. Fuller thought he'd heard transmissions over his shoulder mike but was concentrating on the scene. "We got to get them out!" he yelled to firefighter Will Peterson, who was standing next to him, shouting commands into his radio.

Fuller began moving toward the Mercedes some fifty yards away.

"Wait!" Peterson yelled over the chaos. "No one can go down there! *No one!*"

"We got trapped victims!"

"One spark, one charge, and the whole area goes. First we need a perimeter to push everybody back! *Way the Jesus back!* The leak and vapor buildup down there is extreme. We've got to ground against a static charge, then foam the whole area."

Peterson nodded at the people who were running to the scene from the police and press helicopters, waving at them to stay back.

"Mike, you've got to keep these people back!"

But the woman's distant screams ripped into Fuller. His stomach twisted. Seeing that wreck. Seeing those people alive, *inside a time bomb*. It was more than Fuller could stand.

The man behind the wheel was trying to kick out the windshield. Fuller took stock. Help was coming fast but it might be too late. Fuller couldn't bear another moment. He ran to his car for a fire blanket and a rubber baton. As he gathered them, his car radio blared a Netcom repeat of a Code 6 and a network-wide alert for ROPE to look out for and stop a fleeing multiple homicide suspect believed to be on the northern out-skirts of Santa Cruz . . .

". . . occupants described as white male, Simon Lepp, and white female, Molly Wilson, silver Mercedes 450 SL, rented from Golden Pacific Luxury, California license . . ."

Fuller took in the details, then rushed to the pinned car, ignoring Peterson's warnings because he believed he could get them out through the rear window.

One of the men from the helicopters, Tom Reed, was running ahead of the other, Walt Sydowski, as they followed Fuller. Sydowski flashed his star to Peterson as he and Tom ignored the firefighters' warnings to keep back.

As they neared the Mercedes, the woman's screams increased over the sirens and addi-tional choppers. *"He's going to kill me!"* The man was kicking hard at the car's windshield when it all suddenly focused for Fuller.

This was more than a wreck.

Fuller knew.

The Code 6. Silver 450 SL, a Golden Pacific Luxury plate frame around the California license. White male Simon Lepp. White female. "He's going to kill me!" Molly screamed.

Fuller heard the windshield pop.

Lepp scurried out from behind the wheel, over the hood, yanking at Molly, who tried to resist. Finally, he pulled her out of the vehicle. "Stop, police!" Fuller shouted over the noise. Dropping the blanket and baton, he hopped the guardrail behind the car.

"Hold it right there, Lepp!" Sydowski came around Fuller from another angle.

"Simon, it's over. Let her go!" Tom yelled.

Lepp ignored them, slid his arm around Molly, who struggled as he hurried her down the road. The air reeked of gas, the fumes were choking, making their eyes tear. As they moved deeper into the "ignition zone," Molly glanced over her shoulder at Tom, Sydowski, and Fuller, her eyes pleading.

"Help me! Please help me!"

Fuller drew his weapon. "Freeze!"

The couple halted. Pivoted. Lepp was pressing his gun to Molly's head. His other arm tightened around her neck in a choke hold.

"Put your gun down and she'll live."

Fuller tightened his grip and steadied his aim at Lepp's head.

One spark would incinerate them.

"Simon, it's over. Let her go," Tom shouted as he, Sydowski, and Fuller closed their circle on Lepp. Fumes filled their nostrils. Fuller inched forward. "Sir, place your weapon on the ground now!" They were forcing Lepp to move backward. "Sir, you can smell the gas. Place your weapon on the ground!"

The gun remained at Molly's head.

"Nobody moves or her death will be on *your* hands!" Lepp shouted.

Tom saw the terror in Molly's eyes.

"Everything's going to be all right," he said.

"Nobody takes another step!" Lepp shouted.

"Simon, one spark and we all die." Fuller moved closer.

Lepp inched back, not seeing the huge C-shaped tire fragment from the rig. It came alive when he stepped on it, whipped hard around his calves, knocking his feet from under him. As he fell backward, his hold on Molly loosened.

"Run!" Sydowski shouted.

Molly bolted toward the emergency crews.

The impact of Lepp's hand hitting the ground launched his rubber-gripped Smith & Wesson down the gas-slick asphalt of Highway 1 where it disappeared under the tanker. The others tried to tackle Lepp.

He was too fast and scrambled to his feet, running headlong to the tanker.

"Let him go!" Sydowski shouted. "Let him go! He can't escape! Sydowski pointed to the police helicopters, then urged Tom and Fuller to race to safety.

Lepp came upon the tanker, ignoring the sloshing of gasoline under his shoes. Gagging from the fumes, he searched for his gun.

Tom and the others were running toward Peterson. Firefighters were sending a protective water curtain in their direction as they fled. Adrenaline pumped through the men as they gained distance, twenty yards, thirty yards, forty . . . Lepp found his gun, seized it, and blind with fury, whirled toward the three men and squeezed the trigger.

The concussion wave hefted Tom, Sydowski, and Fuller ten yards toward the firefighters. Airborne helicopters vibrated dangerously. The flash fireball shot skyward some thousand feet, singeing the air and momentarily pushing the surrounding temperature to nearly twelve hundred degrees.

Simon Lepp was vaporized.

Firefighters and paramedics helped Tom, Sydowski, and Fuller to their feet. At the command post specially suited hazmat crews began working on securing the site. Traffic was gridlocked at the Fishhook interchange as scores of emergency and news vehicles arrived.

At the edge of the cordon, paramedics were making a preliminary examination of Molly.

433

She raised her head to Tom and Sydowski. Tears streamed down her face.

Local television news captured much of the dramatic standoff. Details and rumors rippled through the press pack as the sky rumbled with more helicopters from Bay Area TV stations. Some were going live. Tom and Sydowski stayed with Molly at the scene.

Tom put his arms around her, comforting her. They watched the aftermath until Molly suddenly jerked away. She clawed at her finger, removing the ring Lepp had forced on her. Taking a few steps toward the inferno, she raised her hand to hurl it at the flames but something held her back.

It was Cliff's ring, not Lepp's.

Molly tightened her fingers around it, stood there helplessly, and wept. Tom and Sydowski consoled her, their faces painted by the glow of the flames.

"It's over, Molly. It's finished," Tom said.

She sobbed into his chest as they watched columns of black smoke ascend to the darkening sky.

79

The doctors at Dominican Hospital in Santa Cruz kept Molly overnight for observation. The sisters fussed while a female deputy watched over her.

Ted Hall and Sal Vermosa, Santa Cruz County detectives, soon arrived to take her statement to share with San Francisco. Vermosa punctuated his requests with "Now, ma'am, can you recall if . . ." while Hall, a kind white-haired man with a big stomach, reminded Molly of the type of guy who was Santa at children's Christmas parties.

Molly refused all press requests for interviews, never switched on her TV set. She called her father in Texas, assured him she was okay.

"No, Dad. I don't want you to come to see me in California."

"But why, Molly? I think I ought to be there."

"Because I need to come home."

At dawn, Molly rose from her hospital bed and sat near the window where she reflected on her life and the tragedy until Tom came to see her. They spent much of the morning trying to come to terms with what Simon Lepp did.

"I'll never understand what happened," she said.

"Don't even try."

"But was it me? Did I trigger something in him?"

"Don't think like that. He was sick."

"But he sat beside us. He worked with us. *I dated him*. How come we didn't see it? He might have been shy, but he seemed *normal*."

"No one saw it. Sydowski tracked down Simon's aunt last night. Seems he withdrew from everything after his parents died some years ago. She said he'd had a history of psychological trouble since he was a boy but his mother kept it secret. No one picked up on how serious his problems were."

"He told me he'd killed a girl, or a woman and her boyfriend."

Tom nodded.

"They're reopening the case of Amy Tucker and Kyle Chambers. Simon had dated her in high school and she jilted him."

"Oh no."

Molly thought of them, then the others Lepp had murdered. And how close he'd come to killing her. She cupped her hands to her face. Tom rubbed her shoulders and stayed with her a long time.

Sydowski and Turgeon picked her up the

following morning. They respected her request not to take the same route that had brought her to Santa Cruz. Still, the faces of Cliff Hooper, Ray Beamon, and Frank Yarrow haunted her.

She closed her eyes.

In the days that followed, Molly still refused all requests for interviews. With Irene Pepper gone, the *Star* no longer pressured her to write about her ordeal. But Molly wanted to talk to Tom. It led to a dramatic four-part series he produced on the murders, THE KILLER AMONG US. All four editions sold out. The *Star* syndicated it and four hundred dailies across the U.S. reprinted it. The stories were among the most powerful features Tom had ever written and there was talk that it would be a contender for a Pulitzer. After it ran, Molly told Tom and Ann over dinner at their house that she was considering writing a book about her ordeal.

"I think it could be a good thing for you," he said. "It might be an exercise in self-healing. Help you sort out everything so you can move on."

A few days later, Molly packed her little Ford Focus. She was headed for Texas to visit her father and start her book.

Sydowski and Turgeon took a few days off after closing the case. Turgeon visited her sister in New York, where she grappled with self-doubts about continuing to be a cop.

Sydowski spent time with his old man, his birds, and at cemeteries in Colma and Lodi where he'd stand alone over the graves of his friends, asking why they had to die this way.

He'd search the horizon for an answer.

It was a mystery he would never solve.

AUTHOR'S NOTE AND ACKNOWLEDGMENTS

I would like to thank Audrey LaFehr, who guided this book through punishing seas to a safe port. I have also benefited by the help of many other people. Among them: Wendy Dudley, Mildred Marmur, Jeff Aghassi, Laurie Parkin, Steve Zacharius, Doug Mendini, Michaela Hamilton, Joan Schulhafer, and everyone on Kensington's hardworking sales team. Thanks to Barbara, Laura, and Michael. And to Ann LaFarge. I especially appreciate the kind support of John and Jeannine Rosenberg, Donna Riddell, Mary Jane Maffini, Linda Wiken, Sleuth of Baker Street, Beth Tindall, the Florida gang, and booksellers everywhere.

Above all, I thank you, the reader. Hope we meet again soon.

ABOUT THE AUTHOR

Rick Mofina is the author of *If Angels Fall, Cold Fear, No Way Back,* and *Blood of Others,* which won the Arthur Ellis Award for Best Novel. He is an Ottawa-based journalist whose work has appeared in such publications as the *New York Times* and *Reader's Digest.* Please visit his Web site: www.rickmofina.com.